THE
DH

THE DH

THE TRIPLE THREAT · BOOK 3

JOHN FEINSTEIN

A YEARLING BOOK

Text copyright © 2016 by John Feinstein
Cover photographs copyright © 2016 by Shutterstock

All rights reserved. Published in the United States by Yearling, an imprint of Random House Children's Books, a division of Penguin Random House LLC, New York. Originally published in hardcover in the United States by Alfred A. Knopf, an imprint of Random House Children's Books, New York, in 2016.

Yearling and the jumping horse design are registered trademarks of Penguin Random House LLC.

Visit us on the Web! randomhousekids.com

Educators and librarians, for a variety of teaching tools, visit us at RHTeachersLibrarians.com

Library of Congress Cataloging-in-Publication Data is available upon request.
ISBN 978-0-553-53582-2 (trade) — ISBN 978-0-553-53583-9 (lib. bdg.) — ISBN 978-0-553-53584-6 (ebook) — ISBN 978-0-553-53585-3 (pbk.)

Printed in the United States of America
10 9 8 7 6 5 4 3 2 1
First Yearling Edition 2017

THIS IS FOR FRANK MASTRANDREA,
WHO DESERVES A HAPPY ENDING AFTER SO
MANY YEARS OF ROOTING FOR THE METS.

THE
DH

I

"I won."

Matt Gordon's grin was so wide as he put his lunch tray down that he didn't even really need to say the words. Alex Myers knew exactly why he was grinning, but none of the others at the table—Jonas Ellington, Christine Whitford, and Max Bellotti—had a clue. That was because Matt hadn't told his secret to anyone in school except Alex.

"Won what?" Jonas asked.

"The appeal of my suspension," Matt said. "I'm eligible again. I'm out of purgatory."

"You mean you can play football next fall?" Christine said.

Matt nodded. "Yup. . . . And I can play baseball right now." He looked at Alex. "You ready to be the number two pitcher on the team, Myers?"

Alex smiled, but he raised an eyebrow. That comment was

very un-Matt. Like Alex, Matt Gordon was an outstanding athlete. He had been the starting quarterback for the Chester Heights football team and would have been an all-state player if he hadn't been suspended during the state playoffs for taking steroids. Alex was a big part of the reason Matt had resorted to steroid use: When Alex showed up as the team's third-string quarterback, Matt recognized that Alex—just a freshman—was better than he was. He had panicked, and had resorted to taking the drugs that cost him the chance to play for the state title.

The suspension handed down by the Pennsylvania High School Athletic Association was for one year. Now Matt filled everyone in on what had been going on since then.

"I appealed on the grounds that the penalty was too harsh, that I'd never actually tested positive, I came forward on my own, and since then I've tested clean on eleven random drug tests." He shrugged and grinned some more. "I won. The arbitration board voted two to one in my favor. So, to quote Schwarzenegger, I'm back."

"He said, 'I'll *be* back,'" Max said, teasing.

"Whatever," Matt replied. "I'll *be* at baseball practice this afternoon."

Everyone congratulated him, but Alex noticed Christine frowning the way she did when something was bothering her.

"Look, Matt, I'm happy for you," she said. "But I'm confused. You *did* test positive—you just didn't get caught because Jake switched your blood sample for Alex's."

Alex broke in. "Christine, it doesn't matter," he said. "All that matters is Matt won the appeal."

Alex didn't really want to relive what had happened four months earlier: At the behest of Matt's father—football coach Matthew Gordon—Jake Bilney had switched Alex's blood test for Matt's to make it look as if Alex, not Matt, was the one taking steroids. Matt had come forward and admitted his guilt the week of the state championship game. Coach Gordon had been fired, and Bilney had transferred.

Alex really wanted to move on.

Matt waved a hand. "It's okay, Alex," he said. "You're right, Christine. But legally, once the tests were compromised by the label switching, they couldn't be used against me. The board had to base its decision on my tests since then."

Christine tipped her head, considering. "Okay. Well . . . that's good for you." She stood up. "There's still time for me to get a story into this week's *Roar*. I'll go see Coach Hillier right now."

Tom Hillier was the advisor for the student newspaper, the *Weekly Roar*. He'd also become the football coach after Matthew Gordon was fired.

She walked away, drawing looks from most of the boys in the cafeteria. In Alex's opinion, Christine was the prettiest girl in the school. He was biased because she was his girlfriend. Clearly, though, he wasn't the only one who thought she was pretty.

"She seems a little miffed," Matt said. "What's that about?"

"Nah, she just wants to get the story in," Alex said.

"You sure that's all?" Matt asked.

"Totally," Alex said, hoping he sounded more convinced than he felt. He'd picked up a weird vibe from Christine too.

He watched Christine stop to talk to Patton Gormley, one of his teammates from the basketball team. The basketball season had ended the previous Friday, with Chester Heights losing to West Philadelphia in the second round of the sectional playoffs. The Speedboys had beaten the Lions by thirty points in a regular-season game, so the 72–65 loss to them in the playoffs had been disappointing but also a sign of how far the team had come.

Basketball season might have just finished, but Alex was so ready for baseball. He was an excellent quarterback and a very good point guard, but he thought baseball might someday be his best sport. He had been almost unhittable as a Little League pitcher. He knew high school would be different, but he was still confident.

And now Matt Gordon was going to be his teammate again. He'd been a great teammate in football—Alex's biggest supporter, even though they played the same position. Maybe . . .

"Alex," he heard Jonas say. "Quit staring at your girlfriend."

"Why shouldn't he stare at his girlfriend?" Matt said. "She's hot."

"Yeah," Max said. "Even I stare at her sometimes, and I'm gay."

They all laughed, and Alex felt himself relax. Why, though, did he feel unrelaxed?

■ ■ ■

Alex was starting baseball practice a week late because basketball had gone so long, but he knew Coach Birdy would understand—because Al Birdy had been the assistant basketball coach.

In fact, it'd been Coach Birdy who had helped Alex and Jonas get through a rocky start in basketball after they'd missed the opening practices because they were still playing football. Coach Evan Archer wasn't a big fan of football and had made life difficult for Alex and Jonas when they first showed up.

Alex expected that the transition from basketball to baseball would go more smoothly, even though there were just four days before the opening game of the season. But he had no idea how Coach Birdy would feel about Matt showing up for practice.

He also had no idea how good a pitcher Matt might be. Matt hadn't played baseball the previous two seasons because his father had wanted him to focus on football. Even though Matt didn't talk about it very much, it was clear that Matthew Gordon Sr. was no longer an influence in his son's life—at least when it came to sports. When Matt had told Alex that he was appealing his suspension, Alex had asked him what his father thought about it.

"I don't know," Matt had answered. "And I don't really care."

Enough said about that.

Matt was considerably bigger than Alex, but Alex was the one with the golden arm—which was why Matt had nicknamed him Goldie as soon as he'd seen him throw a football. Matt could throw a football just about as far as Alex could, but he wasn't nearly as accurate. Alex figured the same would be true in baseball: Matt would throw very hard; the question would be his control.

Alex was wondering about all these things when he heard the bell ring. He was stunned that his last-period class was over and Mademoiselle Schiff hadn't called on him once. His French teacher had a remarkable knack for catching him when he was daydreaming and nailing him with a question.

"Nice going in there," Christine said as he exited the classroom. She was waiting for him. Her backpack was slung over her shoulders, and her long dark hair was pulled back in a ponytail. Alex thought he could hear kids snickering as they passed by.

"Nice going what?" he said. "I didn't say anything."

Christine smiled her megawatt smile. "I know. I guess you didn't hear Mademoiselle Schiff say that she was going to congratulate you on the basketball season but figured it was a waste of time since you obviously weren't paying attention . . . again."

Alex felt his face grow warm. "She said that?" he said. "In English or French?"

Christine laughed. "Both," she said. "First she said it in French, and then she said it in English. You never looked up."

Alex groaned. French was his worst subject. Part of it was that it was last period; by the end of the day, his mind tended to wander in the direction of practice—first football, then basketball, and now baseball. It was also *hard*. In class, Mademoiselle Schiff was a taskmaster. No English was spoken except in special circumstances, like proving a student wasn't paying attention. The homework was consistently difficult and always took a long time.

"I'd better go back and talk to her," Alex said.

Christine reached up and put her hand on his shoulder. "Go to practice," she said. "I don't think she's mad. Send her an email tonight."

Alex thought a moment and then nodded, and they started down the hallway. He didn't want to be late for his first day of baseball practice—when he was already a week late.

"Did you get the story about Matt into the *Roar?*" he asked.

"Oh yes," she said. "I spent the rest of lunch writing it."

She slowed for a second, then stopped walking. "How do you feel about all this?" she said, surprising him.

"About Matt?" he asked.

"Of course about Matt," she answered.

He shrugged. "I'm happy for him," he said. "Like he said, he never did actually test positive, so . . ."

"Stop with the 'for the record' answer," she said. "I'm not asking you as a reporter. I'm asking as your friend."

He would have preferred "girlfriend."

"That *is* my answer," he said. "You're Matt's friend too. What's *your* answer?"

"He was punished for taking steroids," she said without hesitating. "He *did* take steroids. He cheated, regardless of whether there's an official test that proves it or not."

"He paid a price—"

"One game!" she said loudly, then lowered her voice when she saw people giving her looks. "He missed *one* football game—that's it."

"It was the *state championship* game," Alex said. "He also

■ 7 ■

stood up and told the whole school what he'd done and dealt with the public humiliation that came with it."

"One game," Christine said again. "In the NFL, a first-time offender gets four games, automatic."

Alex stared at her.

"What's bothering you about this?" he asked. "Why are you so upset?"

"I'm not sure," she said.

With that, she turned and walked away.

Al Birdy had asked the three members of the basketball team who wanted to play baseball to meet him in the dugout of the baseball field as soon as their last class was over. Watching Christine walk away from him, Alex realized he was going to be late. He hustled to his locker to drop off his books and then worked his way to the back of the school building, where the athletic facilities were located.

Chester Heights had plush offices for the football coaching staff but almost no space for any of the school's other coaches. Coach Birdy shared an office with three other coaches. That was why he had asked his new players to meet him in the dugout. There, they would have a few minutes of privacy while the rest of the team was still in the locker room getting dressed.

Alex was the last of the group to arrive. Coach Birdy was

already in workout clothes and was sitting on the dugout bench. Jonas Ellington and Patton Gormley sat on either side of him. Matt Gordon sat on one of the dugout steps. He had apparently been invited to the meeting too.

"Have trouble finding the field, Myers?" Coach Birdy said with a grin as Alex huffed up, slightly winded after walking very fast to get there.

"Sorry, Coach," Alex said. He started to say, *I had to talk to a teacher,* but he figured that beginning a new season with a lie wasn't a good idea.

Coach Birdy waved a hand at him, clearly not bothered.

"We were just about to get going," he said. "What I wanted to say is that everyone understands why the three of you who were playing basketball missed practice last week. I'm just going to put each of you into drills at your positions today. If you have a question, ask somebody."

He looked at Matt. "Gordon, you're different. Once we get all the guys assembled out here, I'd like you to explain what happened and why you're joining us now. Any problem with that?"

Matt shook his head. "No, Coach," he said. "I appreciate the opportunity. I'd like everyone to understand why I'm eligible to play."

"You don't have to go into detail," Coach Birdy said. "The basics should do."

Matt nodded.

Alex understood what Coach Birdy was saying: No one really wanted to hear a blow-by-blow of Matt's hearing.

"Gordon, Myers, Gormley—we don't have enough catchers to keep everyone throwing at one time. We've now got seven pitchers and three guys who catch. So you'll take turns—twenty pitches in each rotation up to a total of sixty. Do *not* try to throw hard. Your arms are bound to be stiff and tight."

He turned to Jonas. "Ellington, you fall in with the other outfielders. When we take BP, you go last. Same for you other guys when your positions are hitting. No big deal—I just don't want the other guys thinking anyone is jumping ahead of them." He paused. "Okay?"

They all nodded. "You've got lockers assigned to you, and I had Mr. Hall put some workout clothes in there for you. So you should be all set." He looked at Alex. "You have a glove, Myers?"

Alex realized the other three guys in the dugout had their gloves. In his haste to get to the field, he had left his in his school locker.

"It's, um, in my locker," Alex said.

"Won't do you much good there, will it?" Coach Birdy said. "Go get it, and when you get out here, if we've started stretching, you can give me three loops around the field. Being late once—okay, I'll let you slide. Twice in one day—you gotta run."

Alex was embarrassed. He was standing there thinking of a response—maybe something clever like *Sorry, Coach*—when he realized Coach Birdy was talking to him again. "Myers, are you gonna stand there staring at me or get going?"

"Going, Coach," Alex said, noticing that Matt, Jonas, and Patton were all about to fall over laughing.

He began sprinting back across the soccer and lacrosse field in the direction of the school, thinking to himself, *Am I ever going to start a season without getting into some kind of trouble?*

The answer, at least since his arrival at Chester Heights, was no. This time, though, was different, because he had no one to blame but himself.

■ ■ ■

The rest of the team was stretching when Alex, glove now in hand, got back. He was already winded from running all the way to his school locker, back to the baseball lockers, and then, after changing into the gray sweats hanging in the locker with his name on it, back out to the baseball field. Coach Birdy could see that. The March weather was still cool, probably in the mid-fifties, but Alex was sweating pretty hard.

"Just give me two," he said softly.

Alex set out along the foul line near the dugout and began running. At least he didn't have to run steps the way he'd had to during football season.

"Pick it up, Myers!" he heard someone yell from the middle of the infield, where all the players were stretching. Several others joined in the heckling before Coach Birdy cut them off by blowing his whistle. Alex was on the warning track in the outfield by then, but he could hear Coach Birdy clearly: "Anyone who thinks Myers needs coaching can join him." That quieted things down quickly.

Once he finished his two laps, Alex started stretching.

When they were finished, Coach Birdy called everyone to the pitcher's mound.

"Okay, guys, as you can see, we've got four new players out here today," he said. "I told you last week about Myers, Ellington, and Gormley. They're all last string until we see what they can do." He turned to Alex for a second. "Myers, I know you're used to that."

Everyone laughed, remembering how Alex's football career at Chester Heights had started as a last-string quarterback and tackling dummy the previous September.

"We also have another addition today that none of us were expecting." He looked at Matt Gordon, as did everyone else. "Rather than me trying to repeat what Matt explained to me this morning, I'm going to let him do it. Matt, the floor—the mound—is yours."

Matt Gordon was the coolest customer Alex had ever met. He hadn't flinched at all when he stood in front of the entire school and admitted that he had taken steroids and that his father had switched his blood test with Alex's. But now he actually seemed nervous. Or maybe Alex was imagining it?

"Thanks, Coach," Matt said. He paused and glanced around, as if trying to decide what to say next.

"Look," he finally said. "All you guys know what happened during football season. I confessed to taking steroids, and the state board suspended me from playing any varsity sport for a year."

Another pause. "That was unfair—at least, I thought it was unfair. An entire year? I wanted to play baseball this spring, no matter what my dad said. Plus, I wouldn't have been able to play football next fall."

The confident Gordon grin returned for a moment. "And don't worry—Goldie's going to be our QB. I just want to block for him."

That got a laugh and seemed to loosen Matt up a little.

"I decided to appeal the suspension. There's a board you go before when you do that. A friend of my mom's is a lawyer, so she helped me out. She made the point that I had never actually tested positive—that my punishment was based solely on my own confession—and the board should take that into account. Well, they did. As of this morning, I'm eligible again as long as I continue to submit to random drug tests. And for the record, I've had eleven of them since November and I'm clean."

He looked at Coach Birdy as if to say, *Is that enough?* Apparently it was.

"Okay," Coach Birdy said. "Let's break up into positions and get loose. Like I said, new guys go last for now till we see what you can do."

Alex saw Bailey Warner, who he knew was the number one returning pitcher from last season, start jogging in the direction of the right field line.

"Come on, Goldie," Warner said with a grin. "Let's see what you've got."

■ ■ ■

Alex, Matt, Patton, and Johnny Ellis, who was the team's relief specialist, waited their turn while Warner, Ethan Sattler, and Don Warren threw their twenty pitches. Rick Bloom, whom Alex had noticed jogging up to join the circle while Matt was talking, was their pitching coach. Mr. Bloom, who taught biology, had pitched in college, though Alex wasn't sure where.

"How'd I do, Goldie?" Matt asked quietly while they watched the first three pitchers loosen up.

This time, Alex couldn't resist saying, "Okay, really— who are you and what have you done with Matt Gordon?"

"What are you talking about?"

"Since when are you worried what other people think?"

Matt smiled at him, then shrugged. "Since I knocked myself off that pedestal I used to live on."

Alex thought about that for a second. It made sense, even if it still felt strange to hear Matt sounding like a high school junior and not Peyton Manning or Tom Brady.

"Okay, guys, you're up," Alex heard Coach Bloom say. "Myers, Gordon—no heroics. No need to throw your arms out the first day. Gormley, I'll catch you so we don't get too far behind."

They all nodded.

Alex's arm always felt loose, but he put very little into his first ten pitches. He felt good. He began to pick it up and, in his peripheral vision, could see that Matt—who was next to him—was doing the same thing.

"Last one, guys," said Coach Bloom. "If you feel up to it, you can let this one go a little."

Instinctively, Alex glanced over his shoulder at Matt— who had the famous Matt Gordon grin on his face. Alex turned back, went to his motion, kicked his leg, and threw his fastball at about 90 percent. He heard the mitt of Arnold Bogus, who was catching him, pop. A split second later, he heard another pop. That was Matt's fastball smacking into Lucas Mann's mitt.

The two friends looked at each other.

This time, Matt didn't smile. "It's on, Goldie," he said. Then he turned away and went to the bucket, where bottles of water awaited.

Alex stared after him. *Who are you?* he thought. *And what have you done with Matt Gordon?*

Then the answer came to him: *You're the guy with something to prove.*

After everyone had gone through the various drills at their respective positions, Coach Birdy put the players through a couple of rounds of batting practice. He did the pitching himself, not wanting any of the pitchers to throw any more than they already had.

The pitchers went last and, not surprisingly, all were pretty good hitters. At the high school level, pitchers were often the best athletes on a team, and it wasn't uncommon for the starting pitcher to hit third or fourth in the batting order.

Only one of the pitchers wasn't a pretty good hitter: Matt Gordon. He was a *great* hitter. For one thing, he was a switch-hitter. When he stepped into the batter's box, Coach Birdy stepped back for a moment, surprised.

"You hit lefty, Gordon?" he asked.

"Switch-hitter," Matt answered. "You're throwing righty, so I'm hitting lefty."

Coach Birdy nodded and threw a batting-practice fastball—straight and without a lot of steam on it—right down the middle. Matt swung and hit the ball about 900 feet over the right field fence. At least it seemed like 900 feet to Alex. The fence was 300 feet away, and the ball was still going in an upward arc when it cleared the fence.

Most of the other players waiting their turn to hit were either loosening up with bats or playing catch along the sidelines. But everyone and everything stopped as the ball exploded off of Matt's bat.

"This one's coming in a little bit faster," Coach Birdy said.

Matt nodded. The next pitch didn't go over the right field fence—it went over the center field fence, which was 340 feet away.

Each hitter was supposed to get eight swings and then lay down a bunt. Seven of Matt's swings produced drives over the fence. The eighth was a screaming line drive that one-hopped the wall in right-center.

"Think you can keep a bunt in the ballpark?" Coach Birdy joked before his ninth pitch.

Matt smiled but said nothing—just laid the bunt down and sprinted to first base.

Jonas was standing next to Alex, watching Matt's hitting display. "His father didn't let him play baseball?" he said quietly. "What was he thinking?"

Alex had been wondering the exact same thing. Matt Gordon was a very good football player. But it seemed like he was a *great* baseball player.

Matt jogged over to join them while Patton Gormley stepped in to hit and fouled the first two pitches off.

"Mr. Ruth, I presume?" Alex joked.

Matt shrugged and grinned. "Well, Babe Ruth was a great pitcher who could hit, so that's about right."

"Babe Ruth was a pitcher?" Jonas said.

"He came up that way," Matt said. "Pitched for the Red Sox when they won the World Series in 1918. He was a twenty-game winner twice in the major leagues. Had an ERA of something like two-point-three. The Yankees decided he was too good a hitter not to be in the lineup every day, and, well, you know the rest."

"Yeah," Alex said. "Seven hundred and fourteen home runs later, he retired."

"Yup," Matt said. "There's a reason people talk about 'Ruthian feats.'"

"That was pretty Ruthian right there," Alex said.

"Just batting practice," Matt said.

"Yeah, well, I didn't see anyone else hitting balls nine hundred feet," Alex said.

"Maybe four hundred," Matt answered, grinning broadly now.

"Myers!"

It was Coach Birdy. He was pointing at the batter's box. Alex was up.

He stepped in and took a Ruthian swing at Coach Birdy's first pitch, but he got on top of it and hit a meek ground ball toward second base.

"Easy, Myers," Birdy said. "Just meet the ball."

Alex took a deep breath, relaxed his grip, and focused. He

hit the next pitch hard—a line drive into right field for what would be a solid single.

Seven pitches later, he laid down his bunt and sprinted to first. He had hit the last six pitches solidly, with one going to the warning track. None had left the ballpark. There was only one Babe Ruth at Chester Heights.

■ ■ ■

Coach Birdy had them all run three laps of the field after two rounds of batting practice, then sent them home after telling everyone there would be an intrasquad scrimmage the next afternoon.

"When you get to the locker room tomorrow, I'll have the teams posted," he said. "We've only got twenty guys, so everyone will play throughout. Everyone hits each time through the lineup.

"We open Friday, fellas, so we need to figure out who's starting pretty quickly. Let's get it in."

They circled Coach Birdy, and Jeff Cardillo, who was the team captain and shortstop, held his arm up and said, "Beat the Statesmen!"

They all repeated after Cardillo and headed for the locker room.

"Who're the Statesmen?" Alex asked.

"The team we're playing Friday," Matt said. "Wilmington South—the Statesmen."

Alex hadn't even thought about which school the opener might be against.

They all dressed and headed for home. Matt hadn't been

quite as prodigious at the plate during the second hitting rotation, but he'd been close. Alex had finally hit a ball out of the park, but he guessed the pitch had come in at about 70 miles an hour.

Riding home on his bike, he wondered what it was going to be like to play with the "new" Matt Gordon. During football season, even while his insecurities about his play at quarterback were driving him to take steroids, Matt had never appeared to lack confidence, and he had been steadfastly supportive of Alex.

That wasn't the Matt he had seen today. This Matt wanted to show everyone he was better than they were every time he threw a pitch or took a swing. His presence would undoubtedly make the Lions a better team, but Alex wondered if it would be much fun being around him. Then again, maybe Matt would relax once he'd proved how good he was.

Wheeling his bicycle into the driveway, Alex saw that there was company for dinner. Evan Archer's car was parked in front of the garage. Archer was Chester Heights' basketball coach. He was also—for lack of a better term—Alex's mother's boyfriend. Alex had trouble using the word "boyfriend" to describe someone who was dating his mom, but what else would you call him? Man friend? Nope. Friend? No, that didn't get the job done, either. He usually avoided it or said, "Yes, my mom is still dating Coach Archer," when the subject came up. He even had trouble with that: Moms weren't supposed to date.

On the other hand, dads weren't supposed to be *engaged*

when they weren't yet divorced. Alex's dad had announced to Alex and his twelve-year-old sister, Molly, that he was engaged when they visited him in Boston over Christmas. He had explained that there would be no wedding until he and their mom were legally divorced—if only to avoid jail, Alex figured. The worst part was that he and Molly had both hated their dad's fiancée at first sight.

At least he liked Coach Archer. They'd gotten off to a rocky start, but he'd proved to be a good guy—and a good coach. And it was pretty clear that his mom, unlike his father, wasn't rushing into anything.

Coach Archer was standing in the kitchen, glass of wine in hand, when Alex walked in through the garage door. "Your mom's upstairs changing," he said. "She spilled some wine on her pants." He smiled. "Actually, I spilled the wine on her."

"How'd you manage that?"

"Clumsy, I guess," he said. "How'd the first day of baseball go? Hope the coach didn't give you a hard time for being a week late."

Alex laughed. "No, I gave myself a hard time," he said. "I showed up without my glove, so I had to go back and get it. I was late in the first place for our meeting, then even later because of the glove."

"Good start," Coach Archer said. "Two laps around or three?"

"Two," Alex said.

"I'd have given you five," Coach Archer said.

"I know," Alex answered.

Alex's mom walked into the kitchen. She was thirty-nine and, Alex knew, quite pretty. Molly looked more and more like her every day. Some of Alex's friends had started to ask about Molly—which horrified him. They were in the ninth grade, and Molly was in the seventh. But she looked older because she was tall, about five foot seven, and his buddies had begun to notice.

"How'd it go?" his mom asked.

"He was late and got into trouble," Evan Archer answered, grinning wickedly.

Linda Myers glared at him for a second. "Well, if anyone should know about getting into trouble today, it's *you*," she said—but she was fighting a grin.

She looked at Alex. "Chicken, rice, and asparagus for dinner," she said. "That work?"

"Absolutely," Alex said.

He filled her in on Glove-gate and then told them both about Matt Gordon.

"Al told me this morning that he'd been cleared to play," Coach Archer said. "He said he had no idea if he was any good. I guess that question got answered."

"I just hope he calms down a little once he settles in," Alex said. "He wasn't Matt today."

"Give him some time," his mother said. "You didn't like Evan at first, either—remember?"

"That was different," Coach Archer said. "I *was* being a jerk. Gordon's a good kid who made a bad mistake. He'll be fine."

"I hope you're right," Alex said. "I hope you're right."

Alex's mom picked up her wineglass and pointed at the bottle of wine sitting on the kitchen island.

"Think you can pour me a glass without ruining another pair of pants?" she said to Coach Archer.

"I'll give it one hundred and ten percent effort," Coach Archer said, picking up the bottle.

As promised, Coach Birdy had posted lineups for the red and blue teams on the locker room wall by the time everyone began arriving for practice on Tuesday. Bailey Warner, Alex, and Johnny Ellis—the relief specialist—were listed as pitchers for the reds. Matt, Ethan Sattler, Don Warren, and Patton Gormley were on the blue team. Each was scheduled to throw forty pitches.

"I don't want any of the pitchers throwing too much," Coach Birdy explained when they gathered on the field. "It's still March, and it's cool. Plus, we've got a game on Friday, and I don't want Bailey throwing more than eighty pitches in the first game. Which probably means we'll need at least a couple of guys to come in behind him."

Bailey Warner was the number one returning pitcher, so he would start the opener. That made sense. Alex wondered who would start game two the following Tuesday.

For the scrimmage, Coach Birdy had the pitchers batting last in the rotation. Alex knew that wouldn't be the case when the real games began—especially when Matt was pitching. In the second inning, Warner was close to his allotted forty pitches when Matt came up with men on first and second and nobody out. None of Warner's first three pitches came close to the plate.

"Come on—give me something to hit!" Matt growled, stepping out of the batter's box.

Warner said nothing. He checked the runners and threw what looked to Alex like his best fastball, right down the middle. That was a mistake. Matt, batting righty because Warner was a lefty, turned on the pitch and hit a wicked line drive toward the left-center field gap. Alex figured it was going to drop in for a two-RBI double, but the ball kept rising.

And rising. It cleared the wall by about a foot as everyone stood and stared.

Jonas, who was playing center field for the reds, had raced into the gap as if he could make a play on the ball. He had no chance. Now he stood and watched as it sailed over the fence.

Matt jogged around the bases. He didn't showboat—just put his head down and circled the infield quickly. Warner watched him, hands on hips, saying nothing. Coach Birdy, who was umpiring behind the plate, turned to Alex as Matt touched home plate.

"You're in, Myers," he said. "Warner, that was forty-one pitches. Come on out."

"You couldn't have gotten me out at forty?" Bailey said as he walked in the direction of the dugout. Everyone laughed. At least, Alex thought, Bailey still had his sense of humor intact.

Alex was glad to face the top of the order to start his stint on the mound, if only because it meant he didn't have to pitch to Matt. Andy Hague was leading off for the blues, and happily for Alex, he swung at an outside fastball on the second pitch and grounded it weakly to second base. That helped quiet Alex's jitters. He struck out the next two batters and walked into the dugout feeling very pleased with himself.

He got a few pats on the back, but most of the talk was about Matt's home run off of Bailey.

"Did you see that?" Jonas asked, without even saying what "that" was.

"I was right here, Jonas," Alex answered. "It would've been hard to miss."

"Dude was wasting his time playing football," Jonas said, ignoring Alex's stab at sarcasm. "I mean . . ."

"Yeah," Alex said.

He was trying to think of something else to say when he heard Coach Birdy's voice: "Myers, you're on deck. Grab a bat."

Alex had forgotten he was due up second in the inning. Ethan Sattler had pitched the first two innings for the blues, but now it was Matt's turn on the mound. Alex watched from the on-deck circle while Brendan Chu, the starting right fielder, took a strike down the middle, then hit a weak ground ball right back to Matt, who quickly threw him out at first.

Alex stepped into the batter's box. He hadn't seen enough of Matt the previous day to really have a sense of how hard he threw—although the two fastballs he'd thrown Chu had whizzed in with plenty on them.

Alex dug in and waited for the first pitch. Matt came out of his windup and whipped a pitch that appeared to be headed right for Alex's chin.

He bailed out quickly, bat flying, only to hear Coach Birdy say from behind him, "Strike one." Matt had thrown a curveball that had broken right across the plate. As Alex got up, feeling a little embarrassed, Matt said loudly, "Never seen a curveball before, Myers?"

Alex had certainly never seen a curveball like that one before. Not very many Little League or junior high school pitchers threw breaking balls, and those who did had very little control of them. Matt's next pitch started at Alex's chin again. This time, he hung in and managed to tap a weak foul ball off the end of his bat. Strike two.

Alex stepped out for a moment to gather himself. He wondered if Matt would throw another curve or a fastball. He guessed fastball. Sure enough, the next pitch didn't start out at his chin but right down the middle of the plate. Alex swung his bat in a perfect arc to connect with the pitch as it crossed the plate, belt-high.

Only it didn't cross the plate, belt-high or anyplace else. Instead, it took a last-second dip, breaking out of the strike zone and away from his flailing bat. Alex twisted himself into a pretzel, hitting nothing but air.

"That's called a slider," Matt yelled as Alex slunk from the plate.

The only good news for Alex was that no one else on the reds could touch Matt, either.

They played six innings in all. Alex gave up a run in his second inning on a double by Jeff Cardillo, a stolen base, and a sacrifice fly. He might've been pleased with the way he'd pitched if not for feeling completely inadequate compared with Matt. After they were finished, Coach Birdy told them they'd play another intrasquad game the next day and then have a light practice Thursday.

As they all headed to the locker room, Matt came up to Alex. "Remember what I said about you being the number two starter behind me?" he said.

"Yeah," Alex said, ready to admit defeat.

"I was wrong," Matt said, surprising him. "Warner's better than you too. At best, you're number three. Better work on your hitting."

With that, he picked up his pace, leaving Alex in his wake—again.

■ ■ ■

Wednesday's practice went a lot like Tuesday's, and Coach Birdy told them he would post Friday's starting lineup the next day. Alex figured Bailey Warner would be the starting pitcher. Jonas was clearly the team's best outfielder. Matt would be in the lineup someplace, but where? Matt had told Coach Birdy his best nonpitching position was shortstop, but the team's captain—Cardillo—was the shortstop. Alex usually played the outfield when he wasn't pitching, so he was hoping he'd start in left field, if only because Billy Kellner couldn't hit at all, even though the only person on the team faster than Kellner—from what Alex had gleaned in three days—was Jonas.

When he and Jonas got to the locker room on Thursday, the lineup, as promised, was posted. Jonas was leading off and playing center field. Warner was hitting third and pitching. No surprises there. Matt was hitting cleanup and playing shortstop. *That* was a surprise. Cardillo, batting second, was playing third base.

"A little Jeter/A-Rod thing, I guess," Jonas said. "Except here the starter got moved, not the new guy."

When Alex Rodriguez was traded to the Yankees in 2004, they put him at third base, even though he'd been a Gold Glove shortstop in 2002 and 2003, for the simple reason that the Yankees weren't moving Derek Jeter. This time, Coach Birdy had done the opposite, moving the veteran in favor of the new arrival.

Alex looked at the rest of the lineup. Kellner was playing left field and batting ninth. He, Alex, wasn't starting. Reading his mind, Jonas patted him on the back. "Coach's just giving the senior the chance to start the opener," he said. "You'll start Tuesday. No doubt."

Alex wasn't so sure. He'd done okay during the two intrasquad games, but he hadn't overwhelmed anyone. If Matt was right and he was no better than the number three pitcher, he wouldn't get many chances to start. Since most of the regular season consisted of Tuesday and Friday games, having just two starters was enough for most teams. Offensively, he'd been okay, but—again—nothing special.

Alex understood that there were a lot of juniors and seniors on the team. They weren't stars—except for Cardillo, who seemed to get on base every time he came up and was a very good fielder—but they had experience. Alex had to remind himself he was a freshman. He hadn't even played a game yet. He had to be patient, the way he had been during football season.

"I guess I just have to wait my turn," he said to Jonas.

"It'll come soon," Jonas said. "I guarantee it."

■ ■ ■

Alex's turn came a lot sooner than he had thought it would. Bailey Warner struggled right from the start against Wilmington South. It was a chilly, breezy afternoon, and there couldn't have been more than a couple of hundred people sitting in the bleachers. Chester Heights' baseball field was formally called Roy Campanella Field, in honor of the Hall of Fame catcher, who had grown up in Philadelphia.

Alex wondered how Campanella would feel about the honor if he were still alive: There were bleachers that stretched from just outside third base to just outside first base and seats—benches—that, when full, might hold a thousand people. They were nowhere close to full when Coach Birdy turned to Alex as the top of the fourth inning began and told him to get loose.

The score at that point was 5–5. Both Warner and Wilmington South's starter had been knocked around early. The Statesmen had gotten three runs off Warner in the top of the first, but those runs had been answered quickly when Jonas and Cardillo both singled and, after Warner flied out to deep left, Matt crushed a home run over the right field fence in the first at-bat of his career. He had driven in two more runs with a double in the bottom of the third to tie the score again.

Alex jogged down the right field line with Coach Bloom, who caught for the pitchers when they warmed up during the game. He was nervous. For one thing, it had never occurred to him that Warner would get into so much trouble early. For another, the two intrasquad games had put doubt in his mind about his pitching.

It had never once occurred to him that he couldn't do the job at quarterback when he got the chance to play during football season. Maybe that was because Matt had put the name Goldie on him right away, or maybe it was because he could see how much better he threw the football than the other quarterbacks every day in practice.

In basketball, he'd known from the first day he practiced with the varsity that he was the team's best point guard. But this week had been different: He wasn't close to Matt Gordon as a pitcher or as a hitter, and he wasn't sure if he was even as good as Bailey Warner, who, at the moment, was having trouble getting anyone out.

That trend continued in the fourth. Warner walked the first two men he faced. He was tiring and afraid to throw strikes.

Coach Bloom stood up from his catching crouch. "You ready, Alex?" he asked.

"I guess so," Alex said, not exactly sure what "ready" meant.

Coach Bloom turned to the dugout and held his hand up

to indicate to Coach Birdy that Alex was warmed up. Coach Birdy started out of the dugout instantly. He walked over to the umpire for a moment, which confused Alex.

"He's double-switching," Coach Bloom explained. "You want to throw a couple more?"

Alex shook his head. He'd get five warm-up pitches when he got to the mound. That would be enough—he hoped.

Coach Birdy left the umpire and walked to the mound. He waved at Billy Kellner in left field and took the ball from Warner. Now Alex understood. Warner was a better hitter than Kellner, so he would move to left field and Kellner would come out. Coach Birdy waved his right arm at Alex.

"You're up," Coach Bloom said. "Go out there and have fun."

Yeah, sure—fun, Alex thought. He nodded, forced a smile, and jogged to the mound.

The good news for Alex was that he got through the fourth inning. The bad news was Chester Heights was down, 9–5, and his coach had been ejected from the game.

Coach Birdy had said very little to him when he arrived at the mound, simply handed him the ball, saying, "You gotta throw strikes. Don't walk the ballpark."

Alex knew what the phrase meant: Warner had walked, by Alex's count, five hitters—including the last two. That was a big part of why he was out of the game.

Alex did what he was told. His first pitch was a strike, a fastball down the middle. His second pitch was also a fastball down the middle. The Wilmington South hitter, a chunky righty, blasted it in the gap between Jonas and Warner. As fast as Jonas was, he had no chance to cut the ball off. It rolled to the wall for what would have been a triple if the batter had any speed. Instead, he jogged into second as two runs scored.

Matt had raced into the outfield to take the throw from Jonas after he ran the ball down. Seeing the runner wasn't going anywhere, Matt jogged to the mound, still holding the ball.

"This isn't Little League, Myers," he said, handing him the ball. "You have to pitch to the corners. You throw the ball down the middle like that, they're going to crush you."

"I know," Alex said. "Coach said to throw strikes. . . ."

"On the corners," Matt said, nodding. "Don't be afraid. Your stuff is good enough to get outs. But you have to make the batter work. Okay?"

Alex nodded. There was a little of the old Matt in the pep talk. He liked that.

He got the next two batters out, but working the corners against the cleanup hitter, he walked him on a 3–2 pitch. Alex thought the pitch was a strike.

"Where was that, Ump?" he asked, walking to the front of the mound.

"High," the ump answered.

"High?" Alex replied. "The guy's, like, six four. How could that pitch be high?"

The ump walked out from behind the plate and pointed a finger at Alex. "If you want to be an umpire, son, go train for it. If you want to be a pitcher, get back on the mound and shut up."

Out of the corner of his eye, Alex saw Coach Birdy starting from the dugout. He put up a hand to indicate he was okay, turned his back on the ump, and went back to the mound. He was steaming. The pitch had been a strike.

He was still angry when he threw his next pitch, and it

cost him. Not focused, he threw a fastball down the middle. As soon as he released the pitch, Alex knew he had messed up. Sure enough, the batter turned the pitch around so fast that all Alex saw was Warner turning his back in left field to watch it fly over the fence.

That made it 9–5. As the guy jogged the bases, Alex really wanted to scream at the umpire. Before he could make that mistake, Coach Birdy—perhaps reading his mind—arrived at the mound.

"You can't let one bad call distract you like that, Alex," he said. "You know that. It's no different from basketball. Umpires make mistakes. You have to let it go."

"But, Coach, I was out of the inning. . . ."

"I know," Coach Birdy said. "Doesn't matter."

Alex nodded. Coach Birdy turned to leave. As he did, though, he pointed a finger at the umpire. "At least admit you missed it," he said. He wasn't shouting, but in the emptiness of the ballpark, everyone could hear him.

The umpire took off his mask and walked toward Coach Birdy. "You too?" he said. "I'll take it off the kid because he's emotionally wound up. Not you."

Coach Birdy had been walking in the direction of the dugout. Now he stopped and turned to meet the approaching umpire.

"You missed it," Coach Birdy repeated. "You think you're umpiring high school games because you're a great umpire?"

"You think you're coaching high school games because you're a great coach?"

Coach Birdy smiled. "No, I'm coaching high school games because I'm a history teacher and I like baseball."

The two men were now nose to nose. Alex wondered if he should intervene, then thought better of it.

"Well, you'd better find another game to watch today," the ump said, "because you are *out* of this one." He gave the ejection sign, arcing his right arm into the air and pointing at the sky. Coach Birdy, who had always been the calming voice in the basketball locker room, completely lost his temper for a moment.

"Are you kidding me?" he said, now right in the ump's face. "You're throwing me out because I stood up for one of my kids after you blew a call? The game's about the kids, pal, not about you and your overblown ego!"

Alex didn't hear the ump's response because Coach Bloom had raced from the dugout to pull his boss away. Alex ran in while Coach Bloom stood between them and the umpire just in case Coach Birdy decided to make another charge.

"You'd better get him out of here!" the ump was yelling at Coach Bloom. "One more word and I promise I'll recommend a suspension in my report!"

Matt was on the scene now, having charged in from shortstop when the argument started to get out of control.

"Go back to the mound," he told Alex. "Don't say another word to this guy."

The ump looked at Matt for a moment, as if expecting him to argue too, but Matt just put his arm around Alex and walked him back to the mound.

Coach Bloom got Coach Birdy off the field. As Coach Birdy left, heading, Alex figured, for the locker room, the ump walked behind the plate, put his mask back on, and pointed at Alex.

"Play ball," he said.

That, thought Alex, *is what we're all trying to do*.

■ ■ ■

Alex got out of the inning with no further damage, but by then it was too late. Given a four-run cushion, Wilmington South's starter got his second wind. Matt crushed another home run, a two-run shot in the sixth to make it 9–7, but Johnny Ellis, who relieved Alex in the seventh, gave up an additional run, and the final score was 10–7. Alex went to left field for the seventh to replace Warner, but the game ended in the bottom of the inning with him in the on-deck circle when Oliver Flick popped to second for the last out.

As the players began to line up for the postgame handshake, Alex was tempted to run over and say something more to the home plate umpire. He decided against it. There was a good possibility the guy would work more of their games before the season was over.

In the handshake line, Alex came face to face with the cleanup hitter. "Dre Byers," he said as they shook hands. "Between you and me, that was strike three back in the fourth."

Alex wasn't sure what to say. He settled for "Alex Myers" and "Thanks for saying that."

"We've had that guy in the past," Byers said. "He's not very good, and he's got a temper."

"Nice combination in an umpire," Alex said.

Byers laughed. "No kidding. Good luck the rest of the season."

"You too," Alex said.

He couldn't help but sigh. In football, he'd gotten knocked

cold in the season opener. In basketball, he'd made a play that led to his coach getting ejected in his first game. And now, in baseball, he'd been in the middle of *another* dustup that led to his coach getting ejected.

Jonas walked up behind him. "If I ever coach and you have a son, do me a favor and tell him to play a different sport," he said.

"You're always here for me, aren't you?" Alex said.

"Someone's got to do it," Jonas said. "You keep getting your coaches kicked out of games."

He was clearly pleased with himself for his humor. Before Alex could respond, he saw Christine Whitford and Steve Garland, the sports editor of the *Weekly Roar*, approaching. Except that Christine, after giving him a quick wave, peeled away to talk to Matt, leaving Alex with Garland.

"Have you given any thought to just showing up for the third game of each season?" Garland said.

"You too?" Alex asked. "Is it my fault the ump missed strike three? The kid I threw the pitch to just told me it was a strike. How is that my fault?"

"Little uptight, Alex?" Garland asked.

"Yeah," Alex admitted. "Just a little."

■ ■ ■

Steve Garland was a good guy, a good reporter, and a good writer. During football season, he had been the one person in the school willing to call Coach Gordon out for running up scores, for being a bully, and for taking credit for plays he hadn't called.

He asked Alex to walk through what had happened,

which Alex did, including what Dre Byers had said to him a few minutes earlier.

"Were you surprised that Coach Birdy got so upset?" Garland asked. "He's not exactly what you'd call a hothead."

Garland was right about that. "You should probably ask him what happened," Alex said. "But yeah, I was a little surprised." He paused for a second. "But Coach didn't say anything except 'Just admit you missed it.' It was the ump who amped up the whole thing. *He* was the hothead."

"You didn't recognize him?" Garland asked.

"Recognize him?"

Garland nodded. "Remember when the basketball team played at Mercer back in December? He was the ref who tossed Coach Archer."

Alex gasped. Garland was right. It hadn't even occurred to him that a basketball ref would umpire baseball, but then again, why wouldn't he?

"Wow" was all he could think to say.

"You think he had it in for you guys?"

Alex thought that one over for a minute. He knew where Garland was going, and he also knew he should be careful here. "I'm not sure," he finally said. "Anyone can miss a call. The guy *does* have a temper. But we didn't lose because of him. We lost because we played lousy."

"Except for Gordon," Garland said.

Matt had been three-for-three, with two homers, a double, and a walk, and had driven in all seven Chester Heights runs.

"Yeah," Alex said, glancing to his right, where Christine

and several other reporters were talking to Matt. "Except for Matt."

"Did you know he was this good a baseball player?" Garland asked.

"I had no idea," Alex said. "He told me during the winter that he was good, but I didn't expect this."

"Coach Birdy says Matt's pitching on Tuesday. Can he pitch like he hits?"

Alex thought about that for a minute also. "He might be a better pitcher than he is a hitter."

Garland looked closely at him, as if deciding whether Alex was serious.

"Really?" he said.

"Really," Alex answered.

"If that's the case," Garland said, "you're going to have a lot of pro scouts showing up pretty soon."

Alex looked again in the direction of Matt and the reporters. They were gone—except for Christine. She and Matt were still talking. And she had put her notebook away.

"You're overreacting."

"Am I? What were the two of you talking about when I walked over yesterday?"

Christine Whitford frowned at Alex. "Nothing."

"Then why did you both get so quiet when you saw me coming?"

Christine sat back in the booth. It was noon on Saturday, and they were having lunch at Stark's, their favorite hamburger place. Alex hadn't meant to sound accusatory when he asked Christine about her interview/conversation with Matt. But he suspected it was coming off that way.

"We didn't 'get quiet,'" she said. "You're paranoid."

"You sure? He didn't ask you out?"

She glared at him for a second—a look he'd seen before. It told him he'd said something he shouldn't have.

"No, he did not ask me out," she said. "He knows you and I are going out, and he's your friend. And wasn't he the one who told you last fall to ask me out?"

That was true. Alex had been nervous about asking Christine out, and Matt had pushed him in the right direction. What she probably didn't know was *how* he had pushed: "If you don't ask her to the dance, I will," Matt had said.

"Yes, he did," he finally said. "But that was a different Matt."

Her eyes narrowed. "What do you mean?"

Alex sat back. In truth, beyond wanting to see her, this was the reason he'd asked her to meet him for lunch. Normally, he might have included Jonas and Max Bellotti and perhaps even Matt.

But he wanted to talk *about* Matt, so it was just the two of them.

"He's changed since the fall," Alex said. "He even said to me that he feels different because the whole PED thing knocked him off his pedestal. He wants everyone to know that he's the best baseball player in the history of Chester Heights."

She smiled—which made him happy, because it showed she wasn't mad at him anymore, and because she had one of the world's greatest smiles.

"I don't know much about Chester Heights' history in baseball, but from the little I've seen, he might be close."

Alex grunted. "And you haven't seen him pitch yet."

She took a long sip from the vanilla milk shake she had ordered. "So I've heard," she said. "Okay, he wants everyone to understand he's a great baseball player—that he might be better at baseball than football. What's wrong with that? How does that mean he's changed? He doesn't seem different to me."

Alex thought for a moment. Everything she was saying made sense. It wasn't as if Matt had turned into some kind of a jerk overnight. It was more subtle than that, something he felt in his gut but couldn't articulate.

"I'm sure he's the same with you," he said.

"So . . ."

"So . . . you're not a better quarterback than he is."

He said it without thinking. She gave him a look that told him she thought he was out of his mind. But he wasn't.

And then, on Monday afternoon, the old Matt Gordon showed up for practice.

He and Alex were waiting their turn to throw on the side when Matt said, "Goldie, you know how to throw anything but a fastball?"

Alex thought another put-down was coming, so his answer was defensive. "I can throw a curve," he said.

Matt nodded. "I saw. You throw that kids' curve, with your index finger up in the air. Dead giveaway, especially to good hitters at this level."

Alex's dad had shown him how to throw a curve when he started Little League, admonishing him to use it only when he really needed it because throwing too many curves could put strain on a young arm.

"How else do you throw it?" Alex asked.

"Here, let me show you," Matt said.

He had the baseball he was going to throw when his turn came.

"Instead of holding your index finger out like you're pointing at something, just rest it next to your middle finger. You're still going to use the middle finger to push the ball out of your hand—that's what gives the pitch its break. But the batter won't see the finger sticking up and won't be looking curve. Just try a few when it's your turn."

Which it was a minute later. Alex was throwing to Lucas Mann, the starting catcher. He started with some fastballs and then said, "I'm going to try a few curves."

"Try away," Mann said.

Alex carefully gripped the ball the way Matt had shown him. The first two that he threw came nowhere near home plate. Matt, throwing next to him, apparently noticed what was going on.

"You're gripping it too tight," he said, pausing in between pitches. "Remember the old baseball saying 'Try easier.'"

Right, Alex thought. *Try easier.* He loosened his grip and snapped his arm ever so slightly as he released the next pitch. It arced across the plate, right where the batter's knees would have been.

"Great pitch!" Mann yelled. "Do it again."

Alex did. He threw a dozen in all, not wanting to push his arm too hard, and eight of the last ten were pretty close to perfect.

When they were done, Mann took off his mask and pointed at Matt. "If the pitching thing doesn't work out, Gordon, you can be the pitching coach," he said.

Everyone—including Coach Bloom, who was catching Matt—laughed.

It felt like old times.

■ ■ ■

Tuesday afternoon's game was against Mercer, and as Alex warmed up with Jonas before the game, he noticed that the stands were a lot fuller than they had been the previous Friday. Mercer had brought several busloads of students from their campus in central Pennsylvania, so that was part of it. The basketball team had played at Mercer in December, and Alex vividly remembered riding through the Mercer campus and thinking they had taken a wrong turn and arrived at a small, elite, big-money college.

But that didn't account for the whole crowd. Word had gotten around school about how good a player Matt Gordon was, and since he was pitching, the Chester Heights student turnout was high. And then there were the men in sports jackets and open-collared shirts sitting directly behind home plate.

When Coach Birdy called them into the dugout, Alex pointed with his glove in the direction of the men and whispered to Jonas, "What do you think—college scouts?"

Jonas turned and looked briefly. "Nah," he said. "Matt's just a junior. Why would they be here when he's got another year of high school?"

"Happens in basketball all the time," Alex countered.

"Too soon for people to know anything," Jonas said. "He's only played one game."

"Then who are they?"

Before Jonas could answer, Coach Birdy was calling for their attention.

"You've all seen the lineup," he said. "Depending on how the game goes, I'll try to sub more than I did on Friday. We're giving some different guys a start today. That doesn't mean the rest of you won't be playing. So stay ready."

Alex was one of those different guys, starting in left field ahead of Billy Kellner. He was hitting fifth, right behind Matt. Patton Gormley would be the first man up in the bullpen if Matt got into trouble.

If Alex had any doubts about the men being scouts, they went away when Matt threw his first pitch. Even from left field, Alex could see a half dozen radar guns pointing at Matt as he went into his pitching motion. A radar gun was a scout's calling card. Alex knew this from watching games on TV and from baseball movies—most notably *Trouble with the Curve*. His dad called it a Clint Eastwood movie. To Alex, it was more of an Amy Adams movie. But that was beside the point.

Matt's first pitch whistled in so hard that Alex could hear Lucas Mann's glove pop. The crowd oohed at the sound. Two pitches later, Mercer's leadoff man slunk back to the bench, having not come close to making contact.

The second guy went down in much the same fashion.

Mercer's third hitter, Dave Krenchek, was a friend of Alex's—sort of. In the opening game of the football season, Alex had been sent in to kneel down and kill the clock in the final minute, with Chester Heights leading Mercer, 77–0.

Krenchek had been unhappy—justifiably—with the way that Coach Gordon had run up the score, and he took it out on Alex, knocking him cold.

Krenchek had apologized instantly and had called the next day to make sure Alex was okay. The two had struck up something of a long-distance friendship. Krenchek, it turned out, was a very good basketball player and had played a key role in Mercer's early-season win over Chester Heights in hoops. Since he was batting third, Alex figured he was one of Mercer's best hitters.

And he did have the best at-bat of the inning—he managed to foul off two pitches before striking out. In all, it took Matt eleven pitches to get through the first inning. The Lions fans in the bleachers roared.

■ ■ ■

Mike Albers, who was pitching for Mercer, was almost as good as Matt. He matched zeroes with him for five innings—not overpowering people the way Matt was, but keeping the Chester Heights hitters off balance with a variety of breaking pitches. Alex was as baffled as anyone and struck out twice.

Matt walked one Mercer hitter—Krenchek, in the top of the fourth—but had not allowed a hit through six innings. Albers had given up two hits—a screaming line drive by Matt in the second that went for a double and a bunt single to Jeff Cardillo in the fourth. He had also walked Matt twice, not wanting to throw anything near the plate after his hit in the second inning.

Alex led off in the bottom of the sixth. Coach Birdy had been telling everyone to take at least one pitch from Albers.

"Almost all of his pitches break out of the strike zone," he had said. "Make him throw you a strike before you swing."

Alex did as he was told, and sure enough, what looked like a slider broke low and away at the last possible second for ball one. Albers threw the same pitch again, and Alex took it for ball two. Alex stepped out of the box to look down at Coach Birdy, who was coaching at third base. Coach Birdy went through a series of motions, touching his uniform, his cap, and his face—all of which meant nothing until he pulled on his left ear. That meant the next movement he made was the sign Alex was to pay attention to.

Alex was surprised when Coach Birdy tipped his cap. That was the "hit away" sign. He had expected to be told to take at least one more pitch.

He nodded, then stepped back into the box, thinking, *He's expecting Albers to throw a fastball at 2–0. That's why he's telling me to swing away.*

And on cue, Albers threw a fastball on the outside edge of the plate. Alex was smart enough to not try to turn on it— Albers didn't throw as hard as Matt, but he threw hard—so he took the ball to the opposite field. He didn't hit the ball hard, but his soft line drive sliced over the first baseman's head and landed a couple of feet fair as the right fielder scrambled to get to it.

Alex was thinking double the moment he saw the flight of the ball and bolted from the batter's box. His number one asset as an athlete was his golden arm. But his number two asset was his speed. He was around first base before the right fielder got to the ball and easily beat the throw into second.

The Chester Heights fans, who had done most of their

cheering when Matt was striking people out, were on their feet. They suspected—as did Alex—that one run would be enough.

Alex looked at Coach Birdy to see what sign he was sending to Brendan Chu and to him. Not surprisingly, he wanted a bunt to get Alex to third. Mercer, naturally, was expecting the same thing, and the third and first basemen began creeping in as Albers came to the set position. Albers's first pitch was high and inside—a pitch that was almost impossible to bunt. Chu hit the dirt, but as he went down, the ball hit his bat and dribbled in front of the plate.

It was, unintentionally, a perfect bunt. Alex took off for third. By the time Albers realized what had happened, all he could do was pick the ball up and toss it to Krenchek at first to retire Chu—who was still lying on his back.

"Great bunt, Brendan!" Alex yelled, standing on third. "That'll teach 'em not to brush you back!"

Albers was standing on the mound, hands on hips. He turned and looked at Alex. "You get a bloop hit and you think you're the next David Ortiz?" he said.

"I think I'm on third base," Alex answered.

Before Albers could respond, his coach jogged to the mound—no doubt to calm him down. Coach Birdy grabbed Alex by the elbow while time was out. "No more talk," he said. "Be ready to take off on a ground ball or to tag up on a fly ball."

Lucas Mann, the catcher, was up. He had looked helpless in both of his previous at-bats. This one was no different. Albers didn't even bother with a breaking pitch, blowing Mann away with three straight fastballs. That left it up to Jonas.

"Be ready," Coach Birdy said quietly.

He turned and began sending a signal to Jonas. Alex understood what he had been saying. He wanted Jonas to take the first pitch, then bunt. Given Jonas's speed, if he got the ball down at all, he would be a tough out at first base. He had tried a bunt in the third but had put too much on the ball, sending it right back to Albers. Even then, he'd only been out by a step.

Albers seemed to want to throw fastballs now. His first pitch was down the middle for strike one. Alex wondered if that would change the strategy. Jonas, wondering too, stepped out and looked at Coach Birdy, who simply stared back at him. No change.

Alex figured Albers would throw a breaking pitch, since he was ahead in the count. He did, a vicious slider that broke down and away. But Jonas had anticipated it and was leaning down and across the plate with his bat. He was able to push the ball down the first base line, between Krenchek and Albers.

Alex raced for home plate.

Krenchek had to come in to field the ball, which left first base uncovered. Alex knew Krenchek's only play was to try to get him out at home.

Krenchek's throw and Alex arrived at the same moment. The catcher's left leg was pulled back to keep Alex from hooking a toe onto the back of the plate, but Alex spied a gap—between the catcher's legs. He slid and felt the catcher's glove, with the ball in it, hit his leg at the exact moment his foot touched the plate.

"Safe!" the umpire yelled.

"*What?*" the catcher screamed. He jumped up and began yelling at the umpire as Albers and the coach charged at him too. Alex was starting to get up when Albers pushed him out of the way.

"Hey!" he yelled at Albers. The two began pushing and shoving each other while both dugouts emptied—either to separate Alex and Albers or to look for a dance partner of their own.

Alex and Albers were so tangled up neither could even think to throw a punch.

"Hey, man, nothing personal. I was trying to get to the ump," Albers said, relaxing his hold.

Alex backed off too. "Gotcha. No sweat," he said.

He meant it. The score was 1–0, Chester Heights. That was all that mattered.

Remarkably, no one from either team was ejected after the skirmish, and the umpire didn't toss anyone from Mercer for arguing the play at the plate. Apparently he had a lot less ego than the guy who had worked the Wilmington South game.

Alex kind of wished someone had gotten tossed, because Albers regained his cool and got the last out to end the inning.

Matt went out for the seventh to try to finish off the win—and nail down his no-hitter.

Krenchek led off and, after working the count full, managed to hit a looping fly ball to shallow left. Alex had been playing deep, thinking that if Krenchek did connect with one of Matt's fastballs, his size and strength, combined with the heat on the pitch, would drive the ball a long way.

But Krenchek's bat hadn't hit the ball cleanly, and after

looking as if it might really take off, the ball began to die. Alex froze for a split second, not sure whether to break back or in. When he realized the ball wasn't going very far, he sprinted in and dove, his body horizontal to the ground, glove extended as far as he could reach. For a moment, he thought he was going to catch it, but the ball hit the tip of his glove and rolled away. He knew at that instant that Matt's no-hitter was gone, and he wanted to pound the ground in frustration. Instead, he scrambled to his feet, picked the ball up, and got it back to the infield quickly enough to force Krenchek to put on the brakes and retreat to first base.

Alex was upset he hadn't made the catch but consoled by the fact that he'd held Krenchek to a single. He looked in at Matt, who was standing to the side of the mound, hands on hips, clearly not happy. He started to shout *Sorry, Matt*, but stopped himself. For one thing, he'd done everything possible to make the play. For another, they still had three outs to get.

Coach Birdy, understanding that his pitcher might need a minute after having lost the no-hitter, trotted to the mound and put his arm around Matt. Alex could see Matt nodding, and then Coach Birdy went back to the dugout.

Matt's first pitch to Mercer's cleanup hitter went straight to the backstop. Krenchek took second on the wild pitch. Obviously, Matt was a little rattled. Alex wondered if Coach Birdy would come back to the mound. If he did, he would have to change pitchers. Matt walked around the mound in a circle, as if gathering himself. Watching him, Alex thought back to football season, when it seemed as if nothing rattled Matt.

His next pitch rode inside and hit the Mercer batter squarely on the arm as he tried to dive out of the way. He was up quickly and jogged to first. This time, Coach Birdy did come out of the dugout. Alex saw Matt wave him back, but it was too late. Alex was trying to imagine the conversation—Matt was extremely agitated—when he saw Coach Birdy signal in his direction.

Alex was surprised. Johnny Ellis was the relief specialist. And Patton Gormley had been an option to pitch in this game too. But Coach Birdy wanted him, so he trotted to the mound and saw Kellner running out to left field to take his spot. Matt was waiting, the ball still in his hand. He glared at Alex as he handed him the ball. "Don't screw this up," he said—and left the mound to a standing ovation from the crowd.

Coach Birdy and Lucas Mann were on the mound. "You okay?" Coach Birdy asked Alex, who was still a little bit in shock from Matt's tone.

"Fine," Alex said.

The home plate umpire was approaching. "Come on, Coach, let's get this done before dark," he said.

"Work the corners," Coach Birdy said to Alex. "You don't have to throw your fastball a hundred. Just throw to Mann's glove."

Alex nodded.

"Play for a bunt," he added. "That's the right move for them."

He was correct, of course. A good bunt would move both runners into scoring position with one out.

Alex recognized the first hitter he faced as another basketball player—Mercer's point guard, Tom O'Toole. Smartly,

O'Toole took the first pitch, then bunted the next pitch perfectly, forcing Alex to field it near the first base line. Alex got the out at first, and the runners advanced.

Coach Birdy came a step out of the dugout and held up four fingers, indicating he wanted Alex to walk the next hitter intentionally to load the bases. That would set up a force play at home or a potential game-ending double play on a ground ball.

Alex threw four pitches outside and then faced the number seven hitter in the order, a left-handed batter whom Matt had blown away with fastballs in his first two at-bats. Alex worked him carefully, knowing that a single would probably drive in two runs. But at two balls and two strikes, he got antsy. He didn't want to put himself one pitch away from walking in the tying run, so he knew he had to throw a fastball and make sure it was over the plate.

He threw a good pitch, in the strike zone, but down near the knees. He got exactly what he was hoping for, a one-hop ground ball right up the middle. He reached for the ball, gloved it, and started to come home for a force play at the plate on Krenchek. But he could see that Krenchek had somehow gotten a great jump from third—probably because Alex hadn't been paying enough attention to him—and was now bearing down on Mann. They could get the out there, but there would be no chance for a double play.

He made a split-second decision and turned and saw he had plenty of time to get the runner at second. Cardillo was charging toward the bag to take the throw. Alex threw the ball right at the bag, fully expecting Cardillo to flash across it, glove the throw, and then throw to first to end the game.

Cardillo got there, but for some reason, so did Oliver Flick, the second baseman. One of the cardinal rules of baseball was that the shortstop always took a throw from the pitcher in a double-play situation because he'd be going toward first base, whereas the second baseman would be going away from it. The play was much easier for the shortstop.

And yet there was Flick, cutting in front of Cardillo to try to take the throw. The two collided and the ball ticked off Flick's glove and rolled into center field. Jonas hadn't thought for a second that the play was going to be messed up and was standing frozen to the spot. Krenchek had already scored, and so had the runner from second. By the time Jonas realized what had happened and gotten to the ball, the runner who should have been forced at second was on his feet and was all the way around third. Panicked, Jonas uncorked a throw that was about ten feet over Mann's head and ten feet to his right. The third runner scored standing up, and since the hitter had already rounded second while the fielding follies were playing out, he was awarded third and an extra base since Jonas's wild throw had gone into the stands.

Instead of a double play to end the game, Mercer had scored *four* runs on a one-hop ground ball to the mound. Their fans celebrated wildly while everyone from Chester Heights stood wondering what in the world had just happened.

Alex was standing on the mound in complete shock too when Coach Birdy arrived. "This isn't your fault," he said. "But I'm going to get Ellis in here."

Instinctively, Alex turned to head back to left field. "Let Kellner finish there," Coach Birdy said softly.

Alex understood. He was done for the day.

So was his team. Ellis got the last two outs, but Albers, given a second chance he never expected, retired the Lions one, two, three in the bottom of the seventh. Final score: Mercer 4, Chester Heights 1.

As they went through the handshake line, Krenchek found Alex. He put his arm around him and said, "We were lucky. You missed making that catch on my ball by an inch."

Alex couldn't think of a response. Krenchek continued for another moment. "I was surprised I even made contact. Boy, is Gordon good." He paused and squinted. "Hey, where is he?"

Alex had been near the front of the line. Now he turned to look at his teammates, who were lined up behind him. Matt Gordon was nowhere in sight.

■ ■ ■

As soon as Alex had shaken the last Mercer hand, he saw Christine standing by the dugout. Kim Gagne, who had covered the football team in the fall, was talking to Coach Birdy a few feet away from Christine. Alex was surprised that Christine and Kim were the only media members in sight. He'd noticed some TV cameras during the game.

"Are you guys the only ones here?" Alex asked, gesturing in Kim's direction as he walked up to Christine.

"We're the only ones still *here*," she said. "Everyone else went after Matt."

"Where did he go?" Alex asked.

Christine pointed at the school building. "The locker room. As soon as the last out was made, he took off."

"I guess he was upset," Alex said.

"Ya think?" Christine said, giving him her now-familiar "too stupid to live" look.

For once, it bothered Alex. "Look, I don't really care how upset he was," he said. "You stick around for the handshakes. He'd have led the parade if he'd pitched the no-hitter or even if we'd won the game. You can't have it both ways."

"It wasn't exactly a routine loss, though, was it?" Christine said. "If you hadn't frozen on Krenchek's fly ball, he might have had the win *and* the no-hitter."

Alex had to give Christine credit for understanding the subtleties of the game. But the implication that *he* had somehow cost Matt the no-hitter and his team the game stung.

"Look, the ball was right at me, and it was one of those shots that looks like it's well-hit off the bat and then dies," he said.

"I'm not blaming you," she said.

"Yes, you are," he said. "And I'm sure Matt is too. Which isn't fair."

"How about the double-play ball that turned into Keystone Kops?"

"That was *not* my fault. Did you ask Oliver about it?"

She shook her head. "He took off too. Steve will try to talk to him after he's talked to Matt—if Matt's talking to anyone."

"I'm surprised they didn't send you," Alex said. "I'm sure he would have talked to you."

Christine narrowed her eyes for a second, then took a notebook out of her pocket.

"I need a quote from you on Krenchek's hit and on the blown double play," she said. "And I haven't got time for your sexist cracks. We're getting our stories in for tomorrow's *Roar*. They pushed the deadline back, but I've only got until seven."

Alex figured it had to be close to six now.

"Can you write that fast?" he asked.

"If you stop stalling, I can," she said.

He sighed and mumbled something about it only being the second game and how they still had some fielding kinks to work out. But Matt had been a star, blah, blah, blah. It had been a long afternoon.

Most of the guys were showering by the time Alex got back to the locker room. Jonas was already out of the shower and putting his clothes on.

"You okay?" Jonas asked.

"Christine acted like I blew the game," Alex said. He looked around. "Where's Matt? In the shower? I want to talk to him."

Jonas shook his head. "You aren't going to talk to him now. He talked to all the media guys, came in here, changed, and bolted. Didn't even shower."

"What'd he say to the media?"

Another head shake. "No idea. I didn't stop to listen. I *did* hear someone say that the scouts had him at ninety-four on the radar gun."

An average major league fastball came in at somewhere

between 90 and 92 miles per hour. The hardest throwers could hit 96 or 97 consistently, but there weren't too many of those. The Mets' Matt Harvey and the Nationals' Stephen Strasburg had been in the 98-to-99 range before each had hurt his elbow and been forced to have Tommy John surgery. Great finesse pitchers—Alex's favorite was Tom Glavine because he was from Billerica, the same Boston suburb where Alex had grown up—could get away with throwing 85 to 87.

For a high school junior to throw a fastball at 94 miles per hour was extraordinary.

"Did they say he was hitting ninety-four consistently or just on one pitch?" Alex asked.

"No idea. I just heard somebody say 'The kid hit ninety-four' as I was walking by."

Alex sat down heavily on the bench in front of his locker. He saw Oliver Flick approaching, a towel around his waist.

"Myers, I'm really sorry," he said. "I thought Jeff was deep in the hole and couldn't get to the base for the force." He shook his head. "I really blew it. You had the game won, and I screwed it up."

"No worries, Oliver," Alex said. "I know you didn't do it on purpose. We all make mistakes. I probably should have caught Krenchek's shot to start the inning. If I'd had that one, none of the rest of it happens."

Flick, who was a senior, put out his hand, which Alex shook.

"You're a class act, Goldie," he said. "I wish I could say the same for your pal the user."

That, Alex thought, *is a cheap shot.* He gave Flick a look and said, "What are you talking about?"

Flick shrugged. "Ask the other guys. Soon as he came in here, he pushed me up against the wall and started asking me if I'd ever played baseball before and what the eff was I thinking. I tried to explain, but he just stormed off."

Cardillo, who had also just come out of the shower, patted Flick on the shoulder. "I'll talk to him, Oliver," he said. "I'm the captain. I'll smooth this out."

"Let me do it," Alex said. "We're friends—I'll do it."

Cardillo raised an eyebrow. "You sure?" he said. "Probably won't be an easy conversation."

"I'm sure," Alex said. "I'm very sure."

He had a lot he wanted to talk to Matt Gordon about.

■ ■ ■

Alex thought about calling Matt that night but figured the next day—in person—would be better. Plus, it would give Matt some time to cool down. It wasn't like him to behave the way he had with Flick, and Alex wondered if something else was going on. He knew that things had been tense at home after football season, but he'd seemed okay during basketball season. Of course, Matt didn't play basketball.

Because Matt was a junior and Alex was a freshman, they didn't have any classes together. So as soon as the bell rang to end fourth period, Alex bolted from his history class and headed straight for the cafeteria. He didn't even pause to put his books in his locker.

He was standing just inside the doorway when Matt came

in, walking with Christine. That didn't thrill Alex, but he didn't have time to worry about it.

"Matt, got a minute?" Alex asked, hoping he sounded casual.

Matt was surprised to see him standing there. Normally, they all gathered at their table in the corner.

"Now?" he asked. "I'm kinda hungry, Goldie."

Alex was glad to hear Matt use his football nickname. It seemed like a good sign.

"It'll take five minutes, max," Alex said. "Need to ask you something."

Matt shrugged. Christine's eyes were narrowed in her "What's going on?" look, but she said nothing. "Meet you at the table," Matt said to Christine, and he walked back into the hallway.

The two of them were like salmon swimming upstream, with the rest of the school going into the massive cafeteria. Matt led the way to an empty classroom.

"This okay?" he said.

Alex nodded, and they walked inside. Matt leaned against the teacher's desk, and Alex stood awkwardly a few feet away.

Matt folded his arms and looked at Alex expectantly. "You have the floor," he finally said.

Alex took a deep breath. He hadn't really thought about where he wanted to start. He remembered something his dad had told him about the tactics he used when cross-examining a witness in court: "Start with the easy stuff. Make the witness comfortable."

So he started with the easy stuff. "Listen, I'm sorry I didn't get to that ball yesterday," he said. "I just didn't break on it fast enough. . . ."

Matt held up a hand. "Don't give it a second thought, Goldie," he said. "If there's one thing I know about you, it's that you always give a hundred percent. I was just a little hot about losing the no-hitter. I know you tried. It's not your fault that you aren't much of an outfielder."

Whoa! Alex had been thinking the old Matt was back . . . until the last line.

"Not much of an outfielder?"

Matt shrugged. "Remember when I told you last fall you were a great quarterback?" he said. "I was telling you the truth. I'm telling you the truth now. Your legs are fast, but you don't read the plays quick enough. That's what happened on that play. You broke wrong for a split second. I'm going to suggest to Coach that he move you to first. We need your bat in the lineup."

"First base? What about Andy Hague?"

Matt shrugged. "He can DH sometimes. You think he's Mark Teixeira or something?"

"No, but . . ."

"Anything else?" Matt said, looking at his watch.

Alex had gotten sidetracked. And a little bit upset.

"Yeah," he said. "Flick—"

"Already taken care of," Matt said. "Saw him this morning. He explained what happened. I accepted his apology."

Now Alex was *very* upset.

"*You* accepted *his* apology?" he said. "Did you apologize to him for slamming him into a locker and humiliating him in front of the team?"

Matt abandoned the casual, arms-folded, leaning-against-the-desk stance. He walked right over to where Alex was standing. He wasn't that much taller than Alex—about six three to Alex's six one—but he outweighed him by a good thirty pounds.

"What are you trying to say, Myers?" he said, his voice low but menacing. Alex couldn't remember Matt ever calling him Myers, except on the field.

"You're not the only one who lost that game," Alex said. "And I'm confused. You're the best teammate and leader I've ever been around in my life. At least, you were during football season. But now you're different. The Matt Gordon I knew last fall would have gone after anyone who treated a teammate like you treated Oliver. Now you're upset with *me* for asking what's going on?"

Matt took a step back. Then he paced around the room.

"I'm sorry," he finally said. "You're right. Look, you can't understand what it's been like to be me the last few months. I know that's not an excuse, but . . ." He held up a hand as Alex started to say something. "I know what you're going to say, and you're right: I did it to myself."

He had read Alex's mind.

"The thing you don't understand is that makes it *worse*. If I'd gotten hurt, I could just say I was unlucky. If I'd gotten benched unfairly or . . ." He paused and smiled ruefully. "If someone had framed me for taking PEDs when I hadn't—well, then I could look in the mirror and say I got a raw deal.

"But I can't do that. I look in the mirror and say, 'How could you be so stupid?' There's no way for you to know how that feels, Alex, because you've never done anything that stupid—and you probably never will.

"Like I said, I'm not telling you that's an excuse. I'll find Oliver before practice and apologize. And I apologize to you for saying you aren't much of a left fielder. You're perfectly fine out there. You're just a little bit inexperienced—which is understandable. You're only a freshman."

He wound down and sighed. "If I go off the rails again, you'll call me on it, okay?" He put his hand out.

Alex felt as if a massive amount of tension had just been drained from his body. *This* was the Matt Gordon he knew.

"Deal," he said, accepting the handshake.

Matt clapped Alex on the back.

"Can we please go eat now?" he said. "I'm starving."

■ ■ ■

Matt was as good as his word. Alex saw him pull Oliver Flick aside as they were walking from the locker room to the field that afternoon. He had an arm around him, the way he had often put his arm around Alex during football season.

"So," Jonas said. "I guess your talk with Matt went well?"

"I think so," Alex said, smiling.

"Good work," Jonas said. "Wouldn't it be nice to get through a season without becoming some kind of a media circus?"

Alex laughed. Jonas was right. Chester Heights had received national attention during football season because of the whole PED scandal. Then, during basketball season, Max Bellotti had announced publicly that he was gay. Because Max was such a good player and because there had been a near riot at a game brought on by some crazed homophobes, the national media had been all over them again.

The case could be made that a successful baseball season would be one played without the presence of any TV trucks from CNN, MSNBC, or Fox at any of their games.

For the moment, Alex was just glad that a potential crisis inside the locker room had been averted.

He and Jonas joined their teammates soft-tossing to one another as they awaited Coach Birdy's arrival. Given that they were now 0–2, the atmosphere was surprisingly relaxed and loose. More surprising than that, Coach Birdy was a couple of minutes late.

When he did show up, he was jogging, a little out of breath and clearly not happy.

"Sorry, fellas," he said. "Cardillo, get everyone lined up to stretch. Myers, let me see you for a minute."

"What now?" Jonas said.

What now, indeed, Alex thought.

Alex couldn't begin to imagine what Coach Birdy wanted to talk to him about. That's what made him nervous. He remembered the November day when he had been pulled into a meeting with someone from the state high school athletic association, who informed him that he had tested positive for steroids—which, of course, was a mistake. At that moment, though, Alex had felt as if the entire world was caving in on him.

This unexpected meeting turned out differently.

"I wanted to let you know that you're pitching on Friday at Main Line," Coach Birdy said. "Starting, I mean."

"But what about Warner?" Alex asked, confused. Bailey Warner hadn't pitched especially well in the opener, but he'd been the team's best pitcher last year, so yanking him after one start seemed harsh.

"Bailey's hurt," Coach Birdy said quietly. "He was throwing a bullpen with me at lunchtime and said he felt some pain in his shoulder. Could be nothing, but his parents are taking him to see a doctor this afternoon."

In baseball vernacular, "throwing a bullpen" meant throwing about forty pitches between starts. Since pitchers warmed up in the bullpen, any throwing session that wasn't in an actual game was referred to as "throwing a bullpen." The term, Alex knew, was grammatically inaccurate, but it was part of the sport's language, just the way—as his dad had once explained—the term "prevent defense" in football was also technically incorrect. In truth, the defense was trying to prevent *offense*.

In the major leagues, where pitchers generally pitched one day, rested for four, and then pitched again, most would throw one bullpen session between starts to keep sharp. High school pitchers usually pitched on six days' rest, so most threw two bullpens.

"If he's just sore, couldn't he still start Friday?" Alex asked.

Coach Birdy shook his head. "I don't want to take a chance and make things worse for him," he said. "Best-case scenario, he'll pitch a week from Friday. You're it for Main Line. Go stretch yourself out, and when we start to take BP, get over on the side with Mann and throw to him. Coach Bloom will be there with you. Warm up a little and then throw about forty pitches."

Alex was in a state of semishock, but he nodded. He jogged back to where the other guys were still stretching.

He noticed—for the first time—that Bailey Warner wasn't there. He fell in next to Jonas, who bent over in his direction and said, "So, what was that about?"

"I'm starting Friday," Alex hissed. "Warner's hurt."

Jonas straightened up. "Hurt? What happened?"

There was no chance to answer. Coach Birdy was blowing his whistle, and Alex saw Coach Bloom waving at him.

"Myers, Mann—over here," he said.

Lucas Mann obviously had no idea what was going on because he turned to Alex and said, "What'd we do wrong?"

"Nothing," Alex answered. "Not yet anyway."

■ ■ ■

At the end of practice, Coach Birdy filled everyone in on Warner's injury, telling them—as he had told Alex—that he hoped to know how serious it was by the next day.

"It's a long season, guys. And we've got three more warm-up games to get the kinks out before conference play starts. I don't want anyone getting down about starting oh-and-two." He paused a beat and smiled. "That doesn't mean I want to be oh-and-five at the end of next week. We'll play everyone in our league twice. The only wrinkle is that we play both games with Chester at the end of the season—one at home on a Thursday, and the finale at their place on a Friday. Guess they figure they want a team with pitching depth to win the conference, and those games may decide things if we're going as well as I think we will. That's one of many reasons I hope we'll get Bailey back.

"For now, I really believe we're just fine with the guys

we've got. So let's get win number one under our belts on Friday and go from there."

They huddled up, and Cardillo said, "Number one!"

They put their hands in and repeated after him.

As they broke up, Alex felt a hand on his shoulder.

"You okay, Goldie?" Matt Gordon asked. "Arm feel okay after your inning yesterday?"

"Feels fine," Alex answered.

"Good," Matt said. "You just hold 'em to about three runs, and I'll take care of the rest."

Alex looked at him to see if he was smiling. He wasn't.

■ ■ ■

It was a long bus ride to Main Line Prep, and Alex spent part of it sitting with Coach Birdy, who'd called him up to the front of the bus.

"You know the old cliché 'The best pitch in baseball is strike one'?" Coach Birdy asked. "It means don't fall behind the hitters. I'm not telling you to just groove your first pitch to each batter, but until they prove they can hit your fastball, throw it to a corner as best you can and get ahead in the count. If you do that, you'll be fine."

It was a brisk late-March afternoon. In the locker room before the game, Alex started to put on a long-sleeved T-shirt to wear under his uniform. Matt saw him and said, "What are you doing?"

"Trying to stay warm," Alex answered.

Matt shook his head. "Wrong. You wear short sleeves. You wear the long sleeves, you look soft. You wear short sleeves, it makes the batters think you're a tough guy."

Alex thought that was ridiculous. "I don't want to be a tough guy," he said. "I want to be a warm guy."

"Have I ever told you something about competing that wasn't true?" Matt asked.

Alex sighed, reached into his bag, and pulled out his short-sleeved T-shirt.

"Once you throw a few pitches and get the adrenaline flowing, you won't even notice the cold," Matt said. "You'll be fine."

"I'll be fine," Alex said. "And cold."

As usual, though, Matt was right. Alex was chilly as he warmed up, but his arm was loose and the ball felt good coming out of his hand.

Coach Birdy had moved him up to second in the batting order, with Matt hitting third. In the top of the first, after Cardillo had led off with a walk, Alex lined a single to left.

When Matt came up, Alex noticed the outfielders moving back, almost to the warning track. Clearly, they had scouted the Lions. But all the scouting in the world wasn't going to get Matt out. Main Line's pitcher—trying to throw strike one, no doubt—grooved a fastball on the first pitch. Matt hit the ball to dead center field, so far over the fence that Main Line's center fielder didn't even take a step back. He just stood and watched it soar.

As Matt crossed home plate, where Alex and Cardillo waited to greet him, he batted Alex on the head. "If that's not enough, Goldie," he said, "there's more where that came from."

It turned out to be more than enough. Alex took the mound with all the confidence a three-run lead can give you.

Then he struck out Main Line's leadoff hitter on three darting fastballs and never felt the cold the rest of the day. It was 9–0 after five innings—Matt had doubled his next time up and been walked his next two plate appearances—and Coach Birdy told Alex that he was going to let Ethan Sattler finish the game.

"You're up to eighty-two pitches," he said. "No sense making you throw any more in your first start. We'll need that arm."

Alex's arm felt fine. He had given up three hits—all singles—and had struck out eight and walked only one. It wasn't a Matt-like performance, but it was pretty good. He didn't argue, though; Sattler needed a couple of innings of work, and a 9–0 lead was comfortable.

Main Line managed to get to Sattler for three runs in the sixth and even had two runners on in the seventh, but Cardillo made a diving catch on a line drive to end the game. Alex now knew—in a different way—how Matt had felt when his no-hitter and shutout had gone up in smoke on Tuesday.

They all lined up to congratulate one another and shake hands with the Main Line players. Matt was grinning as they walked off the field.

"You know what the good news is about this game, Goldie?" he said.

"That we won?"

"That too," Matt said. "No, the good news is that you're going to be a very good pitcher. In fact, you're pretty good right now."

"Thanks?" Alex said.

"And the best news is that I don't have to take steroids to be better than you," Matt said with a broad grin. "*That's* the best news of all."

■ ■ ■

There were only a handful of reporters waiting for the players when they came out of the locker room. Coach Birdy gave them about ten minutes to talk before herding them onto the bus.

Christine was there, along with Steve Garland and a kid Alex didn't know from the student radio station. There were several other reporters and, Alex noticed, a crew from Comcast SportsNet Philadelphia.

"They're doing a story on Matt," Christine told Alex as they watched Matt talk to Rob Ellis, who co-hosted Comcast SportsNet's morning show, *Breakfast on Broad*.

That was hardly a surprise. Matt's near no-hitter and his prodigious hitting were bound to draw media attention. Throw in the way he had gone down in flames the previous fall and you had a natural story. Alex saw Ellis and crew approaching him.

"Alex, nice going today. You got a minute?" Ellis asked.

"Sure, if you want," Alex said.

"Just to be honest with you, we're going to ask you about Matt."

Alex smiled. "Fine with me," he said.

Ellis's questions were predictable but fair. It was the second-to-last one that gave Alex pause.

"After Matt admitted to taking PEDs last fall, you were very emotional about what he had meant to your football team," Ellis said. "Back then, did you ever think he'd be your teammate again?"

Alex thought a moment. "I honestly had no idea," he said finally. "I hoped that he would be, but I thought that if it happened, it would be next fall in football. But I'm really glad it worked out this way. I had no idea he was this good a baseball player, but I'm thrilled to be his teammate again."

Ellis had one more question.

"Who's the starting quarterback for Chester Heights next season?"

"I think it'll be me," Alex answered.

Ellis nodded and said, "You'll be glad to know Matt said that for sure it would be you."

Alex laughed. It had been close to a perfect day.

But it wouldn't be a perfect night. . . .

Hope Alexander, Chester Heights' reigning diva, was having one of her Friday-night parties. During football season, Hope's parties were an almost weekly event. The rest of the year, she cut back to about once a month. She lived in a house nearly as big as the school, and her parents spared no expense when their baby girl wanted to have her friends over.

Alex thought that Christine was the prettiest girl in the school, but Hope was undeniably the most noticeable. She was about five eleven, with long blond hair, and she dressed in a way designed to stop traffic. More often than not, she did.

Alex hadn't liked Hope much at the beginning of the year, but he had softened on her after Max Bellotti came out. Hope had pretty much thrown herself at Max when he first arrived at Chester Heights. When Max came out, Hope was embarrassed, but she was also one of the first people to show support for him—even when the rest of the school seemed divided on whether they liked the idea of an openly gay star basketball player. Hope's behavior during that period made Alex like her a lot more.

Usually Max would be at Hope's parties, but he was in Detroit for the weekend, visiting his father. That made Alex think about his own dad—and wish he hadn't. He'd barely seen him since Christmas and the great fiancée debacle.

His father had come down for the first round of the basketball playoffs a few weeks earlier, which was nice. Unfortunately, he'd brought the fiancée (neither Alex nor Molly ever referred to her by name), and that had made for another awkward scene. Alex had called his father the next day and, after swallowing hard, had said, "Dad, we want you to visit as often as possible. But not with her."

"Her name is Megan," his dad said.

"Yeah, fine. That's not my point. It upsets me, and it upsets Molly even more."

"I understand, Alex, but you guys are going to have to get used to it. She's going to be your stepmother, which means she'll be part of your life."

That had pretty much ended the conversation, but Alex had thought long and hard about it after they'd hung up. Was there a rule that said you had to get along with a stepparent? He knew kids who didn't deal with stepparents at all. On the other hand, he didn't really want to force his dad to make a choice between the fiancée and his kids.

Because the way it looked now, he'd already chosen the fiancée.

■ ■ ■

The night began to go south not long after Alex, Christine, and Jonas arrived at the party. Alex had gone off to get a Coke for Christine, but when he returned, she was nowhere in sight.

"Right there," Jonas said, pointing at the dance floor in the massive living room.

Alex looked and saw Christine dancing with Matt.

"No big deal, dude," Jonas said, reading the jealousy on Alex's face. "Matt came over and said, 'Hey, I feel like dancing—what do you say?'"

"I'm guessing he wasn't talking to you," Alex said.

"Come on. They're friends—that's all," Jonas said. "He knows the deal. He just felt like dancing."

"There are about a hundred girls in this room he can dance with."

"True . . . ," Jonas said.

"Hey, Jonas, dance with me."

It was Kim Wilkens, who was the captain of the volleyball team and almost as pretty as Christine.

"Sure," Jonas said, clearly happy that Kim had asked him to dance *and* for an excuse to not continue the conversation.

Alex stood alone, sipping his Coke, still holding the one he'd gotten for Christine. The song ended, and Christine and Matt came over to where he was standing. They were flushed and smiling. Without saying a word, Alex handed Christine her soda.

"That looks all flat," Matt said. "I'll go get us a couple of fresh ones."

"Yeah, get me one too," Alex said, handing Matt his almost empty cup. "Mine's gone flat too."

As soon as he said it, he realized the words had come out more snidely than he'd intended because Matt and Christine both gave him a look.

Matt walked off without a word.

"What's with you?" Christine said.

"Nothing," Alex said. "I go to get you a Coke and two minutes later you're on the dance floor with Matt."

"And . . . ?" she said.

Alex shrugged. "And I guess I thought you'd wait for me to come back."

She put her hands on her hips, which, Alex knew, meant she was angry.

"You gotta stop with the jealousy thing, Alex. Matt knows you and I are dating, and by the way, I know we're dating too. Matt and I are *friends*."

"Yeah, sure," Alex said, knowing she was right but still not *feeling* right about it all.

Matt returned. Just as he did, the DJ put on an old Billy Joel song that Alex recognized, "Uptown Girl."

"Hey, I love this song," Matt said, putting the Cokes on a nearby table. "Come on, Christine."

Christine glanced in Alex's direction, as if deciding what to do.

"I get this one, Matt, okay?" Alex said.

Matt furrowed his brow. "Come on, Goldie. I asked her first," Matt said. "You can get the next one."

"No, *you* can get the next one," Alex said, realizing he was raising his voice. "She's *my* girlfriend."

Matt smiled. "Lighten up, Goldie. It's just a dance."

"He's right, Alex," Christine said, stepping in between them. "It's just a dance." She slipped her hand into Matt's. "Come on, Matt, let's go."

And they went, leaving Alex with three Cokes, wondering if everyone in the room could see how flushed his face was with anger.

■ ■ ■

That could have been—should have been—the end of it. But Alex couldn't let it go.

When Christine and Matt returned a few minutes later, Matt obviously wanted to clear the air. "She's all yours, Goldie," he said. "I didn't mean to horn in."

"Excuse me? I'm *not* all his, Matt," Christine said, her eyes flashing. "First of all, I'm not all anyone's. Second, I really don't want to spend time with him right now. I'm going outside for a while."

"It's kind of cold out there," Alex said.

But Christine was already walking away.

"Well, thanks for that," Alex said, turning on Matt. "Now you've got my girlfriend mad at me."

"Whoa, Goldie." Matt put his hands up in mock defense. "I think *you* got your girlfriend mad at you by overreacting. All I did was dance with her a couple times. Wasn't even a slow dance."

Matt had that in-control grin on his face, which only made Alex angrier.

"Right. So you don't think she's pretty. You wouldn't want to go out with her."

"I told you back in the fall I'd like to go out with her," Matt said. "I also said I'd butt out because you liked her and she liked you. And you know what, buddy? She *does* like you. But *you're* screwing it up—not me."

More of the grin. Alex lost control. Later, he wouldn't even be able to explain what came over him. But he found himself swinging a wild right-handed punch in the direction of Matt's head. If it had landed, it probably would have hurt Alex's hand more than the side of Matt's head.

Even caught by surprise, Matt easily ducked the punch. "Goldie, cool down," he said, the grin gone. "Don't do this to yourself."

Alex took another swing. This one Matt blocked with his arm. Then, as Alex flailed at him again, he bent down slightly and punched Alex in the stomach—not especially hard, but hard enough to knock the wind out of him and cause him to pitch forward onto the floor.

Matt held out a hand to help Alex up.

Alex was still trying to get his breath back, but he pushed Matt's hand away. "I'm fine," he said. "Leave me alone."

He was aware of the fact that everyone was now staring at them. The music had stopped. Matt was still standing there, hand out.

"Come on, Goldie," he said quietly. "Let me help you up and you can go to the bathroom and put yourself back together."

Alex decided the sooner he was off the floor, the better, but his stomach hurt enough that he wasn't certain he could get up on his own. He reached up, and Matt pulled him to his feet. Matt then pulled him close enough so he could whisper.

"I'm sorry," he said. "You left me no choice."

Alex said nothing. He pulled his hand free and walked straight to the front door. He had no idea where he was going, but he knew he had to get out of there as soon as possible.

■ ■ ■

"Alex, it's only a little after ten o'clock. Why do you need to come home now?"

Alex had decided he really needed to go. He was angry at Christine and at Matt. But he was even angrier at himself. He had overreacted and upset Christine and had gotten himself knocked to the floor in front of everyone—a humiliating experience all around. So he'd called his mother.

"Mom, I'm just really tired," he said. "Can you please come and get me?"

"What happened?" his mom continued. "Something's wrong—I can hear it in your voice."

"Mom, please."

She sighed. "Molly's asleep. I can't just leave her here alone. You're going to have to wait until Sandra comes to get you guys."

Sandra was Jonas's mom. The thought of riding home in the same car with Christine—which would be the normal routine—terrified Alex.

"She can't have been sleeping that long, Mom," he said. "It's a Friday. Can you please wake her up? Or just leave her? She'll be okay."

There was a long pause. "If I do that, Alex, I don't want to hear 'Everything's fine' when we get home. I want an explanation—a real one—about what could be so bad that I have to wake your sister up to come get you."

"Okay," he said. "I promise."

"Give me fifteen minutes."

She hung up. Alex sat down on the front steps to wait. It was a brisk March night. It was going to be a long fifteen minutes.

Alex had been sitting for about ten minutes when he heard the door open behind him. His first thought was that someone was leaving, so he stood up to get out of the way. His second thought was worse—that it was Christine. It turned out to be neither. It was Jonas.

"What in the world is wrong with you, dude?" he asked.

Alex turned and walked onto the circular driveway, hoping that Jonas might take the hint and not follow him.

"Hey," he said. "I asked you a question."

"It's really none of your business," Alex said, looking over his shoulder and seeing Jonas right behind him.

"No? I'm your best friend, and it's none of my business? I'm the guy who listens to your moaning and groaning about Christine all the time, and it's none of my business?"

Alex stopped and turned to face Jonas. "I don't moan and groan all that much."

Jonas laughed. "Really? If she talks about how good her hamburger tastes at Stark's, you think she's gonna run off with the cook. If she says 'Thank you' when someone opens a door for her, you think she's flirting."

Alex knew Jonas wasn't really wrong. He *had* been convinced once that a guy taking their tickets at a movie theater had been hitting on her when he said "Enjoy the film."

"Okay, okay, so I overreacted a little," he finally conceded.

"A little?" Jonas said.

"You didn't even see what happened," Alex said. "What do you know?"

"I know everyone in there is talking about how you lost your cool," Jonas said. "I know Christine's sitting on a couch with Matt comforting her because she's so upset. Do I need to know much more?"

For a split second, Alex was tempted to go inside and find out exactly what was going on. Fortunately, he realized that was a bad idea. It was probably the first smart decision he'd made all night.

"Look, thanks for being worried," he finally said as he saw headlights turning in to the driveway. "I'll call Christine in the morning and apologize."

"You'd better," Jonas said. "And you'd better cool your act down. I don't know what's going on with you or Matt right now, but I'm not in love with it."

Alex almost laughed. His mother was pulling up. He could see Molly sitting in the front seat.

"I'll call you tomorrow," he said, giving Jonas as much of a smile as he could muster. "Thanks."

He climbed into the car. It had been a long night.

■ ■ ■

Remarkably, it helped to talk to his mother after they got home and Molly went back to bed. She listened as he told her what had happened and then smiled and patted him on the head lightly when he finished.

"I know it doesn't feel at all this way right now, but this is normal fourteen-year-old stuff," she said. "Christine is your first girlfriend and also your first real crush. My guess is all of this makes your head hurt because it feels so important."

"Mom . . ."

She put a hand up. "I know. It *is* important," she said. "I completely get it. Eric Witsken was my first crush. I was thirteen. There was no doubt in my mind that I was going to marry him."

"What happened to him?"

"I have no idea," she said, smiling. "We ended up going to different high schools—he went to a private school—and I never heard from him or anything about him again. By then, I was madly in love with Jerry Richman."

"So you're saying if Christine breaks up with me, it's no big deal?"

She shook her head. "I'm not saying that at all. But I don't think she's going to break up with you. She likes you, I'm guessing, just as much as you like her. Feeling jealous— even when there's no reason to feel jealous—is perfectly normal. You just can't let it overwhelm you the way it did tonight."

"So what do I do?"

"Jonas is right. You call her in the morning. You say you're very sorry and ask her to have lunch with you at Stark's."

She smiled. "And don't lose your mind if one of the other boys in there looks at her twice or if she smiles at someone. She's a nice person, so if she smiles at someone, it doesn't mean she's flirting."

Alex knew she was right. But knowing it when Christine was dancing with someone else would be harder. He stood up, bent down, and kissed his mom on the cheek. He was grateful she was around.

■ ■ ■

Alex waited until nine o'clock to make the call.

Christine answered right away, which he took as a good sign.

"I'm really sorry about last night," he said. "I was out of line. I just . . . get jealous, and I know I shouldn't."

"Apology accepted," she said. "How's your stomach?"

He had hoped that maybe she hadn't heard about Matt's one-punch knockdown. It was unlikely, he knew, but a guy could dream.

"It's fine. Honestly, I'm more embarrassed than anything else."

"Well, you should be," she said.

He sighed. She was right, but did they really have to talk about it? He'd apologized; she'd accepted. Time to move on . . . to lunch.

"How about Stark's at eleven-thirty?" he said.

There was a pause. "I can't today," she said finally.

"You can't?"

"I'm going to the hockey game this afternoon with my dad."

"I thought Sunday was your day with your dad."

Christine's parents were divorced—had been for a while. Christine lived with her mom but was close to her dad, who was an editor at the *Philadelphia Daily News*.

"It is, but we change up sometimes, and you know I like hockey."

He did know that. "Okay, then. Have fun. Maybe tomorrow?"

Another pause. "How about if I text you later?"

He could feel that little chill that always ran through him when he was scared or thought something was wrong.

"Is something wrong?" he asked.

Another pause.

"I'm not sure," she said. "I need a little time to think. Give me a little space, okay?"

Now it was Alex's turn to pause.

"I . . . ," he started, choosing his words carefully. "I'm not sure what that means. I thought you accepted my apology."

"I did," she said. "And I do. I'm not mad at you. I just need to think about some things."

He wanted to press her, ask her what things she needed to think about, but he decided that would make things worse.

"Okay," he said. "Text me later."

"I will," she said.

■ ■ ■

She didn't.

Alex watched the hockey game on TV—the Flyers lost to the New York Islanders—and then spent the next couple of hours staring at his phone, as if he had some kind of special vision that would make a text magically appear.

His mom fixed dinner and brought it into the living room so he could watch the NCAA basketball regional championship games when they started. By then, it was six o'clock. The hockey game had been over for more than two hours.

Finally, Alex couldn't help himself.

How was the game? he texted, hoping to not sound over-eager but knowing that Christine would see right through him.

A few minutes later, a text finally appeared on his screen. *Game was fun, but Flyers lost. Stark's at 11:30 tomorrow?*

Alex felt as if a thousand-pound weight had been lifted from his shoulders.

He texted right back: *Great. See you then.*

With that, he took a bite of the chicken his mom had made and settled into the couch to watch the second basketball game. For the first time in twenty-four hours, he felt the tension drain out of his body.

■ ■ ■

That feeling lasted until about 11:40 the next morning.

For once, he arrived before Christine—who was almost freakish about being on time—walking into Stark's at 11:25. It was virtually empty on a Sunday morning, and he grabbed the booth in the back where he and his friends liked to sit.

Christine walked in two minutes later, dressed in jeans, a sweatshirt, and sneakers. Her hair was tied back in a pony-tail. She didn't smile at him as she sat down, simply slid into the other side of the booth and said, "You're early."

"So are you." He smiled, hoping to get a return smile.

He didn't. In fact, he didn't even get a response. Just silence while the waitress came over to fill their glasses with water.

When she left, Alex figured it was his move.

"Look," he said, "I know you were upset with me on Friday night—"

She put up a hand.

"I already accepted your apology when we talked yesterday. We don't need to go over all of that again. Look, Alex, I know you're a good guy, and I know that even good guys have a bad moment or a bad night. I get all that."

Alex knew there was a *but* coming but couldn't think of a way to stop it.

Christine plowed on.

"Friday wasn't just a onetime thing, though. I mean, it *was*, in terms of you picking a fight with Matt and acting crazy. . . ."

"I wasn't that—"

She put up a hand. He stopped.

"Your jealousy is pretty relentless. I can feel it the way you look at me if I talk to *any* guy—at lunch or after French class or even when I'm interviewing other players. Every time I go anywhere near Matt, I feel like you're going to explode."

"He does like you, you know."

She took a deep breath. "I know he likes me. Alex, a lot of guys like me. And you may not have noticed, but a lot of girls like you. You're a star. You're good-looking. You're a good guy."

"But I'm not interested in any of them."

"And I've been trying to tell you since our first date in December that I'm not interested in anyone else, either. The difference is, you don't trust me enough to believe that's true. *That's* what bothers me. And, for the record, we're *fourteen*.

"I know you feel insecure about things right now because you feel like you've lost your dad. But you can't not trust me just because right now you don't trust your dad."

Holy cow, Alex thought. *Where did that come from?*

"When did you get your degree in psychiatry?" he asked—then wished he hadn't.

Surprisingly, she didn't get angry. She smiled—for the first time all morning.

The waitress came to take their orders.

"I'm not staying," Christine said. "I'm sorry. Alex, you should order a hamburger."

Alex was starving. But he felt a little bit sick to his stomach when he heard Christine say she wasn't staying. "You want me to sit here alone and eat?" he asked.

"I'll sit with you if you want," she said.

Alex didn't wait for her to change her mind. He ordered a hamburger and a vanilla milk shake.

The waitress, after giving them both a funny look, walked away.

"I'll stay if you want me to," Christine said again. "But

you may not want me to. Look, what I've been trying to say is this: I like you—you know that. I didn't want to talk yesterday because I wanted to think about things before I made any decisions."

Alex was starting to feel dizzy.

"I'm not breaking up with you," she said. "But I think we need a break. I'm a little overwhelmed. We're both too young for feelings like that."

Alex felt like he was in a daytime soap opera. "You know, on TV whenever someone says 'I need a break,' that's the end," he said. "When my parents said they were going to 'experiment' with being separated—that was the end."

"I know," she said. "I knew you'd feel that way. But I'm not planning on going out with anyone else. I just need some time."

"You aren't going to go out with Matt?"

She stood up. "See what I mean?" she said. "I just told you I wasn't going to go out with anyone, and you instantly doubted me. That's why I'm doing this."

She patted him on the shoulder and left.

A moment later, Alex's food arrived. He sat and ate it alone—feeling about as lonely as he'd ever felt in his life.

Alex couldn't wait for school on Monday, if only because it would force him to think about something other than Christine. He almost called Jonas to tell him what had happened but realized he didn't want to talk about it. He did tell his mom, and not surprisingly, she told him not to get too down.

"These things happen in relationships, honey," she said. "Christine's right. You're both fourteen. You're both going to have many more relationships before you grow up. I know it doesn't feel that way now, that it feels like the end of the world. But it's not."

She was right—it *did* feel like the end of the world. Alex moped the rest of the day Sunday, trying to distract himself by watching the last two regional finals on television. Even an overtime game between Duke and Indiana couldn't get his mind off Christine.

When he walked into school Monday, he realized that the end of the weekend was a double-edged sword. Not only was he going to see Christine at some point—lunch, maybe; French class, for sure—but he was going to be confronted with questions and comments about what had happened at Hope's house on Friday night.

It started as soon as he reached his locker—with Jonas.

"You square things with Christine?" he asked quietly, looking around to be sure no one else was listening.

"I had lunch with her yesterday," Alex said, hoping that would be enough of an answer.

It wasn't.

"And?"

Alex also looked around, not so much to see if anyone was listening as to give himself time to think about his answer.

"And we're taking a break. At least for a little while."

Jonas rolled his eyes. "Her idea, right?"

Alex nodded.

Jonas closed his locker. "You need some remedial dating advice, my friend," he said. "We'll talk later."

Just then, the five-minute bell rang, so Alex didn't have to respond. Once upon a time, he would have gone to Matt for remedial dating advice. Right now, that didn't seem like such a good idea.

■ ■ ■

He got through the morning by giving one-word answers to the various questions: "You okay?" "How's the stomach?" "What happened?" "You and Matt patch it up?" His answers:

"Fine." "Fine." "Nothing." "Yes." He left it at that and kept walking.

The first real problem came at lunchtime. As Alex walked to his regular table, he saw that Christine was sitting at a table with several people from the student newspaper: Steve Garland, Kim Gagne, Ally Bachinski, and Janie Kappell. In a vacuum, that wasn't a problem—she spent time with those people almost every day. But she *always* sat at the corner table with Alex, Jonas, Max Bellotti, and, most days, Matt.

Only she wasn't sitting there today. Neither was Matt, who came in a little bit late and joined some of the other baseball players at a different table.

"Trouble in paradise, I take it," Max said, nodding in the direction of the table where Christine was sitting. "I heard what happened."

"People in Mongolia heard what happened," Jonas said. "Question is, what does our guy do next?"

Max shrugged. "I assume you've talked to her since Friday," he said, looking at Alex. "What'd she say?"

"She needs space," Alex said. "Apparently I'm relentlessly jealous."

"You *are* relentlessly jealous," Jonas said. "She does have a way with words, by the way."

Max nodded. "He's right. Give her some space. Let her miss you for a while."

"What if she doesn't miss me?"

Max shrugged again. "Then there's not much you can do. Look, Alex, you know she could go out with just about anyone in the school."

"Except you," Jonas said, grinning.

Max laughed. "You know what? She's so good-looking I might switch sides for her."

Alex knew he was kidding, but the comment didn't make him feel any better. Once word got out that Christine and Alex were "taking a break"—and it would—guys would be lining up for the chance to go out with her.

Seeing the look on Alex's face, Max put his fork down and turned serious. "Did she say she was going to start dating other guys?" he asked.

"No," Alex said. "She actually said she wouldn't start dating other guys."

"Then take her at her word," Max said. "She's a very mature girl. You know that."

"What if she *does* go out with someone else?" Jonas asked.

"Then it's a different story," Max said.

That was the story Alex was worried about.

■ ■ ■

Alex heeded Max's advice that afternoon. When French class was over, he was sorely tempted to follow Christine out of the classroom and engage her in some kind of conversation. But when she didn't even glance at him as she was stuffing her French book into her backpack, he decided against it.

Give her space, he said to himself, and he let her leave ahead of him, taking his time to pack up his own books.

Getting back on the baseball field was a relief. Coach Birdy told them all before practice began that Bailey Warner was going to a specialist to try to figure out why his shoulder hurt when an MRI had shown no structural damage. Matt would pitch at Camden South the next day, Alex would pitch the final nonconference game of the year on Friday against St. Mary's, and then Matt would pitch the conference opener against Bryn Mawr Tech the following Tuesday. By then, it would be April, and—everyone hoped—the weather would be warmer.

Matt said nothing during practice about what had happened Friday night or about his decision to sit at a different table at lunch. He was the old Matt, teasing Alex about his golden arm and how it had "finally shown up again" in the game on Friday. Alex laughed along with everyone else and acted as if everything was back to normal—even though it wasn't.

The team left early the next day for the trip up I-95 and across the Ben Franklin Bridge into Camden. The New Jersey suburb of Philadelphia had a reputation for producing great athletes and for being a tough, gritty place. The bus arrived just as school was letting out, and it appeared, at least to Alex, that a majority of the student body was African American. But when Camden South took the field, the team had just one African American player. During warm-ups, Jonas—as if reading Alex's mind—said, "Even here, no brothers playing baseball."

"What's the deal with that?" Alex said.

"Baseball's dead to black people," Jonas said. "I play because what else am I going to do in the spring? But if you asked me to give up a sport, this is the one I'd give up."

That wasn't all that surprising to Alex. Jonas was a very

good baseball player, but he was better at basketball, and even better at football.

Still, he asked the follow-up question: "Why would you give up baseball first?"

"It's not cool," Jonas replied. "It's slow. Would you rather watch a football game, a basketball game, or a baseball game on TV?"

Alex thought about that. He loved going to Fenway Park with his dad, but he didn't sit and watch baseball for hours on end the way he did football or basketball. He loved the game, but compared with football and basketball, it *was* slow.

"Old people like slow," Jonas continued. "Young people want fast."

"You sound like a Nike commercial," Alex said.

Jonas laughed. "Why do you think they make those commercials? Who buys sneakers and gear from them?"

They were interrupted by Coach Birdy telling them to come on back to the dugout. Alex was again hitting second, behind Jeff Cardillo, and playing left field. Matt was hitting third, and Jonas, even though he wasn't a true power hitter, was batting fourth.

"Camden's the best team we've played," Coach Birdy told them. "But we've got Matt pitching. As long as he's out there, we can beat anybody."

Alex wondered if that was supposed to be a pep talk. Did it mean that when he or any of the other pitchers were on the mound, they *couldn't* beat anybody good?

There was no point worrying about it at the moment, es- pecially since Coach Birdy's assessment proved accurate very quickly. Camden South's starting pitcher was Jaime Garcia, a kid who didn't throw as hard as Matt but had about four different breaking pitches—or so it seemed. Alex struck out in the first inning, swinging at a curveball that bounced on the plate.

Fortunately, Coach Birdy was also right about Matt. He matched zeroes with Garcia inning after inning. The only two hits that Garcia gave up were to Matt—a two-out double in the first, which he followed up by striking out Jonas, and a single in the fourth. Matt also gave up two hits through the first seven innings—both to Garcia. It was as if the two of them were playing one game and everyone else was playing another.

Looking into the bleachers—which would seat maybe five hundred—Alex could see plenty of scouts on hand. He wondered if they were there to watch Alex or Garcia—or both.

The score was still 0–0 after the seventh, which meant extra innings. High school rules dictated that a game played on a weekday could go no more than nine innings. Before he went to coach third base in the top of the eighth, Coach Birdy told Ethan Sattler and Patton Gormley to go warm up. Lucas Mann, the number nine hitter, was about to lead off. Garcia was still in the game. As soon as Sattler and Gormley left the dugout, Matt walked over to Coach Bloom, who was sitting on the bench with all of his various charts on his lap.

"Why is Coach Birdy warming them up?" Matt said. "I'm fine."

Alex was a few feet away, preparing to grab a bat and follow Jeff Cardillo to the on-deck circle, since he would be hitting third in the inning.

Coach Bloom tapped his clipboard. "You've thrown ninety-nine pitches, Matt," he said. "We aren't going to push you past a hundred."

"What?" Matt said, raising his voice so the entire dugout could hear him. "How many pitches has Garcia thrown?"

"Doesn't matter," Coach Bloom said. "We're only worried about you."

"How many?" Matt demanded.

"Hundred and eight," Coach Bloom answered.

"And he's still out there!" Matt yelled.

Coach Bloom had heard enough. "Matt, you're in for Hague at first base in the bottom of the inning."

He put his head down to indicate he wasn't going to argue further. Matt stalked away just as Mann swung and missed at strike three from Garcia.

Alex headed for the on-deck circle. Cardillo was dropping a bat and taking one more practice swing before walking to the plate. It looked to Alex as if he was stalling. "Someone needs to calm Matt down," he said softly, still looking at the plate.

"Not me," Alex said.

"Me, then, I guess," Cardillo said just as the umpire walked in their direction, indicating that Cardillo needed to get in the batter's box.

Alex wasn't sure what Cardillo's plan was, but the first thing he did was lay a perfect bunt down the third base line. Camden South's third baseman sprinted in and tried to grab and throw with one hand, but he threw wildly, over the first baseman's head. By the time the right fielder ran the ball down, Cardillo had raced all the way to third.

Suddenly, the Lions had a real chance to score. As Alex headed to the plate, Coach Birdy walked down from the third base coaching box and waved him over. He wasn't going to chance a missed sign.

Coach Birdy put his arm around Alex.

"I want you to swing at the first pitch—regardless of where it is," he said. "My guess is it'll be out of the strike zone because they're going to want to see if you show bunt."

Alex wasn't quite getting it. "Swing and miss?" he said.

"No, not necessarily, but I'm guessing that's what will happen. On the next pitch, I want you to bunt toward third. The third baseman can't come in too far because that'll give Jeff a running start. Just get it down and he'll score."

Alex walked back to the batter's box. Sure enough, the first pitch was well off the plate. Alex saw the first baseman charging and the third baseman cheating in, both looking for a bunt. He practically dove across the plate trying to swing at the pitch. He missed.

Alex stepped out and looked down at Coach Birdy, who flashed him all sorts of signs, none of them indicating anything had changed. He still wanted him to bunt.

Alex stepped back in and noticed that both the first baseman and the third baseman had backed off a little bit. Garcia was pitching from the windup, since Cardillo was unlikely to steal home. As soon as he kicked his leg, Alex squared and ran his hands up the bat. The pitch was going to be a strike, on the inside corner. Alex twisted his body toward third base and, out of the corner of his eye, saw Cardillo starting toward home. He pushed the ball as hard as he could and managed to get the bunt down in the no-man's-land between Garcia and the third baseman.

Cardillo scored easily, and by the time the third baseman got to the ball, Alex had beaten his throw to first. It was 1–0. Garcia stood, hands on hips, clearly disgusted. His coach came out of the dugout and changed pitchers. Matt came to the plate and, on the new pitcher's first pitch, hit a home run to dead center field, the ball sailing well over the fence. He didn't even move as the ball left the park, just stood at the plate, admiring his work.

Alex waited for Matt at the plate to high-five him. *"Now,"* Matt said, "they can let someone else pitch."

Ethan Sattler came in and got Camden South one, two, three in the bottom of the eighth. The 3–0 deficit had broken the home team's spirit.

"Great win," Coach Birdy said in the dugout after the teams had exchanged postgame handshakes. "We're on the bus in twenty minutes."

Alex noticed Christine, Steve Garland, and a number of other media members gathered outside the dugout. They were all waiting for Matt. When Matt walked over to them, he shook hands with Garland and then hugged Christine.

Alex felt the familiar burn. Behind him, he heard Jonas in his ear. "Keep saying it with me, dude: 'She needs space.'"

Alex took a deep breath. "Not sure how long I can keep this up," he said.

"Been two days," Jonas said.

It felt more like two weeks to Alex. Or two months.

Alex was practicing his deep breathing when he saw Steve Garland walking in his direction. Alex could see that Christine—and several other reporters—was still talking to Matt.

"You got a minute, Alex?" Garland asked.

"Sure," Alex said, in a tone that meant, *Okay—but why?*

Garland picked up on it right away.

"I'm prepping a big story on Matt for next week and need some quotes from the rest of you guys. Christine's writing the game story, so she needs to talk to him about today."

It was almost as if Garland was becoming part of the "Give her some space and quit worrying" chorus.

"Sure," Alex said again, hoping he didn't sound uptight. *More deep breaths*, he told himself.

"Did you have any idea Matt was this good?" Garland

asked, turning on his mini tape recorder so Alex knew they were now on the record.

"No," Alex said honestly. "I'd never seen him play, and since he didn't play the last couple springs, I don't think anyone else knew how good he was, either. I'm not sure *Matt* knew how good he was."

Garland smiled. "He seems to now."

Alex let that go.

Garland tried a different tact. "Just now he was saying that he thinks he's better at baseball than football. You agree?"

Alex was going to be careful with that one. "He was—is—a very good football player and was good before he ever took steroids." Alex paused. "You know that, right?"

Garland nodded in agreement.

"He's a natural when it comes to baseball," Alex continued. "He can do everything. You've seen it. I'm not surprised all these scouts are coming to see him."

"Word travels fast," Garland said. "I asked him if he was going to go to college or turn pro, and he said he didn't know yet. What do you think?"

Alex shrugged. "Well, he's got another year to figure that one out."

Garland gave him a funny look. "Another year? Didn't Christine tell you? He's thinking about reclassifying. If he wants, he can go to summer school to graduate and either go to college or turn pro in the fall."

"*What?*"

"You didn't know?" Garland said, surprised. "When Christine told me, I figured all you guys knew."

"I'm not sure Coach Birdy knows," Alex said.

Alex saw a look pass over Garland's face that told him that he hadn't asked Coach Birdy about it yet.

"Talk to you later," Garland said. "Thanks."

He turned, clearly going to look for Coach Birdy. Alex was willing to bet that the only person who had known was Christine Whitford. And he was sure that wasn't relentless jealousy talking.

■ ■ ■

Alex didn't find out until the next morning that his theory had been correct. Steve Garland's story on Matt mentioned that Coach Birdy "appeared to be caught off guard when informed by a reporter that Gordon is considering passing up his senior year"—though the story didn't say, "Gordon had already confided this information to Christine Whitford."

Alex showed the story to Jonas when he found him at his locker. "He tells Christine but not his coach," Alex said. "What does that tell you?"

"Tells me he likes her and she's a good reporter," Jonas said. "Two things we already knew. Does it say anything in there about Christine doing anything to make you think she was lying on Sunday when she said she wasn't going to be dating anybody?"

Grudgingly, Alex had to admit he had a point.

"Maybe I'll ask Christine why she thinks he told her," Alex said.

"Maybe you won't," Jonas said, slamming his locker door for emphasis. "Unless you want to set yourself back another couple of weeks."

Alex hated that Jonas was right but knew that he was.

To his surprise, Matt was back at the lunch table that day.

"So, I guess you guys know that I'm thinking of passing on senior year," he said as he unloaded his tray, which was piled high with two massive roast beef sandwiches and a plate of French fries.

Before Alex or Jonas could say anything, Max jumped in. "I read it," he said. "Why in the world would you do that?"

"Because I have the hammer right now," Matt said. "I can put my name into the draft, and if I don't get offered a lot of money, I can graduate this summer and go to college, or come back here. No reason not to try."

"Do you really want to go live on your own in some little nowhere farm-team town and ride buses all over the place when you're seventeen?" Max said.

"I'd like to live anywhere that's far away from my father," Matt said.

That quieted everyone.

"I get that," Max said finally. "But you'll have the exact same 'hammer' a year from now, and you'll be bigger, stronger, older."

"Smarter," Jonas added.

"Mr. Anderson says teams like players who are young. I won't be seventeen until July. That will make me more attractive and will probably get me more money."

"Who," Alex asked, "is Mr. Anderson?"

Matt hesitated, almost as if he hadn't meant to bring up the name.

"He's a friend," Matt said.

"What kind of friend?" Alex asked. "What does he know about any of this?"

Again, Matt hesitated. Finally, he threw his hands up in the air and said, "Okay, just between all of us, he's an agent. He knows about all this stuff."

"An agent?" Alex said. "You're talking to an agent? That's gotta be against the rules."

"He's not really giving me anything," Matt said. "He's just trying to help me out."

Jonas was the first one to snort in disgust, but Alex and Max weren't far behind.

"Just trying to help?" Jonas said. "Have you ever read about these guys? They're only trying to help themselves."

"What do you mean, not 'really' giving you anything?" Max said, his voice very low.

Matt shrugged. "He's bought me dinner a couple of times—that's all."

Alex banged his hand on the table. He was actually angry. "After what you put yourself through in the fall, how can you possibly go near this guy?" he asked. "First of all, you don't need any help. Your talent is all you need. Second, if you do need any help, you go to Coach Birdy. *He* wants to help you. Not this guy."

"Since when are *you* an expert?" Matt said. Now it was his turn to be angry.

"It doesn't take a genius to know you stay away from agents until you're a pro. What if you jeopardized your eligibility by letting the guy buy you dinner?"

Matt stood up. "I told you guys because I wanted you to

understand why I'm thinking about doing this," he said. "I don't need to be lectured."

"What'd Christine say when you told her?" Alex asked. He couldn't stop himself.

"She said it was an interesting idea," Matt said.

"Did you tell her about the agent?" Max asked.

"What difference does *that* make?" Matt said.

"Why don't you go tell her and see what she says," Alex said.

"Okay," Matt said. "I will."

He picked up his lunch and walked over to the table where Christine was sitting, pulling up a chair so he could sit next to her.

"What in the world was I thinking when I said that?" Alex said.

"That," Jonas said, "is a very good question."

■ ■ ■

It occurred to Alex as he was walking into French class that maybe sending Matt to talk to Christine wasn't the dumbest thing he'd ever done. He now had an excuse to talk to Christine without appearing to be pressuring her.

When class ended—five hours later, in Alex's estimation— he followed her out the door. As soon as he was in the hallway, he called her name. She was a few steps in front of him, walking quickly. Hearing his voice, she stopped and turned around. Her arms were folded across her chest.

"You look angry or something," Alex said. "Am I not supposed to talk to you at all?"

"Of course not," she said, with just a hint of a smile. "What's up?"

"Did Matt tell you about the agent?" he asked.

"Yes, he did," she said. "He said you and Max and Jonas were giving him a hard time about it."

"You think we were wrong to give him a hard time about it?" Alex said. "He could get in a lot of trouble."

Christine shook her head and Alex saw the "too stupid to live" look. "Just to be sure, I sent Stevie Thomas an email because I know he's dealt with agents a lot," she said. "He got back to me just before last period. Talking to an agent is fine for an amateur as long as he doesn't give you money or as long as you don't sign anything that says he represents you."

Alex knew that Christine was friends with Stevie Thomas, the teenage reporter who had become famous for breaking big stories at major sporting events. Thomas was now a high school junior and did some work for the *Philadelphia Daily News*, where Christine's father worked.

"What did he say about an agent buying an amateur dinner?"

Christine looked at him quizzically. "Matt didn't say anything about that," she said. "But I can't imagine one dinner is all that big a deal."

"First, it was two dinners—at least," Alex said. "Second, from what I've heard, when it comes to agents, *anything* can be a big deal. The NCAA has about a million rules."

"If Matt turns pro, he'll never deal with the NCAA," she pointed out.

"What about the high school athletic association?"

She frowned. "No idea," she said.

"Maybe you should ask your friend Stevie about that," he said, then realized he was speaking in a sarcastic tone.

"What do you mean, my friend Stevie?" she said, picking up on his tone the way she always did.

"I'm sorry," he said. "I didn't mean it that way."

She actually smiled. "Okay, apology accepted. But you're right, I should check with him."

She put her hands on her hips, lost in thought for a moment.

"What are you thinking about?" he asked.

"I'm just wondering why Matt didn't mention the dinners to me," she said. "He had to know I'd find out about it since he'd told you guys already."

Alex didn't have an answer for that one. Except . . .

"Maybe he thought that since you and I aren't seeing each other so much, you wouldn't talk to me or Jonas or Max about it."

She thought about that for a minute.

"Maybe you're right," she said.

She smiled at him, that mesmerizing smile.

"Would you like to have lunch at Stark's on Saturday?" she said.

Alex's heart went to his throat. He was tempted to crush her with a hug.

He settled for a smile of his own.

"Sure," he said. "Sounds good."

14

Alex might have danced his way to the locker room if it wouldn't have been completely humiliating. . . . So he tried to play it cool, but he must have had a silly grin on his face when he walked into the locker room because Jonas looked at him for about five seconds and said, "Okay, what happened?"

"What?" Alex said, knowing the giveaway grin was plastered all over his face.

"Something happened with Christine, didn't it?"

"Sort of."

"What does 'sort of' mean?"

"She said she wants to have lunch at Stark's on Saturday," Alex said.

"Whoa!" Jonas said. "Good job. When should I be there?"

Alex started to say something but then realized that Jonas was giving him a hard time.

"Come at about one," he said.

"You're meeting at eleven-thirty, aren't you? Maybe I'll just come with Max and Matt and we can sit in a booth nearby."

"Max," Alex said firmly, "is fine. Leave Matt home."

They both laughed. It occurred to Alex that it had been a while since he had laughed.

■ ■ ■

Coach Birdy had intentionally scheduled a "win" for their last nonconference game. St. Mary's had just started a baseball program and was 0–4. They'd been outscored 31–2 in the four games.

Naturally, it wasn't Coach Birdy who shared those statistics—it was the all-knowing Matt Gordon. "Everyone will play," he predicted as they warmed up before practice on Thursday afternoon. "I'll bet you don't pitch more than three innings, Goldie. He'll get the other guys some innings and make sure you're ready for Tuesday, if needed."

"You think I'll be needed with you pitching?" Alex asked.

"Hope not," Matt said. "But Bryn Mawr Tech's always pretty good."

As usual, Matt's predictions were on target. It was 7–0 when Alex retired the side in order in the top of the third, and Coach Birdy waved him over as he came into the dugout.

"Good job," he said. "I'm going to give you the rest of the day off. I'm taking Matt out too. There's no reason to humiliate these guys."

Alex was disappointed. He had only walked one in three innings and hadn't given up a hit. Given the quality of the opposition, he might have had a chance to pitch a no-hitter if he stayed in.

He started to say something about the no-hitter but changed his mind. "Okay, Coach," he said.

Coach Birdy read his mind. "I know you haven't given up a hit, but I need to make sure you're fresh if I need you to pitch behind Matt on Tuesday. That's more important."

Alex nodded.

Coach Birdy let the team's other four pitchers go an inning each. Everyone played. The final score was 13–2.

"Could've been twenty-five to nothing, if we'd wanted," Matt said as they trudged out of the dugout to shake hands with their bedraggled opponents. Alex noticed the two coaches hugging each other. His guess was that the St. Mary's coach was grateful to Coach Birdy for going as easy on his team as possible.

As soon as they'd gone through the handshake line, Alex saw that several TV cameras had magically appeared next to the dugout.

"What's that about?" he said to Jonas.

Jonas pointed at Matt, who had jogged over to the cameras.

"I think our buddy likes being a media star again," he said. "Christine told me after English class today that the *Daily News* will have a big Sunday piece on how he's resurrected his athletic career as a baseball player."

"But why would they be here for this game?" Alex said. "He had two at-bats, and that was it. He didn't even pitch."

Jonas shrugged. "Beats me," he said. "But the two of you *do* manage to attract a lot of attention, one way or the other. I have a feeling this is just the beginning."

Alex and Jonas took a wide path so they would stay out of the way of the cameras. Even so, Alex could hear Matt responding to a question as they walked by the scrum of cameras and tape recorders.

"I think once conference play begins, I'll be ready to show people my best stuff," Matt was saying. "I don't think anyone has seen it yet."

"Good thing we play baseball outdoors," Jonas hissed.

"Why?"

"Because his ego wouldn't fit anyplace indoors."

■ ■ ■

Christine was waiting for Alex when he walked into Stark's at 11:25 the next morning. The weather had finally started to warm up, and she was wearing a short-sleeved blue blouse, cutoff jeans, and sneakers. Her hair was tied back in a ponytail, which was the way she usually wore it when she was riding her bicycle.

Alex noticed she was already drinking an ice tea, which meant she'd been there a few minutes.

"Pretty eager to see me," he said, nodding at the tea as he slid into the booth, across from her. "Guess you got here early."

For a split second, he thought he'd put his foot in his mouth again, coming across as cocky—when he felt anything but cocky.

But she smiled, which was a relief.

"You're right, Alex. I was awake all night counting the minutes until I'd see you again," she said. Then, still smiling, she said, "Stop trying so hard."

She was right. He *was* trying too hard.

"So, how worried are you about Matt?" she said, a fast transition that caught him off guard.

"Hang on," he said. "Did you ask me here to interview me?"

"No," she said firmly before he could go any further. "I'm asking because I'm concerned about him as a friend and want to know what you think—presumably also as a friend."

She paused for a moment. "I asked you to lunch because I wanted to see you."

If, at that moment, she had asked Alex to reveal all his darkest secrets *and* break into the Pentagon on her behalf, he would have done it.

"Well, you said there wasn't really anything to worry about," he said. "He can talk to an agent—"

"Agents," she said, cutting in. "It isn't just one now. There are about four recruiting him. Do you know how many teams are going to have scouts at Tuesday's game? Twenty—or more. That doesn't even count the colleges."

"How do you know all this?"

She reached to her left and picked up a thick printout from the seat next to her. She tossed it on the table. "This will be up on the web at noon and in tomorrow's paper."

It was the *Philadelphia Daily News* story that Jonas had mentioned the day before. It was written by Dick Jerardi, whom Alex had first met during football season. Alex glanced at the lead:

Matt Gordon honestly thought his athletic career might be over last November, when he was suspended from the Chester Heights football team after admitting to using performance-enhancing drugs. Not only did he have to sit out the state championship game, but his father, Matthew Gordon Sr., was fired as Chester Heights' coach in the wake of the scandal.

"It was humiliating in every possible way," Gordon said. "The worst part was that I did it to myself. I came very close to going to a boarding school somewhere—just to escape from the whole thing. I'm glad now I stuck it out."

Gordon stuck it out because it occurred to him that the suspension could be a blessing in disguise. He had always wanted to play baseball—which he thought was his best sport—but his father had never allowed him to do so. Now, after his suspension was lifted in time for the start of baseball season, he's playing the game he loves most and opening a lot of eyes with his prowess.

"He's one of the best pitching prospects I've seen around here in the last ten years," said one major league scout, who can't be quoted by name because MLB teams aren't allowed to discuss players who still have high school or college eligibility remaining. "He's amazingly mature, has great control for a kid so young, and understands how to pitch. You don't see all that in a high school junior very often."

Alex looked up. The story was very long, and he could see where it was going.

"It goes on forever," he said.

"I know," she said. "It's almost three thousand words. It'll get national attention. You'd better be ready for that on Tuesday."

Alex shrugged. "Like we haven't been through it before?"

She nodded. "True. But I'm worried about Matt. In the fall, he didn't look like the pressure was getting to him, but it did—which is why he took the PEDs. Now he's reveling in the attention, and I'm worried he's going to make another mistake."

"What kind of mistake?"

"I honestly don't know. All the agents are a concern— that's for sure. I talked to Coach Birdy on background the other day, and he said he thinks Matt's crazy to give up his last year of high school. But if he says that to him, it will look self-serving."

"He's right—on both points."

"I know. Problem is, Matt's really got no one to talk to about this. He doesn't speak to his dad, who has apparently moved out of the house. His mom doesn't know anything about this world. So he needs us."

"Us?" Alex laughed. "Matt *might* listen to you. He's not listening to me."

"I've got someone else in mind. . . ."

"Who?"

Christine nodded in the direction of the front of the restaurant. On cue, Stevie Thomas was walking toward the booth.

■ ■ ■

Stevie Thomas was not, by any stretch, physically imposing. He was, Alex guessed, no more than five nine, and he had curly brown hair. That said, he was one of those people who made you like them almost instantly. Alex had met him in the fall during his football crisis. He remembered something Christine had said about him then: "He's usually the smartest guy in the room. But he never gives you the impression that *he* thinks that."

Now Stevie walked to the booth with a smile on his face and his hand out.

"How's the three-sport star?" he said as Alex stood up to greet him. "Sit down, Alex, please. Hiya, Christine."

He slid into the booth, next to Christine.

"Alex, I swear, if you weren't such a good athlete, I'd sign you up to work with me," he said. "Stories have a way of finding you wherever you go."

"You find tons of stories," Christine said.

"I go out *looking*. But Alex is just trying to play ball and ends up smack in the middle of one story after another."

"This one's not really about me," Alex said.

"I know," Stevie said. "It's about Matt. But he's your friend, your teammate, and a lot of what happened to you in the fall was because of him."

Alex didn't really feel like walking through all that again. It was Christine who jumped into the void left by Alex's silence.

"The question is, what can we do?" she asked, looking at Stevie. "We both have a feeling that Matt's headed down a dangerous path with all these agents and scouts. I mean, he's played all of five high school baseball games. . . ."

Stevie paused as Alex's and Christine's hamburgers arrived. He ordered one himself, then sat back in the cushioned seat.

"Yeah, the agents are bad news. Any agent who's chasing around after a high school kid is looking for some kind of quick fix for his business. The first thing Matt should do is ask who their other clients are. I guarantee you none of them are repping Clayton Kershaw or Madison Bumgarner or, for that matter, Bruce Chen."

Stevie knew who Kershaw and Bumgarner were—two of the best pitchers in baseball. He wasn't so sure about Chen.

"Bruce Chen?" he said.

Stevie smiled. "Just retired about a year ago. Pitched in the majors for seventeen years. Point is, I'll bet these guys chasing Matt are small-timers. They're hoping to catch lightning in a bottle with Matt—or any one of the dozen other kids they're probably romancing. Happens all the time."

"So what do we do?" Christine asked.

"An intervention," Stevie said. "I think your friend needs an intervention before it's too late. And, as Yogi Berra might have said, it gets late early when agents are involved. Very early."

Alex had read about interventions. But they involved addicts—people who drank too much or were addicted to drugs.

"Aren't interventions for people with addiction problems?" he said.

Steve smiled. So too, Alex noticed, did Christine.

"An intervention can be about almost anything," Stevie said. "It just means that a group of people who care about someone get together to tell that person they think he or she needs help dealing with a problem. Matt has a problem that he didn't create—except in the sense that he's a very talented baseball player. But based on what Christine's told me, he needs help with all that's happening to him right now. Anyone his age would need help."

"But who can help him?" Christine said. "We're all teen-agers too. Doesn't this need an adult?"

"Adults, yes—more than one," Stevie answered. "I know his dad's not around and his mom doesn't know much about sports."

"And, like you said, Christine, if we involve Coach Birdy, Matt can brush him off, saying he just wants him back to ‚itch next season," Alex said.

Stevie nodded. "Right. You need someone who is an expert on gifted athletes and what they deal with *and* has no agenda."

"Any ideas?" Christine asked.

"Yup," Stevie said. "Bryce Harper."

"Bryce Harper?" they both said together.

Then Christine, speaking for Alex, added, "How are you going to get Bryce Harper to come and talk to Matt?"

"I'm not," Stevie said. "I'm going to take Matt to talk to Bryce. The Nationals are coming to town next week to play the Phillies. We'll do it then."

"Before I even ask how you plan to pull that off, tell me why Bryce Harper," Christine said.

"He was such a phenom that he graduated from high school two years early. Went to junior college for a year because he wasn't draft-eligible yet. Then he was the number one pick in the draft, and five years later, he was one of the best players in baseball—the National League MVP.

"The difference is, his father's been involved every step of the way. They dodged most—if not all—of the pitfalls of being a phenom. I can't think of anyone better to tell someone like Matt that he needs to be careful who he gets involved with."

"Okay, that's a great why," Alex said. "But how?"

"Getting Matt and Bryce together?" Stevie said. "Not that hard. I've dealt with Bryce a couple times. He's actually a very good guy. When the Nats come here, I'll arrange to get credentials for Matt, and I can take him to the clubhouse a few hours before a game so he can talk to Bryce."

Alex couldn't resist. "Can we go too?" he asked.

"Alex!" Christine said. "This isn't about us."

Stevie smiled. "I'm sure I can arrange for another student reporter and one of Matt's teammates to come too. You guys will have to follow my lead when we get there. You can't start asking for autographs or stuff like that."

That was a little disappointing for Alex. He would have loved to have gotten an autograph from Daniel Murphy or Wilson Ramos or Ryan Zimmerman—even though he was a Red Sox fan. But Christine was right. This wasn't about them.

■ ■ ■

Stevie Thomas's presence at lunch meant that Alex and Christine never really got a chance to talk. She mentioned while they were eating that her dad was picking her up and she was spending the rest of the weekend with him. That eliminated any possibility of a movie or any discussion about whether their "break" was over. Alex figured he shouldn't try to force anything.

"Give her space" was his new mantra.

On Monday, Christine told him she'd gotten an update from Stevie. The Phillies were playing an afternoon game on Saturday against the Nationals. Stevie had made arrangements for Matt, Christine, and Alex to get press passes so they could go see Harper in the clubhouse at Citizens Bank Park at ten in the morning.

"Stevie said Saturday is good because it's a day game after a night game, so the Nationals won't be taking batting practice," she said. "Bryce should have time before the game to talk."

"So what do we tell Matt?" Alex asked.

"Basically, I'm going to tell him the truth: Stevie knows Bryce and thought he'd want to talk to him since he left high school early."

"You think Matt will buy that?"

"What's to buy?" she said. "It's the truth. Besides—who wouldn't jump at the chance to talk to a major leaguer?"

Alex decided there was no point debating with her since he was fairly certain she'd be able to talk Matt into going. But he suspected Matt might have a more complicated reaction than she expected.

■ ■ ■

The conference home opener against Bryn Mawr Tech brought out masses of people—fans and the media— especially since Matt was scheduled to pitch.

He didn't disappoint. He gave up two hits all afternoon—a bunt single in the first inning and a long home run in the fourth by Bryn Mawr's cleanup hitter, Malcolm Folley, whom Alex remembered as a linebacker from football season. Folley timed a fastball perfectly and hit it way over the left field fence. Alex started back when the ball came off the bat but quickly realized he would need a jetpack to get anywhere close to it.

But Chester Heights scored three runs in the first inning—two on a long double by Matt that drove in Cardillo and Alex, both of whom had walked. And then in the fifth, Matt—as if to prove he could match anything that anyone else did on the field—hit a home run of his own that also went way over the left field fence.

Matt was still pitching in the seventh, and he ended the game by striking Folley out on three pitches. The first two were fastballs—one a called strike, the other a foul ball straight back. The third pitch was a classic "twelve-to-six" curveball—a pitch that started as if it was going to hit the batter in the head, then broke down and away, crossing the strike zone at about knee height. Folley almost broke his back flailing at it.

The final score was 4–1, Chester Heights. Alex knew that Bryn Mawr had finished third in the conference the previous season behind Chester and Haverford Station, so this was a good win to start the conference season.

Alex noticed that Matt's postgame session was now divided into not one, not two, but three different groups. First came TV and radio—one of the cameras said ESPN. Apparently Matt was going national.

Jonas, who never missed anything, nudged Alex. "ESPN. What do you think about that?"

"Better ESPN than CNN," Alex said, thinking back to the fall. "As long as the story is just about Matt's pitching and hitting, it's fine."

After TV and radio finished, the print guys would close in—no doubt wanting more detailed answers than Matt had given on camera.

And, finally, the acolytes—scouts and agents—would get their turn with the new prince of Philadelphia baseball.

Alex and Jonas were walking past the dugout on their way back to the locker room when Alex noticed Bailey Warner standing on the top step. Alex hadn't seen Warner at all—not even in the hallways—since Coach Birdy had first told them about his shoulder problems. Warner's arm was in a sling.

"Bailey, what's with the sling?" Jonas said. "Where have you been hiding?"

Warner smiled wanly. "I've been around," he said. "I've gotten a couple cortisone shots in the shoulder. The doctor wants me to wear the sling so I'm not tempted to use it and hurt myself. He's hoping that if I rest it completely for about a week, then rehab it, I won't need surgery."

"What kind of surgery?" Alex asked.

"Rotator cuff," Warner said. "They did four different MRIs and still aren't sure why it's hurting me. The doctor finally said that a couple of my rotator cuff bands are probably just worn down from throwing."

"Rotator cuff bands?" Jonas asked.

"Yeah, you've got four in each shoulder that make up the cuff," Warner said. "Sometimes they just wear down, and sometimes they pop. When they pop, you have no choice but to have surgery."

"So does that mean you can't pitch again?"

Warner shook his head. "Means I have to rest. The doctor said give it two, three weeks and then see how it feels after rehab. Meanwhile"—he nodded in Matt's direction—"it doesn't look like you guys need me much anyway."

Alex laughed. "Oh no, we need you. We'll especially need you as the season goes along."

Warner rubbed his left arm against the sling for a moment.

"I thought this was going to be my year to be the number one starter," he said. "Even if I can get healthy, I'll probably be no better than number three. Matt's a star, and from what I've heard, Alex, you aren't that far behind."

"I'm *way* behind," Alex said, not being modest. "And I'm behind you too when you're healthy." On that, he *was* being modest. He thought he might be a better pitcher than Warner based on what little he'd seen. Then again, Warner had probably been pitching with a sore shoulder all spring.

"Thanks for that, Alex. But right now, I just want to pitch," Warner said. "Give me an inning out of the bullpen and I'll be happy."

Someone up in the stands was calling Warner's name.

"Gotta go," he said. "I can't drive with the sling, so my mom's waiting." He paused like he wanted to say more but just said, "Keep it going, guys. Keep winning." Then he turned and walked away.

Alex and Jonas were both quiet. "It's not fair, you know," Jonas said.

"You mean about him being hurt?"

"Yeah, that's part of it," Jonas said. "But it's also not fair that he's been completely forgotten because he's hurt and Matt's now everybody's hero again."

"Bothers you?" Alex said.

Jonas paused. "Yeah—a little bit, at least. Matt cheated. I know why he cheated, and he showed guts admitting it— even though he was gonna get caught anyway. I'm not saying he's a bad guy, but . . ."

"But a cheater shouldn't be a hero?"

"Do you think he should?"

Alex looked back at Matt. The print media had started moving away, and he could see the guys in the business suits and sweat suits—the agents and the scouts—moving in.

"You know, he's been through a lot too," Alex said. "His father's out of his life, and even though he might be a jerk at times, it's tough losing your father."

"You can relate, huh?" Jonas said.

"Yeah," Alex said. "I can relate."

It seemed to Alex that there were two Matt Gordons in his life.

There was Matt the Old—the same guy who had been his friend all fall; who had stood in front of the whole school and taken responsibility for his screwup with PEDs; who had taken the time to teach him how to properly grip a curveball.

Then there was Matt the New—who couldn't seem to get enough attention; who seemed worried only about himself; who thought he was better than everyone, at least in part because he *was* better than everyone.

On Thursday, the day before the game at King of Prussia, Matt the Old made another appearance at practice.

"Your curve's coming along, Goldie," he said as they threw lightly on the side while the position players took batting practice. "But you're gonna need a third pitch. You need a slider. Never been a great pitcher who hasn't thrown one."

Alex was a long way from being a great pitcher, but he knew that in the majors the slider was often the "out" pitch—the one that pitchers used when they most needed an out. The most notable exception, at least as far as Alex knew, was his fellow Billerican Tom Glavine, who had been famous for throwing one of baseball's wickedest changeups.

"How do you throw it?" Alex asked.

"I'll show you," Matt said, taking the ball from Alex. "Here, hold the ball as if you're going to throw your fastball."

As he had done with the curveball, he showed Alex the grip—which wasn't all that different from the way Alex gripped his fastball. He knew it was called a "two-seam" fastball because you gripped the two seams with your fingers side by side. Older pitchers also threw a "four-seamer," which simply meant your fingers went across the seams so each touched the seams twice—for a total of four seams.

"All you do is move your index finger so it's between the seams rather than on the left seam. Gives the ball a different spin. Then you cock your wrist a little more toward where the thumb is on the other side of the ball. The extra pressure on the thumb makes the ball break and dart, and it comes in almost as fast as the fastball. That's why it's so hard to hit."

Alex did as he was told. Since they weren't actually doing any throwing the day before a game, Matt ran down to catch him. "Just throw a few," he said.

The first three slipped completely out of Alex's hand because he was unable to control the ball with his thumb the way he did with his index and middle fingers. The fourth pitch was better—reaching Matt's glove.

"Right!" Matt shouted. "Just ease up a little. Remember what I said about the curve—try easier."

Alex did so, and each pitch got a little better. Matt stopped him after ten pitches.

"Don't want to overdo it," he said. "You need your arm for tomorrow. For now, only use it on three-and-oh when no one's on base and if you miss with it and it's a walk, it's no big deal. Or on oh-and-two when if you throw a strike, the batter's got no chance, or if you throw a ball, it's still one-and-two. You'll need to practice it some more before you start throwing it often."

"Thanks, Matt," Alex said. "Where did you learn all this?"

"From a book," Matt said. "That's where I got the grips. Throwing the pitches was practice. Remember: Try easier."

They heard Coach Birdy's whistle and jogged, with the other pitchers, to the middle of the infield.

Once again, Alex wondered who the real Matt Gordon was. He liked this one a lot.

■ ■ ■

Alex never got to try his slider in Friday's game against King of Prussia. They'd finished mid-conference last year, so Alex hoped he could cruise through to a win. But when he walked into the dugout after warming up, Matt pulled him aside.

"They've got three transfers," he said. "Two of them are twin brothers, and they hit third and fourth."

"How do you know?" Alex asked.

"Because the kid you're pitching against is their starting quarterback," Matt said. "He told me a few minutes ago."

The twins, Jake and Joey Herman, were huge. Alex found out later they'd just moved from California with their mom.

In the first inning, Alex struck out the leadoff hitter but then gave up an infield single to the second batter. The kid hit what Alex figured was a routine grounder to third base. Jeff Cardillo fielded it cleanly and threw smoothly to first. There was one problem: The KOP kid was so fast that he beat the throw.

Then Jake Herman stepped in. Alex had never pitched to anyone so big. He had to be six foot five and weigh at least 230 pounds. But could he hit?

Alex got the answer quickly. After he'd thrown a fastball outside, he came back with another fastball, meant to get inside and on Herman's hands. Clearly, it wasn't far enough inside because Herman turned on it and hit a line drive that Alex thought might go *through* the right field fence. It hit halfway up, and Brendan Chu and Jonas chased it down in right-center. The kid with the rockets in his legs scored easily from first, and Herman lumbered into second.

That was the hardest Alex had ever seen anyone hit a ball—until two pitches later. He got a called strike on Joey Herman, then decided to try to fool him with a curveball off the plate. The pitch caught too much of the plate and didn't fool Herman even a little bit. He swung and hit the ball five miles into the air. It didn't go straight up, though—it kept carrying to center field. Jonas raced back a few steps, then stopped and turned to watch it soar *way* over the fence. Alex figured it would come down somewhere near the Pennsylvania Turnpike.

Alex had faced only four batters and already trailed 3–0. Coach Birdy came out to talk to him.

"You okay?" he said. "Those two guys are both eighteen-year-old seniors. Don't worry about them. Get the rest of these guys out, and we'll even up the score."

Alex, still a little bit in shock, nodded.

"You sure you're okay?"

"I'm fine, Coach."

He was lying. He walked the next two batters and then gave up a two-run double. It was 5–0 by the time he got to the dugout.

The KOP fans were roaring, and the Lions were shaken. But they got a couple men on in the second, which steadied them, even though they didn't come around to score.

Alex regrouped and pitched better after that. He got the first two hitters in the second inning, then unintentionally/intentionally walked both Hermans. The number five hitter singled to drive in Jake, but Alex struck out the next hitter to get out of the inning.

Then he retired the side in order in the third.

As he came to the dugout, though, Coach Birdy said, "Good job, Alex. We're going to put you out in left next inning."

"Coach, I just got 'em one, two, three," Alex said in protest.

"I know you did," Coach Birdy said. "But you've thrown seventy-eight pitches. I couldn't let you pitch more than one more inning anyway because I wouldn't want to risk your arm. Let's give the bullpen some work and make sure your arm lives to pitch another day."

Alex hoped the Lions' bats would get hot in a hurry. But no.

And the bullpen got shelled even worse than Alex had. Each Herman brother hit a massive home run, and the rest of the lineup chipped in too. By the time the carnage was over, King of Prussia had fourteen runs. Chester Heights managed to score twice—in the top of the seventh—making the final score 14–2.

"Too bad they don't have a mercy rule in this league," Jonas said after the last out.

"You aren't supposed to lose this badly in high school, I guess," Alex replied. The mercy rule was in effect in Little League games. If a team fell behind by ten runs, the game ended in order to avoid truly embarrassing scores . . . like 14–2.

Once they'd shaken hands and gathered in the dugout before the bus trip home, Coach Birdy spoke quietly but firmly.

"It was a bad day," he said. "They happen in baseball. We play them back at our place next month; the score might be reversed."

"Only if I pitch," Matt said, loud enough to be heard.

Everyone turned and looked at him. "Kidding," he said, realizing how obnoxious the comment had sounded.

"Gordon, if you'd pitched today, the score might still have been fourteen to two," Coach Birdy said. "They just had a very good day, and we had a bad one. We're one-and-one in conference now, and we go to Haverford Station on Tuesday. They're likely to be as solid as these guys." He looked Matt right in the eye. "You're pitching, Gordon," he said. "We'll find out what you've got. For the rest of you, let's make Monday's practice a productive one. I'll have some things for us to work on."

The bus ride back to school was very quiet. As usual, Alex sat near the back with Jonas. When the bus was stopped at a light, Matt came and sat right across from Alex.

"You know what I said wasn't directed at you, right?" he said.

Alex really wasn't sure. "Well, it was directed at least in part at me, wasn't it?" he said. "I was the one who got us down by six runs after two innings."

"Yeah, but—"

"Yeah, *but*," Jonas interrupted. "You need to stop thinking you're Madison Bumgarner or something. We all know you're good. We see the scouts and the agents. But you don't need to rub our noses in it. Where's the Matt Gordon we'd have all run through a wall for during football season?"

Matt stared at Jonas, and for a moment, Alex thought the two of them were going to really get into it.

"I don't know where he is," Matt finally answered. "Maybe he decided that winning's more important than being Mr. Nice Guy."

"We won twelve football games," Alex said. "A lot of them because of you."

"Yeah," Matt said. "And lost the last one. Without me."

This time, he didn't wait for the bus to stop before getting up and walking back to his seat.

Alex was left feeling like he'd been punched in the gut all over again.

Jonas mumbled under his breath: "Intervention time, for sure."

■ ■ ■

The plan for Saturday morning was for everyone to meet in the school parking lot at nine-thirty. Alex had asked for Jonas to be included too, and Stevie had arranged for it. After what had happened on Friday, Alex wasn't sure it was such a good idea. In fact, he wasn't sure if the whole *outing* was a good idea. He'd never felt so tense about going to a ball game.

Alex, Christine, and Jonas had all ridden their bicycles and were waiting by Stevie's car when Matt pulled up shortly after nine-thirty.

"Sorry, everyone," Matt said as he locked his car. "I hit every light. Least it felt that way."

As they drove toward Citizens Bank Park, Stevie explained to them how things would go.

"We'll all go into the clubhouse, and I'll introduce everyone to Bryce. I told him I was bringing several people in addition to Matt. Then, Matt, we'll leave you to really talk with Bryce, and I'll take everyone else to the Phillies' clubhouse. I thought you might want to meet some of the players."

"No autographs, right?" Jonas asked.

"Right," Stevie said. "You're in the clubhouse with a media credential, so you have to behave like members of the media. They aren't allowed to ask for autographs."

"Why not?" Alex asked, curious.

"It's unprofessional," Stevie said. "Fans can't go in there to ask for autographs, so the presumption is that if you're there, it's because you have a job to do. If you aren't doing a job, you shouldn't be there."

"In other words, we shouldn't be there," Alex said.

"I told the Phillies exactly what we were doing when I asked for the credentials, and I promised that no one would get in the way," Stevie said. "If I'd wanted to bring you in after a game, with writers on deadline, they'd have said no. But before a game, especially a day game, it's a little bit looser."

Stevie had managed to get a parking pass in the media lot, which was directly across the street from the media entrance, but a long way from home plate—at least as far as Alex could see. The guy at the door waved them through when he saw their credentials. That surprised Alex a little. They didn't exactly look like reporters.

They walked down a long hallway that led past the Phillies' clubhouse and finally came to the clubhouse marked VISITORS. They had to sign in there, and then Stevie led them into the biggest locker room Alex had ever seen in his life.

There were several couches in the middle of the room, and a card table and chairs nearby. A number of guys were playing cards, and several others, in varying degrees of undress, were sitting on the couches reading newspapers. If Christine's presence bothered them, they didn't show it. Alex noticed a female reporter standing at Gio Gonzalez's locker chatting with the left-handed pitcher.

Bryce Harper was sitting in an armchair by his locker, headphones on, when they approached. He must have seen them coming, because he took the headphones off and stood to greet Stevie.

They shook hands, and Harper nodded at Stevie's four companions. "Which one's the hotshot pitcher?" he asked. He smiled at Christine and said, "I'm betting you're the hotshot reporter, right? The next Stevie Thomas?"

"The next Susan Carol Anderson, I hope," Christine said, giving Harper her dazzling smile.

"Oh yes, I've met her," Harper said. "She and Stevie are quite the team."

Stevie introduced them all, saving Matt for last. "He's the hotshot pitcher," he said.

"Okay, hotshot," Harper said. "How about if you and I take a walk out to the dugout. No BP today, so it'll be quiet out there."

He picked up his phone, which was in his locker, and held it up. "I'll text you when we're done," he said to Stevie.

"We're going to go by the Phillies' clubhouse," Stevie said.

"Good," Harper said. "Tell their pitcher to go easy on me."

■ ■ ■

As luck would have it, Matt Harrison, the Phillies' pitcher, was standing in front of his locker talking to Dick Jerardi when they walked into the home clubhouse, which was about twice the size of the visitors' clubhouse.

"You could put a hundred guys in here," Alex murmured to Jonas as they walked in.

"Easily," Jonas said.

Seeing a friendly face, Stevie made a beeline for Jerardi, who looked a little surprised to see the four teenagers walking in his direction.

"Hang on—is this the World Series?" he said with a laugh. "I thought Stevie Thomas only showed up for the big events."

"Just visiting," Stevie said. "I think you know these guys from Chester Heights."

"I do," Jerardi said. "Two three-sport stars and a future Pulitzer Prize winner." He turned to Harrison and said, "Matt, when you're ready to write your book, this"—he pointed at Christine—"is who you want to write it."

Alex noticed that Christine had turned bright red. He didn't think he'd ever seen her look embarrassed before. Angry, yes; embarrassed, no.

Harrison put out a hand to Christine. "When the time comes, Dick will know how I can reach you, right?" he said with a smile.

Christine was trying to talk but not doing very well. Finally, she managed to stammer, "Um, sure, yeah. . . . I think he's just joking."

"Couldn't be more serious," Jerardi said. Then he introduced Alex and Jonas. It occurred to Alex that he had never before been in the presence of someone who was paid more than thirteen million a year. The thought made him a little bit dizzy.

"So, what brings you guys out today?" Harrison said. "It isn't to see me pitch—I'm injured."

"Yeah, I know," Stevie said. "Harper says to tell the other guys to go easy on him."

Harrison laughed. "If we go easy on him, he'll hit three bombs today instead of just one or two."

Stevie explained the real purpose of the outing. Harrison turned serious.

"How good is he?" he asked.

It was Jerardi who answered. "I've seen him once, Matt. He's very good—for sixteen. Hits ninety-four, ninety-five on the gun pretty regularly. Good control. If you didn't know how old he was, you'd figure him for eighteen, maybe nineteen."

"What'd you hit on the gun when you were a junior in high school?" Stevie asked.

"Never hit ninety," Harrison said. "But I grew kind of late. Sometimes it's better that way. You put a lot of pressure on your arm throwing in the mid-nineties that young. That's why so many young pitchers end up having Tommy John before they're twenty-five."

Alex knew that Tommy John was a kind of elbow-repair surgery that had first been performed in the 1970s on a very good pitcher named Tommy John. The doctor who invented it, whose name Alex couldn't remember at the moment, had taken a tendon from John's other arm and used it to replace a torn ligament in his pitching elbow. The surgery had now become almost commonplace among pitchers, and in many cases, they actually threw harder after the surgery than they had before.

"That's one reason we thought it would be a good idea to talk to Bryce," Stevie said. "Even though leaving high school early didn't hurt him, he went through some growing pains along the way."

Harrison nodded. "That was about maturing as a person

more than as a hitter, probably," he said. "Plus, he's a once-in-a-lifetime type of talent. Pitchers should never be rushed."

"Matt's a good hitter too," Christine said.

Harrison smiled. "I was a good hitter in high school too," he said. "We were all good hitters in high school."

"So what would *you* tell him to do?" Jerardi asked.

"Go to college," Harrison said. "Enjoy being a kid. Once you turn pro, you're living the life of an adult, even if you aren't an adult. And the minor leagues are rough. Small towns, cheap hotels, bars where you can smell the cigarette smoke before you walk inside. Tell him not to be in a rush."

"You signed out of high school," Christine said—not surprising Alex by knowing Harrison's history. "And you turned out all right."

"Yup, I did," Harrison agreed. "I wasn't quite eighteen when I signed, and I struggled for a few years and I've had a lot of injuries along the way. I could have gone to college, had a good time, and still been here today."

"So do you regret signing early?" Alex said.

Harrison shook his head. "Regret it? No. Like my future biographer said, I turned out all right. But if I had it to do over again . . ." He paused and shrugged. "I would like to know somebody's fight song by heart."

Stevie's phone buzzed.

"It's Bryce," he said. "They're done."

They thanked Harrison for taking the time to talk to them and shook hands with Jerardi. As they walked back down the hallway, Alex asked Stevie if he knew the name of the doctor who had invented Tommy John surgery.

Before Stevie could answer, Christine, who was doing her best Hermione Granger imitation, answered, "Frank Jobe. I think he died just a couple of years ago."

"He did," Stevie said, nodding assent.

"I wonder why the surgery is named for Tommy John and not for Frank Jobe," Jonas said, echoing Alex's very thought.

"Good question," Stevie said. "One that I don't have an answer for right now."

They found Matt waiting for them in the hallway.

"They're having some kind of team meeting, so they kicked everyone out," he said. "Bryce said he was sorry he didn't get to see you guys again."

"So you liked him?" Christine said.

"Oh yeah, good guy," Matt said.

Before he could say anything more, the security guard stationed in front of the clubhouse door walked over to where they were standing.

"You kids need to get out of the hallway," he said. "How'd you get down here anyway?"

Alex realized this was a different guy from the one who had checked their credentials when they walked in. The first guy had been young, African American, and friendly. This one was older, white, and decidedly unfriendly.

"We have credentials," Stevie said, pointing to the badge dangling around his neck and to those the rest of them were also wearing in very plain sight.

The security guard took Stevie's credential in his hands and looked at it closely. Disappointed that it was legitimate, he said, "Okay, then, but don't loiter out here. The clubhouse is closed. You need to move along."

"Actually, we don't," Stevie said. "But we will, since there's no one here we want to talk to anyway."

With that, he turned, saying, "Come on, guys. Let's go upstairs and eat."

Alex could hear the security guy muttering as they walked down the hall. "You ever mess with me again, kid . . ."

They didn't stop to hear the rest.

■ ■ ■

It cost them ten dollars apiece to eat lunch in the press box. The food was reasonably good, and sitting in the dining area, surrounded by various media members, seemed like a very cool thing to Alex. After they all were settled with lunch, Matt filled them in on his conversation with Bryce Harper.

"We got interrupted a few times," he said, biting into a hamburger. "Some publicity guy wanted to make sure he'd do a TV interview before tomorrow's game. Then someone else brought some kids to meet him and get autographs."

"I thought that wasn't allowed," Jonas said.

Stevie jumped in. "They were probably with someone from the marketing department and had dugout passes because they know someone or paid extra money or something. That goes on all the time."

Matt nodded. "That's what Bryce said. Their passes were definitely different from ours."

"Cut to the chase," Christine finally said. "What'd he say?"

"He said what I guess you guys thought he'd say," Matt replied. "He said if I was really good enough to make it to the majors, I would, no matter when I come out of high school or whether I go to college or not. He said he was really lucky because he only spent a year in the minor leagues, but most of the time pitchers need longer than that. And that college is a nicer place to develop as a pitcher than the bush leagues."

"That makes sense to me," Alex said.

"Yeah, I guess," Matt said. "I asked him how long Stephen Strasburg was in the minors, and he said it was less than a year but that he'd gone to college for three years."

"So, are you convinced?" Stevie asked.

"I'm convinced that you guys are trying to steer me in what you think is the best direction," Matt said. "But I'm not convinced you really *know* what's best for me."

"Do you think Bryce Harper knows what's best for you?" Christine answered.

"Honestly?" Matt said. "No." He smiled. "But I do think he'd make a great teammate someday."

■ ■ ■

Stevie told Matt what Harrison had said about wishing he'd gone to college. Matt listened and nodded. "But signing out of high school *did* work out for him, right? Look, I'm not a dummy, I've done some homework on this. There's no guarantee one way or the other."

"Yeah, but if you go to college, you've got a backup plan," Jonas said.

"And if I'm drafted in the first round and I get a bonus of a million dollars, I'll have plenty of money to go to college if baseball doesn't work out."

"Who told you that?" Stevie asked.

"A bunch of people," Matt said.

"Agents," Christine said, pointing a finger in an accusing way at Matt.

"And scouts," Matt said calmly. "Look, I can put my name in the draft if I graduate from high school. If I'm not offered a lot of money, I can still say no and go to college."

"Not if you sign with an agent," Stevie said.

"I don't have to sign with an agent," Matt said. "They're allowed to be 'advisors' until you sign a contract."

"Only if you haven't taken any money from them," Alex said.

For the first time, Matt's answer wasn't quick and easy. He looked at Alex as if deciding how to respond, then said, "Right you are, Goldie."

There was a long silence. Alex saw Tom McCarthy, whom he recognized as the TV play-by-play voice for the Phillies, walking in the direction of the table.

"Stevie Thomas is here?" McCarthy said in the same tone Jerardi had used in the clubhouse. "Did we release Ryan Howard? Have we fired another manager? Is the ballpark on fire?"

"Just a day at the park with some friends," Stevie answered. He was apparently used to famous people not only recognizing him but also knowing of his reporting exploits. Alex thought it must be unbelievably cool to be Stevie Thomas.

Stevie introduced them all to McCarthy, noting they were all from Chester Heights High School.

"Of course," McCarthy said. He pointed to Alex and Jonas. "The freshman hotshots, right? Quarterback and wide receiver." He turned to Matt and said, "And you're the comeback story, right? Fallen quarterback turned pitching phenom."

If the "fallen quarterback" reference bothered Matt, he didn't show it. "I've been watching you for years, Mr. McCarthy," he said, shaking hands.

McCarthy turned to Christine. "And you're the student reporter. I've read you in the *Daily News*. I didn't realize how pretty you were. If you ever decide you'd prefer TV to writing, let me know."

"I prefer writing," Christine said, smiling.

"Understood. Good for you," McCarthy said. "Of course, if Dick Jerardi can do both, anybody can."

Jerardi had just walked up to the table carrying a tray. "The only thing I'll say about you, Tommy, is that no one can accuse you of making it in TV because of your looks," he said without missing a beat.

McCarthy nodded, laughed, and looked again at Matt. "I read in the paper the other day that you're thinking of graduating this summer and going in the draft?"

"Thinking about it," Matt said.

"Well, just remember, it gets mighty hot in Clearwater in July."

Someone was calling McCarthy's name. He waved a hand at everyone to say goodbye and walked off.

"Clearwater?" Matt said.

"It's where the Phillies' rookie league team is," Jerardi said. "You turn pro, that's the kind of place you'll go to start out."

"I won't be there for long," Matt said.

"Let me guess who promised you that," Christine said.

"I'm going to get some ice cream," Matt said. He stood up and walked away.

■ ■ ■

The day wasn't entirely lost as far as Alex was concerned. It was the first weekend of the major league season, and the weather was brisk—an announced fifty-nine degrees at game time—but it was sunny, and the view from the press box was spectacular.

Even sitting in the third row, where there were ample

empty seats, they could see the entire field perfectly. They also had a great view of the Philadelphia skyline since the afternoon was as clear as a newly cleaned windshield.

Alex kept score, the way he always did when he went to Fenway Park with his dad. Bryce Harper hit a mammoth two-run home run in the first inning—already his third in only the fifth game of the season—but that was all the scoring for the Nats. The Phillies got home runs in the fifth from Maikel Franco and Odubel Herrera, then scored again in the sixth on a Stephen Strasburg wild pitch. That was enough. The Phillies won, 3–2.

Alex didn't have any real feelings for either team, but he enjoyed seeing the home team win, if only because he really liked the ballpark. There wasn't much talk among the group during the game. All of them were into it, and Matt and Christine, born and raised in Philadelphia, were intensely involved in pulling—quietly—for the Phillies. Stevie had explained that the rule about no cheering in the press box was taken very seriously.

Alex had heard about the rule from Christine in the past, but she had told him that at high school football games there were always a few people who cheered anyway. Not so in a Major League Baseball press box. That was fine with Alex because it allowed him to focus more closely on the game without the distractions of people jumping up in front of him.

They stayed until the last pitch and then walked quickly back to the car. Since the media lot wasn't that far away, they were able to beat most of the traffic back to I-95.

They made small talk in the car, most of it centered on

whether the Phillies could break out of their doldrums in the coming season. Finally, as Stevie wheeled the car into the school parking lot, Matt changed the subject.

"Hey, Stevie, thanks for setting the whole day up," he said. "I don't want you to think I'm not going to think about what Harper said or about what you guys told me Harrison said, either."

He paused. "It means a lot to me that you guys care about me—even if I've been a bit of a jerk this spring."

They had pulled into the spot next to Matt's car.

"Don't underestimate yourself, Matt," Jonas said. "You've been a *complete* jerk this spring."

He was smiling when he said it, but everyone—Matt included—knew it wasn't just a laugh line.

"I know, Jonas," Matt said. "I'll try to do better."

He popped out of the car with a wave goodbye. As Stevie pulled over to the bicycle rack, Christine asked the question that was on all their minds.

"Think he learned anything?"

"Not a thing," Stevie said.

Alex was only marginally more hopeful. "I think he doesn't *want* to be a jerk," he said. "But there are a lot of people tugging him in a lot of different directions right now."

"Yeah," Christine said. "And a lot of them are tugging him in the wrong direction."

On Monday, Matt rejoined the lunch table, as did Christine, and it felt like old times to Alex. He and Christine hadn't had time for any kind of serious talk since their Stark's lunch a week earlier, but she had been noticeably warmer to him since then, even making a point of complimenting him after French class one day when he had smoothly—for him—recited a fairly lengthy passage from *The Three Musketeers*.

Matt was his old self during lunch, talking about how Chester Heights stacked up in the conference after the loss to King of Prussia. "Those twins are all stars, but I hear the only good pitcher they have is the guy who pitched on Friday—Anderson," he said. "They aren't going to go undefeated. No one will. We'll get another shot at them."

"Do *we* have more than one good pitcher?" Alex asked.

"'Course we do, Goldie," Matt answered. "You had a bad

day. It happens. Did you see what happened to Vince Velasquez yesterday?"

Alex had seen that Velasquez, the Phillies' best starter, had been knocked out by the Nationals in four innings on Saturday—largely because Bryce Harper had homered twice off him.

"Maybe Velasquez went easy on Harper, as requested," Christine said.

"Yeah, right," Matt said. "Point is, if Vince Velasquez can give up six runs in four innings, it can happen to a high school kid."

"Bryce Harper is a little better than the King of Prussia hitters," Jonas countered.

"I don't know," Alex said. "Those twins were pretty good."

They all laughed, and Alex felt as relaxed as he had in a long time. That feeling lasted all the way through Monday's practice, where he worked on his slider and felt like he was getting more consistent with it, and all the way through the start of the game at Haverford Station the next day. With Matt on the mound, the Lions were a different team. The opposition was different too. No one in Haverford Station's lineup resembled the Herman twins in any way, shape, or form.

Matt retired the first eight hitters before issuing a walk to Haverford Station's catcher, the number nine hitter in the lineup. The walk came on a 3–2 pitch that Matt thought was a strike. Even from left field, Alex could hear him shout "Really?" at the umpire as he came down off the mound to take Lucas Mann's toss back to him.

Okay, Alex thought, *let's not start this again*. Matt must have had the same thought because he took the return throw and walked back onto the mound without another word. By then, Chester Heights had a 2–0 lead, thanks to Alex, Matt, and Jonas. Alex had singled with one out in the first, and Matt had promptly doubled to the left-center field gap. Running all the way, Alex had scored. Jonas then poked a single up the middle to score Matt.

Alex's sense was that the two runs would be enough, but in the bottom of the fifth, Cardillo walked, Alex walked, and then Matt hit a long home run to left to make it 5–0.

The only real suspense at that point was whether Matt would finish off his no-hitter this time. He walked two more hitters in the fifth but ended the inning by striking out the catcher, whom he had walked earlier. It was his ninth strike-out of the day.

In the bottom of the sixth, Haverford Station's leadoff man, Eddie Kenworthy—Alex didn't know his name until later—took a called first strike. Then, with the infield playing back, he squared and pushed a perfect bunt between the mound and third base.

Caught by surprise, Matt bounced off the mound, picked the ball up, and turned to throw in one motion. But his back leg slipped, and he threw wildly to first. There was little doubt that Kenworthy would have beaten the throw even if it had been perfect. With the wild throw, he ended up on second. Alex heard the PA announcer say, "That is a single and an E-1." E-1 meant an error on the pitcher—Matt.

As the next hitter stepped into the box, Matt stood on

the back of the mound, hands on hips, staring at Kenworthy, who was standing with one foot on second base.

"You're down five–nothing and you bunt just to try to break up a no-hitter?" Matt said, loudly enough that Alex could hear him from his position in shallow left field.

Kenworthy spread his hands and said, "I'm on second base, pal."

"Yeah, because you're playing —— baseball," Matt said, using a word that was very much banned in the Myers household.

The second base umpire moved between the two players, pointed a finger at Matt, and said, "That's enough, son. Get up on the mound and pitch."

Matt paused for a moment, nodded, and went back onto the pitching rubber. Alex breathed a sigh of relief.

Billy Twardzik stepped in. Twardzik was the only Haverford Station player Alex knew. He was the Hornets' best basketball player by far, and he and Alex had become semifriendly during their two basketball games that winter.

Twardzik had come the closest of anyone to getting a hit off of Matt prior to the Kenworthy bunt, hitting a long fly ball that Jonas ran down in deep center field. Now he stepped in, waving the bat, wanting to get Kenworthy home.

He never got the chance.

Matt's first pitch was a rising fastball that went straight at Twardzik's head. From where Alex was standing, it looked as if Twardzik was just a tad slow trying to duck. No doubt, given Matt's pinpoint control most of the day, he was surprised to see a pitch heading right for him. Alex heard the *thunk* of the ball hitting the side of Twardzik's head. He was wearing a batting helmet that protected his ear, but it appeared the pitch had caught him just below the flap. He went down as if he had been shot, his face in the dirt, arms outstretched.

He twitched briefly and then stopped moving. Alex felt his heart go into his throat. He knew instantly that this was serious. Very serious.

Lucas Mann and the umpire were the first ones to get to Twardzik, with Matt right behind. The Haverford Station dugout emptied, and Alex wasn't sure if it was to see how badly Twardzik was hurt or to go after Matt. There was no doubt in Alex's mind that Matt had thrown at Twardzik in retaliation for Kenworthy bunting to break up the no-hitter.

While the coach leaned over Twardzik, Alex could hear several players yelling "Are you crazy?"—and a number of other things that weren't nearly as polite—at Matt.

Alex saw everyone leaving the Chester Heights dugout and the rest of his teammates heading in the direction of the plate. He began running in too, if only because that's what everyone else was doing. As he reached the infield, he heard the Haverford Station coach say, "We need a doctor!"

A couple of people began heading down from the stands in response. The scene was chaotic, with several Lions holding off several Hornets who were trying to get at Matt.

"It was an accident!" Matt was yelling. "I didn't mean to hit him in the head!"

"You threw at him on purpose!" Alex heard Kenworthy

say. He had rushed in from second base, only to be cut off by Jeff Cardillo before he could get to Matt. "Your control's been spot-on all day—you did that on purpose!"

Before Matt could answer, one of the doctors who had come out of the stands and was now leaning over Twardzik pulled out her phone.

"I'm calling 911," she said. "He's still out. Best case, he's going to have a serious concussion."

"And worst case?" Alex heard the Haverford Station coach ask.

"I honestly don't know," she said. "But we need to get him to the hospital—"

She broke off. "This is Dr. Elaine Somers," she said into her phone. "We have an emergency on the baseball field behind Haverford Station High School."

She paused for a second. "Yes. Player knocked unconscious."

She nodded and clicked off the call. "They said five minutes. Meanwhile, let's turn him on his back—gently. He'll breathe easier that way."

A couple of the Hornets leaned down and gingerly turned their teammate first onto his side and then onto his back.

A second doctor had now arrived, carrying a black bag that Alex assumed he had gone to his car to retrieve.

"Let me check his vitals," he said to Dr. Somers. She nodded and moved aside.

Everyone had stopped yelling and pushing and shoving and was now watching the two doctors. The call to 911 had made it clear that this wasn't the time for a fight.

"His pulse is fine—strong, actually," the doctor announced.

Alex could see a trickle of blood coming out of Twardzik's ear and from his cheek.

The doctor did some more checking. "He's breathing okay. A little labored but steady."

Alex heard a siren in the distance. Jonas was standing next to him. He noticed that Steve Garland and Christine, who he knew had been watching from the press box, were now standing a few yards away. There were also a couple of TV cameras recording the scene. No one seemed inclined to tell them to stop.

"Man," Jonas said softly. "What in the world was Matt thinking?"

"He *wasn't* thinking," Alex hissed back.

He glanced over at Matt. He still had a wall of teammates between him and the Hornets, but the shouting had stopped. Matt had his cap off, and it looked to Alex like he was staring into space.

The siren grew louder. A moment later, an ambulance came around the end of the bleachers and down the left field line. The two coaches yelled for everyone to clear some space, and players from both teams hustled out of the way as it pulled up. Two men jumped out of the back and quickly removed a stretcher. The driver also came around.

"Who's the doctor here?" he said.

"I made the call," Dr. Somers said. "It was Dr. Allynson who checked his vitals."

The driver looked at Dr. Allynson. "What've you got?" he said.

"Hit in the head with a pitch about seven minutes ago," the doctor said. "He's still out, but his breathing is okay and his heart's very strong."

The two men with the stretcher were now both kneeling next to Twardzik. Alex couldn't see exactly what they were doing, but he heard one of them say, "He's coming out of it a little bit. Let's get him up and moving ASAP."

They lowered the stretcher down to the ground and gently moved Twardzik onto it. Alex could see that his eyes were open now, but they looked glassy and unfocused.

"Who wants to go with him?" the driver said. "We can take one adult in the back of the ambulance."

"I'll go," Haverford Station's coach said. "What hospital we going to? I want to call his parents."

"Penn," the driver said. "It's closest and the best."

The Haverford Station coach looked at Coach Birdy while the two EMTs were wheeling the stretcher to the back of the ambulance.

"Al, what should we do?" he asked.

"We'll figure it out later," Coach Birdy said. "I don't know what to say, Rod. I'm sorry. Anything we can do to help at all, just let me know."

Rod nodded and jogged over to the ambulance.

Coach Birdy turned to the home plate umpire. "Obviously, we aren't playing any more baseball today," he said.

The umpire nodded. "I'll leave all decisions on how to proceed to the schools and the conference," he said. "If you do resume the game, though, your pitcher is ejected."

"I know that," Coach Birdy said. "I'll deal with all that."

The ambulance was pulling away, siren blaring. A lot of people had now come out of the stands.

There was little conversation between the two teams. Alex finally walked over to Matt.

"What happened?" he asked, knowing his tone was incredulous.

"I lost my mind," Matt said. "For one second, I lost my mind. And look what I've done."

He had tears in his eyes. "What have I done?"

Alex didn't know the answer to that one.

Even though there were media people all over the place, Coach Birdy ordered all the players back to the locker room as soon as the ambulance pulled away. "I'll deal with the media," he said. "All of you get dressed and be on the bus in fifteen minutes. You can shower back at school."

"Coach, we'd like to know how he's doing," Jeff Cardillo said, meaning Twardzik.

"I know, Jeff," Coach Birdy said, raising a hand. "I want to know too. As soon as I finish here, I'm going to go to the hospital. When I know something, I'll text all of you."

"I'd like to go to the hospital too," Matt said.

For a moment, Coach Birdy said nothing, thinking about what Matt was proposing. Finally, he shook his head. "Not tonight, Matt," he said. "Let's find out how serious this is, and then maybe you can go see him tomorrow—if he's still there. Right now, let's just leave it to his family to be there for him."

Matt didn't argue. He still had a sickened look on his face. It occurred to Alex that if *he* felt queasy about what had happened, he couldn't possibly imagine how Matt felt.

As the team started to leave for the locker room, several camera crews began racing in Matt's direction. Coach Birdy cut them off.

"Guys, I'm going to be the one talking to you today," he said. "I want to get the kids out of here and back home as quickly as possible."

There were protests, but Coach Birdy was firm. One TV guy was angry. "Coach, he might have just killed someone. He should talk to us."

Alex saw Matt visibly sag when he heard those words. Coach Birdy pointed a finger at the TV guy and said: "First, the young man was conscious when he left here. Second, how dare you make this about what *you* want for the six o'clock news. The kid's sixteen, and he's shaken up enough as it is."

"Maybe he should have thought about that before he threw the pitch," the TV guy said.

For a moment, Alex thought Coach Birdy was going to start a fight. He took a step in the TV guy's direction, and the TV guy—not so brave now—retreated quickly. It was Steve Bucci, whom Alex recognized as Channel 3's sports anchor, who stepped in front of the guy with the camera.

"Cool it, Tim," he said firmly. "Coach, we apologize. This is a tough situation. We'd be grateful if you'd take a few minutes to talk to us."

That calmed things down. Coach Birdy walked to a

spot where everyone could gather around him. The players headed—finally—toward the locker room. Cardillo had an arm around Matt as they walked.

"You weren't trying to hurt him," Alex heard him say. "You were throwing inside to make a point. They'll all know that when things settle down and he's feeling better."

"I don't know what's wrong with me," Matt said. "One minute, I feel great about things; the next, I'm mad at the world."

"Lots going on in your life right now," Cardillo said. "Don't be too hard on yourself."

It was the right thing to say, Alex thought. Throwing inside was part of baseball. But he remembered reading a book once in which Tony La Russa, the Hall of Fame manager, had talked about just this: "Below the shoulders is fine. Make a point. Get a guy off the plate. But when you throw at someone's head, you're messing with their career—and maybe with their life."

That thought chilled Alex. Especially as a pitcher.

One of the reasons he preferred baseball to football was that you didn't take the kind of pounding in baseball that you did in football.

The fact was, it *hurt* to play football, no matter who you were. Alex was lucky, as a quarterback, that he didn't get hit very often. The linemen took a beating on every play, and running backs and receivers often got slammed so hard that Alex was stunned when they got up and walked away.

Baseball wasn't like that. There was the occasional collision at home plate, and every once in a while a runner might come in hard sliding into second or third base.

Alex had never been hit by a pitch in Little League. At that level, if a pitcher threw inside in any way, he was apt to be ejected.

Now he understood why there could be fear in baseball too. He'd seen guys get hit, and he knew it had to hurt—there was a reason a baseball was also referred to as a "hardball." And when someone who could throw as hard as Matt threw at someone, it was dangerous. Especially, as La Russa said, above the shoulders. Then you were endangering someone.

Alex knew that only one player in major league history had actually been killed when hit by a pitch, but lots of others had been hurt very seriously.

In truth, though, he hadn't given it much thought except when his dad told him about Tony Conigliaro, a Red Sox star in the 1960s, who was never the same player after getting hit in the head with a pitch and who died young.

Now he'd seen it up close—even from the outfield it had felt very close. It scared him.

A lot.

■ ■ ■

Alex was sitting at the desk in his bedroom shortly after eight o'clock, trying to focus on reading *The Three Musketeers* in French—impossible under the best of circumstances—when his phone buzzed. It was Coach Birdy, at last.

The message didn't fill Alex with relief: *Billy is conscious, though groggy. Docs are going to run more tests tomorrow.*

More tests. That didn't sound too good. Alex had read

enough about professional athletes who had suffered head injuries to know that if all was well, the wording was more along the lines of "He's being kept overnight for observation." That was different from "more tests."

He was staring at his phone when it rang. Not surprisingly, it was Christine.

"You got Coach Birdy's text?" she said.

"Hang on," Alex said. "*You* got Coach Birdy's text?"

"He put Steve and me on the list because we're trying to beat the deadline for tomorrow's paper. We actually pushed it back to get more information."

"What do you think?" Alex asked.

"I think it doesn't sound very good," she said, confirming his initial fears.

"I wonder how Matt's doing," he said, suddenly realizing that the text would probably land harder on Matt than on anyone else.

"I don't know," she said. Then she added, "I called you first."

His phone was telling him he had another call coming in. He looked at the screen. It was Matt.

"Matt's calling me," he said. "I'll call you back."

He switched over to Matt.

"This is really bad," Matt said without saying hello.

"More tests," Alex said. "Could just be a precaution."

"No," Matt said. "You don't understand. It's not just that. I got a call from Billy Twardzik's father."

"Really?"

"Yeah. He said the doctors think Billy might have

bleeding on the brain and they may have to do surgery. He said if that's true or if he's hurt seriously, he's going to sue me and the school. He was going crazy."

"Bleeding on the brain. My God, Matt."

"I know. I don't know what to do. My mom is freaking out. The only income we have right now is what she makes teaching kindergarten. We can't afford a lawyer. And her friend who helped with my appeal isn't equipped to take on something like this at all."

"Slow down," Alex said. "You're not nearly at that point yet."

"Yeah . . . yet," Matt said. "I gotta go. Call coming in I need to take."

He clicked off. Alex was in a state of semishock. Then it occurred to him that he knew a lawyer, someone he was going to see that weekend: his dad.

Alex and Molly were supposed to take the train to Boston Thursday afternoon for the long Easter weekend. He wondered if Matt could wait until then for some answers.

■ ■ ■

Matt was nowhere in sight at lunch the next day. Max slid into his usual seat and announced that Matt hadn't been in their third-period chemistry class. Christine arrived with more bad news: The conference had told Coach Birdy that Matt was suspended indefinitely—at least until they knew more about how serious Billy Twardzik's condition was.

"I guess it's a good thing we aren't playing Friday," Jonas said. "Maybe by then Twardzik will be okay."

"Even if he is, Matt's not playing for a while," Christine said. "He pretty much admitted in front of everyone that he threw at him. He can't backtrack now and say the pitch slipped or something."

"Someone should call him and see what's going on," Alex said. He told them what Matt had told him the night before.

"He must be completely freaking out," Jonas said. "You should go call him right now. Find out why he's not in school."

Alex grabbed a few more bites of his pasta, then headed for the door. Once he was outside the cafeteria, he walked out a side door leading to a small garden where kids often went looking for a quiet place to study when the weather was nice.

It was raining lightly, so no one was around. He took out his phone and dialed Matt's number. There was no answer. He was starting to leave a message when he saw that Matt was calling him back.

"Where are you?" Alex asked.

"I went to the hospital," Matt said. "I needed to know more about what was going on."

"How'd it go?"

There was a grunt on the other end of the line. "Not well. I managed to get to the family waiting room. He has a sister and I told her who I was and she was actually very nice. She was telling me they were still hoping the bleeding on his brain might stop without surgery when his father came over and started yelling at me. I was trying to tell him how sorry I was and that it was an accident—"

"Matt, you shouldn't say anything like that—"

"I know, I know. I was sort of panicked because he was so angry. He told me if I didn't get out, he'd call security. I basically ran out of there."

"You know, Matt, my dad's a lawyer and I'm going to see him this weekend. . . ."

"It's okay. I know you don't like these agents hanging around me, but a couple of them are lawyers and they said they'd help me out, if need be."

"*Matt!* If you don't pay them, you're probably jeopardizing your eligibility by taking free legal advice."

"My eligibility doesn't matter, Alex. I'm done."

"What do you mean, you're done?"

"They're gonna suspend me for the rest of the season—I know it. I have to turn pro this summer. I need the money."

"What if Billy's okay and you're only suspended for a couple of games?"

"Then maybe I can improve my draft position. Mr. Anderson says right now I'm late first round, early second round."

"Matt, this is crazy. . . ."

"Gotta go," Matt said. "This is Mr. Anderson right now."

He was gone. In more ways than one.

■ ■ ■

The fifth-period bell was ringing when Alex walked back inside, so he didn't have time to tell everyone about his conversation. He settled for texting them briefly: *He went to the hospital. Not good. He's lost right now.*

Matt wasn't at practice, either. Coach Birdy told the team that he had called to ask permission for the day off. There would be no practice the next day, since a lot of team members were leaving town with their families for the holiday weekend.

"We don't know what Matt's status will be for next week," Coach Birdy said. "Right now, Alex, you should plan on starting against Lincoln on Tuesday. The rest of you pitchers, be ready to go too. If Matt can't play in either game next week, then, Ethan, you'll start against Jefferson on Friday. So you'll be the one guy who *won't* pitch for sure on Tuesday. Everyone else is in the bullpen."

He updated them on Twardzik, but without much detail: "He's still in the hospital, and they're monitoring him. Matt tried to go see him this morning, but only family can visit right now. Coach Meese from Haverford Station said he'll let me know when there's any news."

They went through a desultory practice, taking BP and doing infield drills. Alex threw thirty pitches on the side to keep his arm loose.

When he finished, Coach Birdy called him over. "What are your plans for the weekend, Myers?" he asked. "Is there anyone you can throw to on Saturday? I don't want you going four straight days without throwing."

Alex thought about it for a second. "I'll be with my dad in Boston. I'll ask him."

That was good enough for Coach Birdy. They stayed on the field for about ninety minutes, and he told the players to relax over the weekend and not think about baseball or—as best they could—what had happened the day before.

"We still have a lot of season left, fellas," he said. "We've shown we have the potential to be a good team . . . with or without Matt. If he's out for a little while, we'll figure something out."

As they walked to the locker room, Jonas, always the voice of reality, shook his head.

"With or without Matt?" he said. "We were four-and-three with him. How good will we be without him?"

That was exactly what Alex had been thinking.

20

Alex had been so caught up in everything going on in his life—whether it was the travails of the baseball team, his relationship with Christine, or his nightly wrestling match with *The Three Musketeers*—that he had almost forgotten the trip he and Molly were supposed to make for Easter weekend.

Somewhere in the back of his mind, he knew he was intentionally avoiding the subject—even just with himself—because whenever he thought about it, he flashed back to the Christmas disaster.

When Alex's mom had brought up the possibility of going to Boston for Easter, neither Alex nor Molly had been thrilled with the idea.

"Look, kids," she had said, "I know it's been rough. But the three of you need to work this out. He's still your father, he still loves you, and I know you love him."

Alex conceded that was all true. Molly, who was two years younger than Alex and pretty high-strung, wasn't so sure. "If he loves us so much, why does he spend *all* his time with the fiancée and no time with us?" she asked.

Reasonable question, Alex thought.

His mom, as usual, had the answer. "Because, let's face it, right now he knows that when he sees you, it's going to be uncomfortable. So, yes, he's avoided coming down here, and I've told him that's the wrong thing to do. See what happens this weekend. The ball is in his court. See how he handles it. I'm betting this time will be better than last time."

"Pretty low bar, Mom," Alex said.

"Very low," Molly agreed.

■ ■ ■

Alex and Molly were now veterans of the Acela Express trip from Philadelphia to Boston.

They convinced their mother it was fine to drop them off at Thirtieth Street Station rather than walk them inside and wait for the train. The fact that the station was absolutely packed with holiday travelers, which made parking pretty much impossible, no doubt influenced her decision.

Alex bought a *New York Times* in the station. He did almost all of his reading online, but he'd grown up sharing the *Boston Globe* with his father at the breakfast table most mornings. His dad also read the *Times* each morning. Now Alex read the *Philadelphia Inquirer* in the morning, but not the *Times*. His mom had said continuing their subscription— except on Sundays—was too expensive. So he shelled out $3.50 to buy a *Times* to read on the train.

Not surprisingly, the train was packed. Alex read for a while, then fell asleep. The trip took five hours, and the train pulled into South Station shortly before ten o'clock. As they followed the crowds toward the exit that led to the street, Molly asked Alex if he thought "she" would be waiting with their dad.

"No way," Alex said. "The last thing Dad wants is to get the visit off to a bad start."

"Bet you a dollar," Molly said.

"Done," Alex said.

There were lots of people waiting to meet tired travelers. Alex was scanning the crowd for their dad when he heard Molly shriek, "Oh my God, I win!"

Alex looked where she was pointing. Standing several yards away, behind most of those who were eagerly pushing forward to greet the arriving passengers, was their dad, dressed in a gray suit. And right next to him, wearing a blue dress, some kind of silly-looking hat, and ridiculously high heels, was Megan Wheeler.

"Davey, there they are!" he heard Megan say—her voice somehow carrying over the noise in the station. Alex had literally had nightmares with Megan Wheeler saying, *"Davey, Davey."* His mom had never once called their father Davey. At least not in front of her children.

Alex's dad turned and spotted them, and a smile—an awkward one, Alex thought—creased his face.

The four of them moved toward one another, even though Alex actually had an urge to grab Molly by the hand and find out if there was an overnight train back to Philadelphia. How could their dad *possibly* think this was a good idea?

"Oh, children, it is *so* nice to see you again," Megan Wheeler was gushing. "We must get you up here more than once every four months!"

"Davey" had yet to say a word. As Alex and Molly approached, Megan Wheeler came forward, arms out, and hugged Alex, who felt his entire body go stiff, head to toe, as she wrapped her arms around him. She turned to Molly, who—being Molly—screamed, *"Don't touch me!"*

Alex almost burst out laughing.

Their father found his voice at that moment. "Molly, stop! Megan's just glad to see you guys."

Molly was crying. This was the high-strung part of her taking over.

"Dad, we came to Boston to see *you*, not to see *her*!" she said.

Megan Wheeler was obviously shocked by Molly's reaction to her presence.

"Molly, I just want all of us to be friends," she said.

"Why should we be friends?" Alex said, feeling a sudden urge to defend his sister. "You got engaged to our dad when he was still married to our mom. In fact, I wouldn't be surprised if you were dating him even before we left Boston."

"Alex!" their dad yelled, now in full voice.

"Am I wrong, Dad?" Alex said. He noticed that people were turning their heads to look at them.

"Alex, we're certainly not going to have this discussion standing here in South Station," their dad said. Then, after a pause, he added, "But you've got it wrong."

The hesitant denial pretty much confirmed Alex's suspicions, but he said nothing. He figured he'd already said too much, though, honestly, he didn't feel all that bad.

"Davey, just get me a cab and I'll go home," Megan Wheeler said.

"Megan, it'll be okay," Dave Myers said. "We'll get a bite like we planned, and we'll talk all of this out."

"David, I'd like to go home, please," Megan said. "*Now.*"

Apparently "Davey" became "David" when Megan was mad.

David Myers turned a little bit red.

"Okay," he said. "Let's go."

They turned in the direction of the exit. Alex and Molly stood rooted to the spot, not moving.

Their father turned around.

"You guys coming?" he said.

Alex looked at Molly.

"What do you think, Moll?" he asked.

"As long as she's really getting in a cab," Molly said.

Alex nodded. They started walking. Their father had waited, but Megan was several steps in front. As they pulled even with their father, Alex said to him, "You owe Molly a dollar on my behalf."

"Why?" their dad asked.

"I'll tell you later," Alex said.

They walked in silence from there to the cabstand outside.

■ ■ ■

Alex wasn't certain why they needed to wait in the cab line with Megan, but they did anyway. When her cab pulled up,

■ 173 ■

she gave their dad a quick peck on the cheek, and Alex heard him say, "I'll call you later."

It occurred to Alex as her cab drove away that the idea of getting something to eat—especially now that Megan was gone—was a good one. He was starving.

"Dad, how about if we go eat?" he said as they started walking away from the cabstand.

For a second, their father didn't answer. He was clearly distracted. "What?" he finally said. "Eat?"

"You said the plan was to go eat," Alex said. "We're both hungry. I know we're pretty close to Faneuil Hall—can we go to Regina's and get a pizza?"

They had reached the car, which was parked at a meter.

"Considering the way the two of you treated Megan just now, I don't know if that's a good idea," Dave Myers said, giving his two children a look as he popped the trunk.

Molly started to say something, but Alex put a hand on her shoulder.

"I think if we agree on anything, Dad, it's that we need to talk about this," he said. "And Molly and I are hungry."

Alex saw their dad nodding his head.

"Okay," he said. "Okay."

The drive only took a few minutes, and they got lucky, finding a parking space not far from the waterside entrance to Faneuil Hall. They walked through the arch that led into the outdoor promenade and then into Quincy Market. Even at ten-thirty on a cool spring night, it was bustling, everything open late apparently for the holiday weekend. They made their way past the familiar food stands until they came to Regina's—Alex and Molly's favorite pizza in Boston.

"You know Bertucci's closed in Washington," their dad said as they waited for their pizza to be heated in the oven. He was talking about another pizza place that Alex also liked.

"Really? When?"

"About a year ago. I found out last time I was in D.C. Tried to go there to grab a quick bite, but it was gone. I thought maybe it was just the Dupont Circle location, but when I Googled it, I found out they'd all closed down there. Still open here, though—thank goodness."

It occurred to Alex that their dad was talking to them the way he had when they were still a family—which, remarkably enough, was less than a year ago.

Even though it was cool and breezy, they decided to take their pizza and drinks outside. There were eight slices of pizza, and Alex felt as if he could eat all of them. He settled for four. Luckily, Molly and their dad were happy with two apiece.

They settled down on a bench not far from the statue of the great Celtics coach Red Auerbach. After they'd been eating for a couple of minutes, Dave Myers leaned back and said, "Okay, why don't you two tell me what happened back there at the station."

Molly looked at Alex. As the big brother, he guessed he was the spokesman.

"Look, Dad, we don't know Megan all that—" he started.

Their dad broke in. "That's for sure."

Alex held up a hand. "You asked a question, right?"

Their dad nodded. "Right. Sorry. I'll let you finish."

He did. Alex went through the disastrous lunch back in December and the fact that their father had all but disappeared the last few months and how much they had been looking forward to spending time with *him* this weekend.

When Alex was finished, their dad looked at Molly.

"Moll, anything you want to add?"

Molly was much calmer now, munching on her pizza. Still, she didn't hesitate to tell their father what she thought.

"Dad, how can you like her? She's a *snob*. And she's not nearly as pretty as Mom."

That made Dave Myers laugh for the first time since they'd gotten off the train. "Moll, your mom is beautiful, just like you are."

There was silence for a moment. Then he continued, "I hear what you're both saying. I guess bringing Megan to the station probably wasn't a good idea."

"Probably?" Alex and Molly both said.

"Okay, *wasn't* a good idea," he amended. "But I can tell you our intentions were good. Megan was very upset at how badly things went in December. She *does* want to have a good relationship with you guys, and she thought by coming to the station it would be a way of letting you know that."

"So it was her idea," Alex said.

"Yes, Alex, it was her idea. But if you want to blame someone, blame me. I could have told her no."

"Could you have, Dad?" Molly said. "Really?"

Dave Myers didn't answer that one.

"Look, my office is closed tomorrow. The three of us will have all day together—most of it anyway."

"What does that mean?" Alex asked.

"We're all going to dinner tomorrow night, all four of us," Dave Myers said. "At Ruth's Chris."

Alex groaned. If anything could ruin a great steak dinner, it would be the presence of Megan Wheeler.

They slept in the next morning, and to Alex's surprise, their dad made them breakfast. In the old days, their mom had done all the cooking.

"Okay, here's the plan," he said as he handed Alex and Molly plates with fried eggs and toast on them. Alex could smell bacon sizzling. The day was getting off to a good start.

Or so he thought. As he and Molly dug into their eggs, their dad said, "I have to go into the office for a couple of hours, so I thought—"

"I thought you said the office was closed today," Molly said a split second before Alex said it.

"It is. But I have a backlog of paperwork that has to be done by Monday, and I'm keeping all day tomorrow clear because I've got tickets for us to go to Fenway, and then, since the Celtics are playing at twelve-thirty on Sunday, I thought we'd go to the game, and then I'll take you right to the train station."

That sounded good to Alex. Unless . . .

"Do you have three tickets for the games or four?" he asked.

"Four," their dad said.

"Can't we get *any* time just with you?" Alex said. "We have a lot to talk about."

"We'll have plenty of time," Dave Myers said. "We'd have more time if you two slugabeds hadn't slept so late. We can talk this afternoon when I get back from the office and tomorrow before we go to the Red Sox game."

He was now taking the bacon off the stove. He was clumsy and dropped a strip.

"Sorry," he said.

"Okay," Alex said. "But no more excuses."

"I'm not making excuses," he said defensively. *Too defensively,* Alex thought.

He looked at his watch. "I have to go. I should be home no later than three. Our reservation isn't until six-thirty, so we'll have time then."

"What are we supposed to do while you're gone?" Molly asked.

"Your mom said you both have homework that you brought with you," he said. "It's raining right now anyway, so why don't you get that out of the way."

"You sure you'll be home by three?" Alex asked.

"If I get going right now," their dad said.

"Fine," Alex replied, resigned.

"If you guys want to put the dishes in the dishwasher when you're done, that wouldn't be a bad thing," their dad said.

He walked over and gave them each a kiss on the forehead. He had always done that in the past—Alex was surprised to realize he'd missed it.

"Call if you need me," he said on the way out.

Alex picked up a strip of bacon. Molly was staring at the door. She had eaten her eggs, but her bacon was untouched. Alex knew Molly loved bacon, so he knew something was up. Finally, she picked up a strip of bacon and pointed it at Alex.

"He's lying," she said.

"Lying? About what?"

"About going to the office. He's going to see her."

"What makes you say that?" Alex asked. The thought hadn't even crossed his mind.

"What does Mom call it?" Molly said. "Women's . . ."

"Intuition."

"Yeah, that's it. Women's intuition. I can just tell."

Impossible, Alex thought. He looked at his sister. She wasn't hysterical or acting crazy. She was perfectly calm. And, worst of all, he thought she might be right.

■ ■ ■

They cleaned up the kitchen and got out their books. Their dad's townhouse in the North End was nice enough, but it was new and strange and Alex couldn't get comfortable. He stared at a description in French of yet another D'Artagnan duel and, after about thirty minutes, realized he hadn't read a word.

"Okay," he said. "Let's find out."

"Find out what?" Molly said, looking up from her math book.

"Find out if Dad's really at the office."

Without waiting for Molly to respond, he walked to the phone in the kitchen and dialed their father's direct number at the office. Molly followed him into the kitchen. After four rings, the phone went to voice mail. Alex hung up.

"No answer," he said.

"Doesn't mean he's not there," Molly said. "He could be in the bathroom or just not answering his phone because he's working on stuff."

"He'd see this number come up if he was at his desk," Alex said.

"So wait a few minutes and try again."

"Don't think so," Alex said.

He had a sick feeling in the pit of his stomach. He went to his computer, which was sitting on the table in the family room.

"What are you doing?" Molly asked.

"Looking up a phone number for Party Forever," he said.

"Megan's business? Why would you want that number?"

"Because, remember, she said she works out of her house."

He found the number on Party Forever's website. He picked up his cell phone and walked to the kitchen window. That was the best place in the house to get cell service. He glanced in the direction of the harbor, took a deep breath, and entered the number.

"Why are you using your cell?" Molly hissed, as if someone might hear her.

"She'll recognize the house number and know that something's— Hi, Megan, it's Alex. I'm sorry to bother you. Is my dad there yet?"

There was a pause at the other end of the line. Alex held his breath for a moment. If he was wrong, there was going to be a huge fight when their dad got home, and they would owe him—and Megan—an apology.

"He . . . he just walked in, Alex. Hang on a minute."

Alex wanted to cry. He also wanted to hang up. But there was no time.

"Alex, what's wrong?" he heard their dad say. "Why didn't you call on my cell?"

"Because Molly and I thought you might be lying," Alex answered, his voice quaking with anger and hurt. "And we were right. Stay with Megan, Dad. We'll figure out how to get to the train station."

"Alex, hang on—"

Alex didn't. He hung up.

■ ■ ■

In a twist, Molly was far calmer about what had happened than Alex. He wanted to get a cab to the train station, change their reservations, and go home right away. She persuaded him to pause long enough to call their mother first.

Alex was about to pick up the phone when it began to ring. The caller ID said it was their mom.

"Alex," she said. "I know how upset you are, and you're absolutely right. Your dad is on his way back there right now. Don't leave. Wait for him."

Their dad had obviously called her right away. "Did he tell you what he did?" Alex asked.

"Yes, and I don't even know what to say to you about it, I'm so upset. Which is why I understand why *you're* so upset. He said to me, 'Alex and Molly need to understand that I still love them,' and I told him he had a strange way of showing it and that he needed to prove it to both of you. I think—I hope—he got it. The fact that he said he'd come right home was, I thought, a good sign."

Alex was torn. He was so angry with their father that he wanted him to come home to an empty house. Any explanation for what he'd done was going to sound pretty hollow.

"What can he possibly say to make us feel better about this, Mom?" he asked.

There was a long pause on the other end of the line. "I honestly don't know," their mother finally said. "But at least give him the chance to try. When he's finished, if you still want to come home, call me."

Alex looked at Molly, who was standing a couple of feet away.

"Tell you what, I'll leave it up to Molly," he said. "She's the one who knew right away he was lying. If she's willing to stay and listen, I'll stay and listen."

"Fair enough," their mom said. "I'm home, so call whenever you need me."

Alex hung up and looked at Molly. "You heard?"

She nodded. "Mom's right," she said. "He's still our dad. A bad one right now, but still our dad."

■ ■ ■

They heard the car pull into the garage about twenty minutes later. Alex had thought about packing but decided to wait. Dave Myers walked into the family room carrying a large bag in his hands.

"I thought we should eat," he said. "I stopped at Shanghai Village and got some Chinese."

Shanghai Village had been a family hangout once upon a time, the place they went for dinner most Sunday nights. Alex was certainly hungry. He was always hungry. It crossed his mind that if their dad had been confident enough to stop for food, their mom must have called to tell him she had talked the kids into waiting for him.

"Fine," Alex said, getting up to walk into the kitchen. Molly, without a word, did the same. They silently got out dishes and opened the containers of food, and each got a drink. Then they sat down at the kitchen table. Alex and Molly started eating. It was their dad's move. He understood.

"Look, all I can say is I flat-out blew it—last night and today," he said. "I got caught in between you guys and Megan, and I made two bad decisions."

"No, Dad, you made three bad decisions," Alex said, still feeling as if their dad wasn't getting it. "First was bringing her to the station, second was deciding to go see her today, and third—and by far *worst*—was lying to us about it."

Dave Myers picked up his chopsticks and put some kung pao chicken into his mouth. He took a swig of water.

"You're right," he said. "Three bad decisions. I need to do a better job of finding a balance—"

"What balance?" Molly interrupted, speaking for the first time since their dad had walked in the door. "There's no balance. We haven't seen you for months, and we've been here for all of five minutes and you're already out the door to see her. You obviously still don't get it. We're your kids. Either we come first or we don't come at all. Do you think for one second that Mom would ever tell you to find 'balance' between taking care of us and taking care of her? *No.* It's your fiancée who's using the word 'balance.' We're not her kids, so she has no reason to care about us. *You're* the one who is supposed to care about us."

Alex stared at his sister for a second. She couldn't possibly be two months shy of turning thirteen. There was no doubt in his mind that she was the smartest—and maybe the most mature—person in the room.

"Moll, those are pretty strong words," their dad said. "You know how much I love you."

"No, I don't!" Molly said, tossing her chopsticks down. "Neither does Alex right now. All I know is that since we left Boston, you've hardly come to see us at all, you've gotten engaged to a woman while you're still legally married to Mom, and now, when we come here to supposedly make up for what happened at Christmas, you *lie* to us so you can run off and see *her*!"

Dave Myers looked at Alex as if to say, *Help me out.* Alex was a long way from there.

"Dad, she's right," he finally said. "Let me ask you: Are you willing to call Megan"—unlike Molly, he managed to actually use her name—"and tell her you're spending the rest of the weekend with just us because you have to start fixing your relationship with your kids?"

Now it was their dad's turn to put down his chopsticks.

"I'm going to have to think about that one, Alex. I mean, that's a lot—"

Alex stood up. "Don't bother, Dad," he said. "Don't think about it. It's fine."

He pulled his cell phone out of his pocket and walked to the front door. "I'm going outside to call Mom. Molly, go upstairs and pack."

He didn't wait for their father to respond. It was time to go home.

Their dad insisted on driving them to the train station once he realized that Alex and Molly weren't going to change their minds about leaving.

"We can take a cab, Dad. It's okay," Alex said. "It's only a few minutes away."

"No. I'll take you," Dave Myers said.

There wasn't much talk in the car en route to the station. Alex thought their dad might make one last plea for the two of them to stay, but he didn't. He dropped them at the front of the station, saying only, "I'm *very* sorry about this. I *promise* that I *will* try to fix it."

Alex had a lot of answers for that—most of them beginning *We've been hearing that for nine months now*. But he left it alone. He and Molly walked into the station, which was crowded—it was, after all, Good Friday—but not nearly as crowded as Thirtieth Street Station had been the day before.

Once they had changed their tickets and gotten on the train, which wasn't quite full, Molly fell asleep quickly—no doubt emotionally wrung out. Alex took one more swing at D'Artagnan and friends but was staring out the window when his phone buzzed, telling him he had a text. He almost didn't bother to look at it, figuring it was his dad with another lame apology.

When he did look, he almost wished he hadn't. It was from Coach Birdy. *Billy had surgery early this morning*, it began. *Bleeding on the brain had to be relieved. He came through OK but is in intensive care at least until tomorrow. More when I know more.*

A wave of guilt swept through Alex. He had been so caught up in his family's ongoing melodrama that he hadn't given any thought to Billy Twardzik since leaving Philadelphia. He also wondered how this news would land on Matt. He had never even gotten around to asking his dad about where Matt might stand legally if Billy's family followed through on their threat to sue.

While he was thinking about all this, his phone rang. He looked and saw it was Christine. No doubt she had seen the text.

"Where are you?" she said as soon as he answered.

"On the train, coming back from Boston."

"*Back* from Boston?" she said. "Didn't you just go up there last night?"

"Yes. . . . Long story," he said, not at all eager to tell it.

"Oh God," she said. "Something happened with your dad. Okay, I won't ask you now because I can barely hear you with the train noise. You got Coach Birdy's text, right?"

"Yes," he said. "It's awful."

"Matt called me," she said. "Coach Birdy called him before he sent the text out. He said this is very, very serious. Matt's scared out of his mind. And he's got no one to talk to."

For a split second, Alex thought about saying, *Apparently he has you to talk to,* but he quickly flushed the idea. Not only would the comment be his crazy jealousy talking, it was pretty tasteless at this moment.

Christine continued. "His dad's gone. His mom is clueless. These agents have all of a sudden disappeared. I guess they think he's damaged goods in some way because of what he did."

That surprised Alex. In part because it never occurred to him that agents would care whether an athlete hurt someone, as long as *he* wasn't hurt, but also because Matt had indicated that at least one had offered free legal advice.

"You sure about the agents?" he said. "My sense from Matt was they were still acting like they were his pals."

"I think that changed when ESPN and CNN did stories last night with Billy's parents talking about how shocked they were that anyone could throw at someone's head the way Matt did. Matt's become a huge villain on Twitter."

Alex hadn't been on Twitter much in the last twenty-four hours, but he was sure Christine was right. He tried—again—to picture what Matt might have been thinking when he threw the pitch. He was angry because Kenworthy had broken up his no-hitter by bunting. He couldn't turn to second base and throw at Kenworthy, so he threw at the hitter—Twardzik. It was, to put it mildly, stupid. But even though he'd wondered for a second about Matt's aim, Alex believed—wanted to believe—that Matt had never intended to hurt Twardzik. He had wanted to make him dive out of the way, eat some dirt, maybe even start a fight—but that was all. Matt had changed, but not that much. At least Alex hoped that was the case.

Now Twardzik was in intensive care, his future in jeopardy, and Matt was apparently a national villain, his future in a different kind of jeopardy.

"I don't even know what to say about any of this," Alex finally managed, realizing Christine had been saying "Are you there, Alex?" for several seconds. "This makes the whole PED thing last fall look like nothing."

"You have any plans tomorrow?"

"No," he said. He'd planned to be in Boston.

"Good. We should all take Matt to lunch at Stark's. Then, if they're letting Billy see visitors by then, we'll go see him. His parents won't treat us the way they treated Matt when he went over by himself."

"You sure about that?" Alex asked.

"No," she said. "But we'll try anyway."

"And what makes you sure Matt will go along with this plan?" he said.

He could almost see her smiling when she answered the question. "Because," she said, "I'm going to tell him I want him to do it."

That, Alex thought, *settles that.*

■ ■ ■

Linda Myers, figuring her kids would be hungry getting off the train, took them to Tony's Pizza, which had become the family's favorite pizza place in Chester. Pizza two nights in a row was fine with both Alex and Molly.

Their mom had apparently talked at length to her soon-to-be ex-husband about what had happened, and now, unlike in the past, she wasn't defending him to her children.

"He still doesn't completely understand how wrong he is," she said while they waited for their pizzas. "He knows the lying was just flat-out dumb, but he still doesn't know that his priorities when it comes to you guys and Megan are a mess right now."

She sighed. "I know I've said this before, but you have to be patient with him. I'm not telling you not to be angry, but he's going to come around. Your father's a good man."

"If he's such a good man, how can he be doing what he's doing right now?" Molly asked.

"Because sometimes good people do bad things. And dumb things. Sometimes they lose their way for a while. The past year's been rough for all of us. I'm lucky because I have you guys to keep me sane. I suspect your dad was very lonely when we left."

Alex wanted to ask if their mom thought their dad had gotten involved with Megan Wheeler before they split but decided against it. At this point, the answer didn't matter all that much anyway.

He went to sleep with the pizza rumbling in his stomach and his mind filled with thoughts of his dad, of Megan

Wheeler, of Billy Twardzik, and of Matt Gordon. It hadn't been a good few days.

■ ■ ■

Naturally, Christine was right about Matt. He walked into Stark's two minutes late, with Jonas right behind him. Christine, Alex, and Max were already there, waiting.

"What is this, an intervention?" Matt said, smiling.

Apparently, Christine hadn't revealed the entire guest list to him.

"More like a support group," she said, not bothering to explain any further. "You need your friends right now."

Matt's smile disappeared as he slid into the circular booth that was big enough for five—barely. Jonas squeezed in next to him.

"You're right," he said. "I do need my friends. I also need a lawyer, apparently."

"Did you hear from Twardzik's family again?" Max asked.

Matt shook his head. "No, I heard from a lawyer—some guy named Pollock. He suggested I find a lawyer because the family had asked him to prepare a wrongful injury suit against me personally and against the school."

Alex sighed. He now felt worse about not talking to his father.

"What happened to the agents who were going to help you out?" Jonas asked.

Matt snorted. "Going, going, gone," he said. "One of them told me that if Twardzik is okay *and* I get drafted in the first round, then he'll be happy to represent me. But for the moment, it's bad for their 'image' to be connected to me in any way."

"Their *image?*" Christine said. "Since when does an agent care about his image?"

"It's about attracting other clients, I think," Matt said. "If they're recruiting someone and his family asks, 'Do you represent that guy who hit the kid in the head?' they don't want to have to say yes—unless Twardzik recovers and they can say—'I only signed him after the player had recovered and he assured me nothing like that would ever happen again.' Even then, I'm a risk they won't take unless they think they're going to cash in quickly."

They ranted for a few minutes about what bad guys agents were, then Christine—as usual—brought everyone back to the issue at hand.

"Matt, what can we do to help?" she said.

"I liked your idea about going with me to the hospital," Matt said. "I'd like to try to go and see him and tell him I'm sorry. To be honest, I'm afraid to go alone again."

"It's worth a try," Alex said. "Worst thing that happens is we all get thrown out together."

They finished their lunch and then split up into two cars to drive to the hospital—Matt driving Christine and Jonas, and Alex going with Max. Since it was a Saturday, there was parking around the hospital. Matt had checked that morning and been told that Billy was out of intensive care and in a private room.

When Alex and Max walked in, Matt was at the front desk, trying to act as if they were expected.

"It's William Twardzik," he was saying to an elderly volunteer. "He was moved into room 436 this morning. Can you give us directions to find the room? I haven't been here since he was moved."

The volunteer smiled at Matt and began tapping keys on the computer in front of her. Alex was thinking Matt was pretty smooth—it looked like they were going to at least get up to the room—when he saw the woman's smile disappear.

"Oh dear," she said.

"Something wrong?" Matt said, still trying to sound casual. "I'm pretty sure I've got the right room—"

"Oh no, young man, you've got the right room," the woman said. "But Mr. Twardzik's not there anymore."

"Not there?" Matt said. "They just moved him there this morning. . . ."

"I know," she said. "But it says here that he's back in surgery."

Alex almost gagged when he heard what the woman was saying. Matt was white as a ghost.

"Back in surgery?"

"Yes, I'm afraid so. I can direct you to the surgical waiting area, if you'd like."

"N-n-no thanks," Matt said, his voice very shaky. "We'll . . . we'll check back later."

"Certainly," she said. "I hope everything turns out okay."

Christine threw an arm around Matt as he turned away.

"He's going to be okay," she said. "He will be. Let's all go somewhere around here and talk."

Matt nodded, and they all walked slowly to the door. Once they were outside, Alex made a decision. "You guys go ahead. Text me and tell me where you are when you get there," he said. "I've got a phone call to make."

While the others headed in the direction of a coffee shop Christine knew about, Alex found a small park area and sat down on a bench. It was mid-April, but the day was brisk and windy, so there wasn't anyone else around.

He called his father's cell. His dad answered on the first ring.

"Alex," he said. "Is something wrong?"

Apparently his dad figured the only reason Alex would call him at this point was if there was some dire emergency.

"I'm fine, Dad," he said. "So are Mom and Molly. But I have a problem I'd like to talk to you about if you have some time."

"All you want," his dad said, and Alex was relieved because it felt like Megan—for once—wasn't around.

He walked his father through everything that had happened since Tuesday. It was hard to believe that it had only been four days. . . .

His dad listened, interrupting only a couple of times to ask for details. When Alex finished, his dad let out a long breath.

"Wow," he said. "As we used to say when I was a kid, that's heavy."

"Is Matt in trouble?" Alex asked.

"He could be, I'm afraid," his dad said. "The Twardziks have no claim against the school because every family signs a waiver giving their child permission to play with the understanding that there's no liability for the school—or an opponent—in case of an injury. The only exception to that would be if a coach told someone to intentionally injure a player on the other team, and there's no evidence that happened here."

He went on, "So, you said that Matt admitted in front of witnesses that he threw at him on purpose but didn't mean to hit his head." He paused for a second. "Did he say he was trying to hurt this kid?"

"No," Alex said. "In fact, he said he *wasn't* trying to hurt him."

"Well, that's one thing in his favor. Still, even if his intent wasn't to injure, his action led to the injury. That's not good. And if there's any permanent damage, then it gets worse.

"And legalities aside, if there's permanent damage, it's going to be hard for Matt to live with himself."

Alex didn't want to ask the next question but, under the circumstances, thought it needed to be asked.

"Dad, what if Billy dies?"

His dad didn't answer that for several seconds.

"Let's not even think about that unless we have to," he said.

"So what should we do now?" Alex said.

"Matt needs a lawyer. Not just because the Twardzik family is making these threats, but because he needs to feel he's got someone on his side who can take care of him in all this. Protect him."

"You got any suggestions? Know anyone?"

"Yeah, I do," his dad said. "Me."

For a moment, Alex didn't understand what his father was saying.

"Alex, you there?" his dad asked.

"Yes. Yes, I am, Dad. What are you talking about?"

"I want you to tell Matt to call me—today," his dad said. "I can help him. I'll come down there if he wants me to, although I'm guessing I can deal with their lawyer on the phone, at least for now.

"I can't help Matt with his guilt. That's a different story. But I can relieve some of the pressure he's feeling."

"Dad, I don't think his family has very much money," Alex said. "His dad's out of work and . . ."

"I know that. I'll do it pro bono. Matt's your friend, and he needs help. This is the least I can do for you right now."

Alex was stunned. His dad was saying he would come to Philadelphia if need be and offer his usually very expensive legal services to his friend for free. This was a very different person from the one who had driven him and Molly to the train station twenty-four hours earlier.

"That would mean a lot to me, Dad," he said quietly.

"Alex, a journey of a thousand miles begins with a single step," his father said. "Think of this as my first step. Have Matt call me as soon as possible."

■ ■ ■

Christine had texted Alex while he was on the phone to tell him that they were waiting for him at a coffee shop called the Drexel, which was three blocks away on the edge of the Drexel University campus. He walked there fast, feeling better than he had in two days. He found them, sat down, and said, "Matt, get out your phone. I'm going to give you a number."

Matt complied. Alex gave him his dad's cell phone number and then filled him in on the conversation he'd just had.

"Wow," Christine said. "That's great of your dad."

"He'd really come down here if I needed him to?" Matt said.

Alex smiled. "Why not? He hasn't been here for months. He could use a change of scenery."

The mood lightened, although their concern about Billy was still palpable. Christine had texted Coach Birdy and asked him to get in touch with Coach Meese so they could get an update when Billy got out of surgery.

They had all ordered ice cream before Alex arrived. Alex ordered a sundae, and Matt went outside to call Alex's dad.

"It's great of your dad to do this," Max said. "I think it will help Matt a lot. But I wish he had someone to talk to about all that's going on."

"Maybe my dad can help with that too," Alex said. "Once upon a time, he was a good sounding board for me."

"Not so much lately, though," Jonas said.

"No, not so much lately," Alex agreed.

Then he had a thought. "But you know what? A journey of a thousand miles begins with a single step."

He smiled when he said that.

■　■　■

Word on Billy Twardzik didn't reach Alex until that evening. He had asked Christine if she wanted to go to a movie since he was back in town, but she was spending the night with her dad and her brother.

"Maybe next weekend," she had said—three words that made Alex feel about six inches taller.

He had gone home and had dinner with his mother and Molly and was watching the Phillies play the Pirates when his phone rang. It was Matt.

"He's out of surgery," Matt said, not bothering with a hello. "They say he's listed in critical condition, but Coach Birdy told me that's routine after surgery like this."

"Any idea if what they did worked this time?" Alex asked.

"From what Coach Birdy told me, they won't know until he's awake—which he's not."

"Who did Coach Birdy talk to?"

"Coach Meese. He's been pretty good through all of this. He even called me a couple times to tell me that he knew I didn't mean to hurt Billy this way."

"That was nice of him," Alex said, a little bit surprised.

"Yeah. It's not like he said 'Don't feel bad' or that there

are no hard feelings, but he wanted me to know that he understood my intent wasn't to hurt Billy, even though he did tell me he was going to ask the conference to suspend me for the rest of the season if Twardzik can't play again."

"Wow. What did you say to that?"

"I told him I understood why he might feel that way but that it sounded pretty harsh."

Actually, Alex didn't think it sounded *entirely* unfair. If Twardzik couldn't play because Matt had been hotheaded, maybe Matt shouldn't play. Of course, if Matt didn't play, Chester Heights' season was, for all intents and purposes, over—especially with Bailey Warner still hurt. He didn't say that, though, because he knew Matt didn't need to hear his friends saying anything negative.

Matt read his thoughts through the silence. "You think I shouldn't play, either, don't you?"

"No, I don't think that," Alex said. "I guess I can just understand why Coach Meese would feel that way."

"Yeah," Matt said.

"What do you think they'll do?" Alex asked.

"Coach Birdy thought the other day that I'd be suspended for five games," Matt said. "But that was before Billy had to have surgery."

Twice, Alex thought.

"I called your dad again," Matt said. "He told me that as soon as we know exactly what's going on with Billy, he'll come down here to see me."

That was news to Alex. "Good," he said.

"He didn't tell you?" Matt said.

"No, not yet," Alex said. "I'm sure he'll call and let us know."

He didn't mind that his dad hadn't called. Actually, it made him feel good. His dad didn't know yet when he was coming down, and he wasn't just calling to let Alex know what a good guy he was for volunteering to give up time in Boston to come down and help Matt. Alex knew that his dad had always done a lot of pro bono work—helping people who couldn't afford a lawyer—but almost never talked about it. He remembered when he was much younger asking his mother why Daddy would work for free.

"Because it's the right thing to do," she had answered.

It had been a while, at least in Alex's mind, since his dad had done something just because it was the right thing to do. He was proud of him. He liked the way that felt.

By Monday morning, there was finally some good news on Billy Twardzik. He was out of intensive care and awake and talking. Most important, the doctors believed he hadn't suffered any brain damage as a result of the bleeding caused by the pitch Matt had thrown. All this news came in a text from Coach Birdy, who was still communicating regularly with Coach Meese.

Alex was relieved when he saw Matt walk into the cafeteria at lunchtime. He'd wondered if Matt would show for school after what had happened over the weekend, but he sat down at the table with a smile on his face.

"You feeling okay today?" Max Bellotti asked.

"Much better," Matt said. "I know you guys saw Coach Birdy's text. I just talked to him, and he told me that Billy really is out of serious danger. Almost as important, he also told me that Billy is willing to see me this afternoon."

"Wow," Jonas said. "His parents are going to allow that, with all the legal stuff they're threatening?"

Matt smiled. "They said their lawyer had to be in the room. So my lawyer is going to be in the room too."

"Really?" Alex said, surprised.

"His plane lands at two o'clock. He's renting a car and picking me up here. He said to tell you he'd like to see you for a couple minutes before we leave. He's going to stay overnight."

Alex was a little miffed that his dad hadn't let him know he was coming to town. Matt read his mind.

"He also said to tell you that this just came up this morning and he'd have texted you but he knows you can't have your cell phone on at school."

"How'd you get in touch with him?" Alex asked.

Matt smiled. "I snuck outside with my phone after Coach Birdy told me what the deal was. Your dad answered right away. He's been amazing, Alex. It means a lot to me."

It meant a lot to Alex too. Still, looking at his phone— which was allowed during lunch—he wished there was a text from his dad.

■ ■ ■

As soon as French class ended, Alex walked toward the parking lot with Christine—who had never met his father. Matt was already there, and so was his father, both standing by the rental car. Alex introduced Christine.

"Very nice to finally meet you," Dave Myers said, shaking hands with Christine. "I've heard a lot about you."

Christine reddened a little bit at the comment, then said, "I've heard a lot about you too."

Then, realizing how that must have sounded, she quickly added: "Matt's filled us in on how great you've been these last couple of days."

Alex's dad looked at his watch. "We'd better get going, Matt," he said. "Don Pollock asked us to try to be there by three."

"Who's Don Pollock?" Alex asked.

"The Twardziks' lawyer. I actually tried a case against him a few years ago. He's a good guy."

"Is he a good lawyer?" Christine asked.

"Very good."

Seeing the look of concern cross Alex's and Christine's faces, Dave Myers put up a hand. "What that means is, I feel confident we can reason with him. If the Twardziks had hired some ambulance chaser looking to make a buck, that would be much worse. Don will look at this reasonably. Plus, now that it's starting to seem like Billy's going to be fine, that makes the idea of some kind of financial settlement much less likely."

"Can they file criminal charges?" Christine asked.

"In theory, the district attorney still can, yes," Dave Myers said. "It's happened in professional hockey in the past. But if it's happened in high school baseball, I've never heard about it. They can make a case that Matt was careless and hot-headed, but they'd have a very hard time making a case that he *intended* to injure Billy."

That was a relief to Alex—and, judging by the look on his face, to Matt too.

"Let's go, Matt," Alex's dad said. "We need to get to Penn.

And, Alex, you need to get to practice. I understand you've got a game to pitch tomorrow."

Alex had almost forgotten about baseball practice and about the next day's game against Lincoln. He had completely forgotten about Coach Birdy's request that he throw over the weekend. Tuesday's game had been about the last thing on his mind.

"Let us know how it goes," Christine said.

"You two will be the first," Matt said, getting in the car. "If there's time, Alex, I'll come back to practice."

"I will too," Alex's dad said. "I'm not flying back until tomorrow. Unless you two object, your mom said it was okay if I take you and Molly to dinner."

Three days ago, Alex's response to that suggestion would probably have been, *No thanks. Why don't you go to dinner with Megan?*

Now he smiled and said, "Sounds great, Dad."

■ ■ ■

When Alex got to the locker room, the mood was somber. The team hadn't been together since the previous Wednesday because of the long weekend, and Matt's absence—and the reason for it—seemed to weigh on everyone.

"Still no official word on his suspension, I guess," Jonas said as he and Alex walked in the direction of the field.

"They have to say soon," Alex said.

"Maybe, if Twardzik's really okay, they won't suspend him," Jonas said in a tone that made it clear he didn't believe what he was saying.

"Five games," Alex predicted. "It'll be five games."

It didn't take long for him to find out that his prediction was off the mark—by a lot.

"Everyone grab a seat in the dugout," Coach Birdy said after they had stretched and warmed up for a few minutes. They all sat on the bench or the dugout steps, and Coach Birdy stood in front of them, his hands on the railing that protected the bench from foul balls.

"I just got word from the conference on Matt a few minutes ago," he said. By the look on his face, Alex knew it wasn't good news. Coach Birdy paused, took a deep breath, and shook his head.

"Matt's been suspended for the rest of the season," he said finally.

"Wha—?"

"No!"

"Impossible!"

"Are they kidding?"

The players were all protesting angrily at once, in part because the punishment was so harsh, in part because they felt bad for Matt, and in part because they realized that without Matt their hopes of a winning season had probably gone out the window.

Coach Birdy put up a hand.

"I know. I know what you're all thinking," he said. "I think it's unfair too. But the guy I talked to on the phone a few minutes ago said that Matt's past was factored into the decision. In fact, the guy told me there's some feeling that Matt's reaction might have been caused by 'roid rage."

"But he's tested for steroids twice a week!" Alex said. "That's impossible!"

Coach Birdy nodded.

"I know, Alex. That's what I told the guy—that he's tested clean for months now. But he didn't seem to care. He just said, 'Well, he can appeal to the state high school association if he wants to, but my guess is they're pretty upset with him after they shortened his penalty already so he could play baseball this spring and this is what they get in return.'"

Alex was exasperated. And angry. Five games, sure. But they had thirteen games left to play—plus the rest of the Haverford Station game, whenever the conference decided it should be completed. Matt didn't deserve this.

"What happens now, Coach?" Jeff Cardillo asked.

"Two things," Coach Birdy said. "They have to officially let Matt know their decision. He can then file a protest if he wants. And, second, we have a game tomorrow to get ready for. Myers, you're starting. Go throw on the sidelines—but not too much or too hard. We're going to need some innings from you." He didn't ask if Alex had thrown over the weekend.

He looked at all of them for a moment, as if trying to decide whether to say anything else. Apparently the answer was no.

"Let's go," he said, and slowly, with very little spring in their steps, they all stood up and took the field for practice. To Alex, it felt like an empty exercise. The season might as well be over.

■ ■ ■

Alex's dad and Matt showed up shortly after five, just as practice was wrapping up.

It was pretty clear from the look on Matt's face that Coach Birdy hadn't yet told him about the suspension. He was smiling—really smiling—and Alex realized that it had been a while since he'd seen him smile like that.

As soon as Coach Birdy saw his suspended star and his lawyer approaching, he waved everyone in from the field. They gathered around, knowing without being told that there was news. Alex's dad delivered it.

"The lawsuit's over—or, more accurately, will never start," he said, which drew cheers from everyone. "Matt spent some time with Billy while his lawyer and I went and had a talk. Billy knows how sorry Matt is about what happened, and his lawyer knows there isn't much of a case. His parents were upset—understandably—last week. I thought they might be looking for some kind of settlement, but that wasn't it. They were just angry."

"They still are, actually," Matt put in, picking up the story. "But Billy told them he just wants to get better and try to play again before the season's over. He doesn't want this to drag on. He's a good guy. If he's back when we play them again, I hope we get far enough ahead that I can groove a pitch to him so he can hit one out."

There was silence when Matt made that comment. He looked around, sensing that something was wrong. He looked at Coach Birdy.

"The suspension?"

Coach Birdy nodded. "I hate to tell you about this now, Matt, I really do, but I just told the guys."

"And?" Matt said. "More than five games?"

More silence. Alex could tell Coach Birdy didn't even want to say the words. "It's the season, Matt," he said, then paused. "I'm really sorry. We can appeal, but—"

"The season?" Matt screamed. "The *whole season*? But he's okay! The doctor said he might play again in a couple weeks. The surgery worked. There shouldn't be any lingering after-effects. I talked to the doctor myself!"

Coach Birdy nodded. "I hear you, Matt," he said. "We'll get the doctor to put that in writing for the appeal. I promise."

Matt's smile, so wide a moment ago, was completely gone. His eyes were glistening.

"I gotta go," he said.

"I'll give you a ride home," Alex's dad said to Matt. Then he turned to Alex. "I'll call you later."

Alex just nodded. Jeff Cardillo's voice reminded him that the entire team was standing there staring after Matt: "Hey, fellas, let's bring it in. We still have a game tomorrow."

He put his arm up as everyone huddled around him.

"Win one for Matt!" he yelled.

They all put their arms in and repeated what he had said. As they put their arms down and started to walk slowly to the locker room, Alex saw Christine standing to the right of the dugout.

"When did you get here?" he asked.

"Just as Matt was leaving," she said. "I tried to get him to talk to me, but he just shook his head and kept going. What happened?"

Alex filled her in—first the good news, then the bad news.

"Well, you guys can win one for him," she said finally, having witnessed the team's cheer. "The problem will be the twelve after that."

She was right, Alex thought. As usual, she was right.

Alex had just finished dinner and was about to go upstairs to do some homework when the phone in the kitchen rang. His mom answered, and Alex could tell right away that it was his dad.

"I'll ask them," he heard her say finally.

She turned to Alex and Molly, who was clearing her plate, and said: "Your dad just now finished with Matt and his mom. He's sorry about dinner, but he would like to take you guys out for some ice cream. How do you feel about that?"

Alex looked at Molly. He had filled both Molly and his mom in on the events of the day during dinner.

"My homework is done," Molly said. "It's up to Alex."

Alex's homework wasn't done. "How soon can he get here?" he asked.

His mom repeated the question and said, "Fifteen minutes."

Alex nodded. "Okay, then."

Exactly fifteen minutes later, their dad was on the doorstep. Their mom opened the door, with Alex and Molly both standing there. She smiled at her ex-husband-to-be and said, "No pressure, Dave, but you need to have them back here in an hour. Alex still has homework to do."

"There's a Friendly's that the GPS says is about seven minutes from here," Dave Myers said. "I'll have them back by eight-thirty."

Alex didn't even know there was a Friendly's anywhere close to their house. In Boston, they'd gone to Friendly's all the time. He loved the Fribbles.

When they got there, Alex ordered a vanilla and Molly asked for a chocolate. Their dad ordered an ice cream cone— just like he always had in the old days.

They sat in a booth near the back, and Alex and Molly waited expectantly.

"First, I owe you both an apology, an unqualified one, for what happened Friday," their dad said. "That was a new low for me—lying to my kids.

"The good news is that it was a wake-up call. I've done a lousy job dealing with this separation and the divorce. Your mom has had to be two parents for the last nine months, and that's on me."

He looked at Alex and smiled. "I'm not going to promise to do better because I know you don't want to hear that again. But here's what I *did* tell Megan before I came down here: You two are my number one priority going forward. I told her she had to deal with taking a backseat and that didn't mean I didn't love her, I just owe you guys a lot better father than you've had since last July."

"How'd she take that?" Alex asked.

Their dad smiled. "Not especially well."

"How 'not especially well'?" Molly asked before Alex could ask the same question.

Dave Myers took a big bite out of his cone, then sighed.

"Well, we've postponed any wedding plans," he said. "In fact, we're taking a break."

Alex felt a chill—a thrilled chill—run through him. He knew that "taking a break" in a relationship at forty-one was a lot different from taking a break at fourteen. When adults decided to take a break, it usually meant the relationship was over. Still, he wasn't about to say that. He didn't need to— Molly did.

"Dad!" she said. "You broke up!"

"Molly, do you have to sound *so* happy?" Dave Myers asked, not denying that his daughter was right. He was smiling when he said it, clearly not angry.

"But did you break up?" Alex asked.

Their father sighed again. "Probably," he said. "I mean, the door's still open. . . ."

"Dad, why her?" asked Molly, never one to hold back. "I mean, what were you thinking? She's so . . ."

"Horrible," Alex filled in.

Their dad either smiled or grimaced—Alex wasn't sure which—and put up a hand to fend them off.

"Look, kids, I understand why you feel that way," he said. "Megan wasn't at her best the couple of times you met her. I think she was probably trying too hard."

"Oh, come on, Dad," Alex said. "She's a snob. She's a phony. She wears too much makeup, and she wanted nothing to do with your kids."

"You aren't wrong about that, Alex," he said. "Look, when you guys left town last year, I was lonely—really lonely. And she was . . ."

"Available?" Molly said.

"Yes, available. And I did *not* have a relationship with her before your mom and I separated. I know that's crossed your minds, but it's not true. She pushed hard for us to be engaged, and I went along. That was a mistake.

"What happened last week made me take a step back. Actually, it was your mom who kind of brought me back to my senses. She said, 'Dave, you *lied* to your children. How could you do that?' She was right. So I apologize, not just for Friday but for the last nine months."

Alex felt as if a hole in his heart had just been stitched up. Molly must have felt the same way because her face was shining with happiness.

"So why don't you get back together with Mom?" she suggested. "You're still married. It's not too late."

Dave Myers shook his head. "It *is* too late, Moll. I'm sorry," he said. "Remember, it was your mom who decided we should separate. I wanted to give it a little longer, but she felt the time was up."

Alex didn't remember that because—he was pretty certain—he had never known that.

"I thought the two of you decided together," he said.

"By the time we told you two, we had decided together," he said. "But it was your mom's idea, and honestly, she was right. We still love each other, but we stopped being *in* love."

Alex understood the difference. He wondered if Molly did. Apparently there was no reason to wonder.

"Dad, don't be in such a rush to be in love again," she said.

Dave Myers leaned forward in his chair and kissed his daughter on the forehead. "Moll, when did you become a grown-up?" he asked.

"When you and Mom split up," Molly said, looking at Alex for confirmation. "We didn't have much choice."

■ ■ ■

Alex was happy to learn that his dad was going to help Matt put his appeal together.

"I'm going to meet Matt and Coach Birdy for breakfast in the morning," he said. "I've got a flight out at noon, but I'll be back whenever they hear Matt's appeal. We'll have to go to Harrisburg, but I'll pick him up and drive him there."

That all sounded good to Alex. He wasn't ready to think he had his dad back, but the last few days had been encouraging. And the fiancée was gone! That alone was reason to celebrate.

Matt showed up at the lunch table the next day looking a little bit grim. Alex had already told Jonas and Max and Christine about the appeal.

"How'd it go?" Alex asked.

"Your dad is going to put it all together in the next day or so," Matt said. "The goal is to file the appeal by Friday so they'll hear it sometime next week."

"What are you going to ask for?" Jonas said.

"Time served," Matt said. "By the time they hear it, I will have missed three games—maybe four if they don't get to it until next Friday. Alex's dad says ask for the moon and hope for the best, so that's what we're doing."

He smiled and turned to Alex. "You ready to carry us for a while, Goldie?"

"I'll need some help—that's for sure," Alex said.

"Well, you've got some, Goldie," Alex heard a voice say behind him.

Alex looked up and saw Bailey Warner standing behind him holding a tray in his hands.

"Bailey!" he said. "What's the deal?"

"The deal is, I went back to the doctor yesterday," Warner said. "The shots and the sling worked. He thinks I can start rehabbing right away. He cleared me to start throwing lightly today—before the game. If everything goes okay and I don't feel any pain, I could pitch as soon as next Tuesday—at least for a couple innings."

Christine put her fork down and put her arms in the air for a second. "If you guys get Bailey and Matt back, you can still make a run at winning the conference," she said.

Bailey sat down. "Yeah, but those are still ifs, aren't they?" he said. "I gotta pitch my way into shape, and Matt . . ." He shrugged. "Who knows—right?"

Matt nodded. "Yeah, exactly," he said. "Who knows."

■ ■ ■

When Alex walked to the mound that afternoon, he felt as if it had been months—not ten days—since he had pitched in a game. Which might have explained why he walked the bases full almost immediately. The third walk, on a 3–2 pitch, was a fastball that Alex thought had caught the corner.

The umpire never moved—ball four.

"Where was that?" Alex asked, frustrated he hadn't gotten the call.

"Low *and* outside," the umpire replied. "Other than that, a perfect strike."

The second part of the comment made Alex angry. He walked off the mound in the direction of the umpire, who took his mask off and walked around the plate to meet him.

"The pitch was a strike," Alex said, pointing with his glove.

"Other than being low and outside, you're right," the umpire said. "Now, you want to get yourself ejected when you're already down a pitcher, or you want to play baseball?"

Fortunately, Lucas Mann had followed the ump out and jumped in between him and his pitcher before Alex could tell the umpire it was none of his business what the status was of the Chester Heights pitching staff.

"It's okay, Mr. Umpire," Mann said. "No one's getting thrown out. Come on, Alex, let's just get back on the mound and pitch."

Coach Birdy had arrived on the scene by now, and he put his arm around Alex and turned him back in the direction of the mound.

"Alex, let's focus on the next batter," he said softly.

"The guy's a jerk," Alex said between clenched teeth.

"I know," Coach Birdy said, nodding and smiling so that if the ump was watching, it would look like he was calming his pitcher down. "But you know what? He's right. We can't afford to have you get yourself thrown out. It was a close pitch—a good pitch. So now you're going to be a hero for getting out of a bases-loaded, no-out jam in the first. Throw strike one to this next batter and you'll be fine. He'll be taking, waiting for you to throw a strike. Just get ahead of him."

Alex nodded. Coach Birdy jogged back to the dugout. Lincoln's cleanup hitter was at least six foot four and weighed, Alex guessed, 225. He looked a lot like a Herman twin. *If I throw this guy strike one*, he thought, *he may not take and he'll hit it eight hundred feet.*

Mann signaled for a fastball. Alex shook him off. Mann signaled fastball again. Alex shook him off again. Mann called time, took off his mask, and jogged to the mound.

"Myers, what are you doing?" he said. "You heard Coach—we gotta get ahead of this guy."

"I throw a fastball down the middle, he might hit it to New Jersey," Alex said. "Let's start him with a slider."

"Can you throw it for a strike?" Mann asked.

"Yeah," Alex said. "I can."

The umpire was on the mound now. "Fellas, there are no lights here," he said. "We need to finish before dark."

What is this guy, a stand-up comic on the side? Alex thought.

He said nothing. Mann went back behind the plate and put down three fingers—the universal sign for a slider. Alex threw it exactly where he wanted to, right on the corner. The ump hesitated a moment, then put up his hand, signaling strike one. Alex breathed a sigh of relief. He was okay now.

Four pitches later, he was out of the inning. The cleanup

hitter smashed a one-hop comebacker to him, and Alex turned it into a 1-2-3—pitcher to home to first—double play. Then the next hitter popped his first pitch up to Cardillo at shortstop.

The Lions sprinted to the dugout, energized by the escape.

"I told you that you were going to be a hero," Coach Birdy said, giving him a high five as he reached the dugout steps. "Lot of guts throwing that slider. I'd have killed you if you'd missed with it."

"Goldie is all guts," Matt Gordon said. He was seated in the dugout—in street clothes—allowed to do so, pending his appeal. If he lost it, he wouldn't even be able to do that. He gave Alex a high five too, then walked to the end of the bench to get some water. Alex knew this was killing him. But still, he was there for his teammates.

Even though at that moment he wasn't part of the team.

As it turned out, Lincoln's first-inning threat was the only time Alex was in trouble all day. Having settled down thanks to the double play and the pop-up, he rolled through the next four innings, allowing just three singles, one more walk, and one run. In the meantime, the Lions were battering three Lincoln pitchers for eight runs. Alex, moved into the third spot in the batting order in Matt's absence, had three straight doubles. He drove in three runs and scored three himself.

As he came into the dugout after the fifth, he wasn't surprised to see Coach Birdy waiting for him. Because of his wild first inning, Alex figured his pitch count was pretty high. "I'm going to let the bullpen finish this one for you," Coach Birdy said. "You may have to pitch a lot the next few weeks, so let's not push the envelope."

"How many pitches have I thrown?" Alex asked.

"Eighty-nine," Coach Birdy said. "That's plenty."

Patton Gormley and Johnny Ellis each pitched an inning of shutout ball, and the final was 8–1. The win raised Chester Heights' conference record to 2–1. There had still been no announcement about how the issue of the Haverford Station game was going to be resolved. Coach Birdy had told the players he suspected the conference was hoping it would have no meaning in the final standings and would just go in the books as "suspended."

"If either Haverford Station or Chester Heights has a chance to win the conference title, then they'll have to do something," Coach Birdy had said. "Let's hope we put them in that position."

Without Matt, that was unlikely. Alex and everyone else understood that the win over Lincoln was hardly a big deal. The Presidents were 0–4 in the league, and it was easy to see why after playing against them.

There was plenty of media coverage for the game, not surprising as it was the first the Lions had played since the Gordon-Twardzik catastrophe a week earlier. Naturally, most wanted to talk to Matt, but he politely explained that while his suspension was under appeal, he couldn't really answer any questions. He did go on camera long enough—Alex saw it later that night—to say that he'd visited Billy Twardzik in the hospital and was very pleased to hear he was scheduled to go home the next day.

"I hope to pitch against him later in the season," he said. "I told him he'd better be ready because I would be throwing nothing but strikes."

That was, Alex thought, a smart way to handle the situation. He was pretty certain his dad had coached Matt on what to say to the media.

Alex got a fair bit of attention himself, although there were a lot more Matt questions than Lincoln questions.

"Alex, if Matt doesn't play again this season, what do you think your team's chances are to compete for a conference title?" was the opening question.

Alex couldn't resist being a little bit of a wise guy. "Yes, we're all very happy that Billy's doing so much better. Thanks for asking," he said. "And yes, I agree, this was a good win for us after what went on last week."

He stopped. Some of the reporters laughed. The questioner, who was clearly a TV guy but not someone Alex recognized, didn't.

"Are you going to answer my question now?" he asked.

"Sure," Alex said. "I have no idea. Time will tell."

The answer was an honest one, but it was also Alex's way of telling the TV guy what he thought of his question. Not that it was a bad question, it just seemed wrong to ask it without even a mention of Twardzik or the day's game.

"Alex," someone else asked, "do you think the suspension is appropriate?"

Alex had anticipated that one. "I'm biased," he said. "Matt's my friend and my teammate. I know he wasn't trying to hurt Billy. But I also know he lost his temper. I think a couple of games—two, maybe three—would be fair. But the whole season? To me, that's not fair."

"Do you think the conference took into account his PED use and suspension last fall?"

This was the same TV guy again.

Alex shrugged. "You'll have to ask them. But I'm not sure what one has to do with the other," he said.

"What if it was 'roid rage that caused him to throw at Twardzik's head?"

Alex was getting angry, but he knew that was what the guy wanted. "You'd have to check with the conference for the exact number, but Matt has passed a lot of drug tests. If he was using any kind of drug at all, he would have tested positive."

And then he had one last thought. "That was a really stupid question," he added. "I gotta go."

He walked away and was halfway to the locker room when he heard someone calling his name. It was Christine. She was smiling.

"Way to go," she said. "You just guaranteed you'll be on every newscast in the city tonight."

Alex didn't really care. "Who was that guy asking the dumb questions?"

"He's a freelance guy," she said. "I think he was here for Fox today. Not sure, though."

"Well, he's a dope," Alex said. "I hope they all show me telling him his PED question was stupid, because it was."

"Of course it was," Christine said. "The same guy asked Matt the same question five minutes earlier."

"Matt should have punched him."

"Yeah, that would have been smart."

"What did he do?"

"He told the guy he'd been tested twice a week since early December—including last week—and he was clean."

"Well, that's essentially what I said."

"Yeah, until you called him stupid."

Alex sighed. They had won the game easily, he had pitched well after the game's first three batters, and he was walking into the locker room with a knot in his stomach because Christine was telling him he had somehow screwed up by calling someone stupid who *was* stupid.

He decided to change the subject.

"Would you like to go to a movie Saturday afternoon?"

She shook her head. "No. My dad has tickets in the *Inquirer/Daily News* box for the Phillies game. You want to come with us?"

Alex smiled. He felt the knot loosening.

"Absolutely," he said.

He walked into the locker room with—he knew—a goofy grin on his face.

As usual, Jonas picked up on the look right away.

"I'm guessing that stupid smile has nothing to do with the game," he said. "Christine, right?"

"Yup," Alex said, happy to share good news. "She invited me to go to the Phillies game Saturday with her dad."

"How romantic," Jonas said, but his grin made it apparent he knew this was a good thing for Alex.

■ ■ ■

The big question at Wednesday's practice was who would be pitching Friday.

Jonas told Alex, "Coach posted the lineup already. Ethan starts. No change in plan there. I guess everyone else except you has to be ready to pitch in."

"Pitch in?" Alex said.

"Sorry, didn't mean it that way," Jonas said, grinning.

Alex had been thinking about the game against Jefferson and how the pitching staff would get through it. None of the team's three top pitchers were available: Matt was suspended, Bailey Warner would be hoping to throw forty pitches pain-free before the game began, and Alex had pitched on Tuesday.

"I could probably go an inning if I had to," he said.

"Which would leave us where for Tuesday against Lansdowne?" Jonas said.

Alex knew Jonas was right. The problem was, if they wanted to contend in the conference at all, they couldn't afford any more losses. King of Prussia, with the Herman twins hitting balls into outer space, was already 4–0, and so was Chester. The two teams would play the following Tuesday, so only one would stay undefeated. Then again, without Matt, any thought of catching either of those teams was probably fantasy anyway.

As it turned out, Jonas's notion that everyone would have to pitch in against Jefferson was accurate. The Jeffs' pitching wasn't any better than the Lions', and the game became a slugfest. Jeff Cardillo tied it in the top of the fourth with a three-run inside-the-park home run. And Ethan Sattler managed to last four innings but gave up six runs and left with the score tied, 6–6.

It was 9–9 in the top of the seventh when Alex came up with one out and no one on. Jefferson's pitcher promptly fell behind him 3–0, and Coach Birdy gave Alex the swing-away sign. Alex lined a grooved fastball into the right field corner and slid into third with a triple. Cardillo singled to left, and Alex jogged home with what proved to be the winning run. Don Warren walked two batters in the bottom of the inning, making everyone a little nervous, but then he struck out Jefferson's cleanup hitter to end the game.

"Big win—great win," Coach Birdy said afterward. "That was the definition of a team effort. We needed everyone to contribute, and everyone did."

Matt had not made the trip to the game. He was allowed in the dugout in street clothes at home, but he couldn't travel with the team to road games. When Alex turned on his phone on the bus trip home, he saw a text from Matt: *Great win. My hearing is next Friday in Harrisburg. You guys have to get through two or three more without me.*

Alex knew that was probably optimistic. Matt was thinking that his father's request that the suspension be reduced to time served—it would be four games by next Friday—would be accepted. Alex showed Jonas the text.

Jonas shook his head. "I don't see it that way," he said. "I think we'll be lucky if they reduce it to ten."

"If we could get him back for the last five, we might have a chance," Alex said.

Jonas shook his head. "You've seen King of Prussia. You think anyone's beating them?"

"Maybe Chester," Alex said. "And if Matt pitches when we play them again . . ."

"And if I grow ten inches by next basketball season, I can play center," Jonas said, giving Alex a look.

He was right. Alex knew he was right. But he didn't want

to think about it right now. He decided to think about going to the Phillies game with Christine and her dad instead.

■ ■ ■

The Phillies lost, but Alex felt like he'd won big-time. Christine's dad was nice, and it was pretty clear that Christine had told him good things about Alex. He even made a comment about his French accent.

"Christine tells me you're the only one in class with an accent as good as hers."

"No one's accent is even close to being as good as Christine's," Alex answered, grinning.

"She's got you well trained, I see," Mr. Whitford said.

It was a good day.

So was Tuesday.

Alex was now starting to pitch with confidence, and it showed against Landsdowne. He actually retired the first nine hitters he faced before a walk and a single in the fourth led to Landsdowne scoring on a sacrifice fly. That was the only run he gave up in six innings.

Meanwhile, Chester Heights pieced together single runs in the second, third, fourth, and sixth. Johnny Ellis pitched the seventh, and the Lions walked off with a 4–1 win.

"Franklin's awful," Matt said as they all headed for the locker room. "You guys will beat them, and then we'll be five-and-one—really, six-and-one, because we were up by five when the Haverford Station game was suspended. That means we'll be tied with whoever loses the KOP-Chester game today, and only one game behind the other guys."

"You have it all pretty much figured out, don't you, Matt?" Jonas said.

Matt shrugged. "It's not like I have much else to do with my free time these days. The point is, we've still got a chance."

"Why are you so sure your suspension's going to be reduced?" Alex asked.

Matt smiled. "I've got a great lawyer."

27

No one on the team had any idea what was going on at Matt's hearing when they boarded the bus for the trip to Benjamin Franklin High School.

The hearing had been scheduled to start at one o'clock to give Matt and his lawyer plenty of time to make the two-hour drive from Philadelphia to Harrisburg.

"Your dad says the hearing will probably take about two hours," Matt had told Alex. "They should have a decision by the middle of next week."

"So if they go with time served, you could—in theory— pitch against KOP next Friday."

"Can't wait," Matt had answered.

Alex hadn't seen his dad that morning, but the plan was for everyone to meet back in Philly after the game for dinner.

"If you guys win, I'll take you, Matt, Jonas, and Christine to the Palm," Alex's dad had said.

"What if we lose?" Alex asked.

"McDonald's," his father answered.

Alex had eaten at the Palm with his parents in New York on trips there in the past. The thought of one of their steaks was a pretty good incentive—if an incentive was needed.

There was important news for the team even without any word from Harrisburg, and that was the name of that day's starting pitcher: Bailey Warner. He had thrown a pain-free seventy-five-pitch bullpen session on Monday and had pleaded with Coach Birdy to get him into the Landsdowne game for an inning. Coach Birdy had turned him down because he didn't want him throwing two days in a row and also because he was thinking of starting him on Friday.

Bailey had practically skipped over to the lunch table on Friday to report that he was starting.

"You going to be on a pitch count?" Jonas asked.

"Yeah, like around eighty," Bailey said. "That should be good for at least six innings."

He was joking. If he made it through five, it would make everyone happy and would mean the bullpen shouldn't be too taxed.

Just as they were getting off the bus, Alex saw a text pop up on his phone. It was from his dad: *Just finished. Heading back. Depending on traffic, we'll try to get to the game. If not, will let you know and we'll meet at the Palm.*

He had made a point of telling the boys to bring a change of clothes with them since there was no point going back to school. The Palm was about a ten-minute cab ride from Ben Franklin. They were going to get their Palm dinner win or lose, but there was no doubt the steaks would taste a lot better after a win.

The good news about Bailey Warner's first start since the season opener was that he threw exactly eighty pitches and was pain-free. The bad news was it took him eighty pitches to get into the fourth inning and he had to leave with one out and the bases loaded. Standing in left field as Coach Birdy walked to the mound with the score tied, 4–4, Alex wondered if Coach Birdy might wave him in. This was a must-win, and the game the next Tuesday against Bryn Mawr Tech was probably winnable, even if Coach Birdy had to resort to the "all hands on deck" approach with the pitching staff again.

That wasn't what Coach Birdy was thinking. He waved Ethan Sattler in from the bullpen, and Alex let out a deep breath—he wasn't sure if it was relief at not being given the ball at that moment or just nerves. Fortunately for the Lions, the bottom of Franklin's lineup was coming up. Sattler gave up a sacrifice fly to give the Lightning a 5–4 lead, but he struck out the number nine hitter to keep the game close.

Alex, due up third in the fifth, raced in from left field. For once, Matt Gordon's assessment of an upcoming opponent had not been a hundred percent accurate: Franklin was a decent team—at least, facing Bailey Warner it was a decent team.

Lucas Mann led off the top of the fifth and walked. Franklin's starting pitcher, a kid named Oscar Flores, was tiring. Their coach went to the mound to talk to him. Two pitchers ran down the right field line to begin warming up. Jeff

Cardillo promptly hit Flores's first pitch into center field for a single, and Mann—who ran like the catcher that he was—stopped at second.

Alex walked to the plate quickly. He sensed that Flores had little left, and he didn't want to give the relievers any extra time to get warm. The catcher went to the mound, blatantly stalling, but was soon hustled back to the plate by the home plate umpire.

Alex stepped in. He checked with Coach Birdy at third base just in case he wanted him to bunt—which he hoped wouldn't be the case. In Alex's mind, there was zero sense in giving up an out to a tiring pitcher. Coach Birdy was thinking the same thing. He went through all sorts of motions, but he never touched his ear, meaning there was no sign.

Flores tried two breaking pitches, neither one close to the plate. Alex thought about backing out on 2–0 to check with Coach Birdy but decided against it. This was a hit-away situation, and he didn't want to chance seeing a "take" sign. Flores had to throw a fastball, and he had to throw a strike.

Stay back, Alex told himself, remembering his tendency to jump at pitches when he was overeager. Flores checked the two runners—who weren't going anywhere, especially with Mann as the lead runner—and finally threw a pitch he didn't want to throw.

It was a fastball, and it was right down the middle. Later, Alex remembered actually thinking batting-practice fastball before he swung, because it was little more than that. He stayed back and met the ball solidly, making sure not to overswing. He didn't need to hit the ball out of the ballpark; he just needed to hit it hard.

In the end, he did both. The ball took off toward left-center field, and Alex, thinking triple, took off as soon as the ball left his bat. He was about to turn at first base when he saw the two outfielders stop running. The ball had carried over the fence for a home run. It was hardly a Matt Gordon moonshot, but that didn't matter—it counted the same. Alex was rounding second base when he saw Franklin's coach heading back to the mound. He had left Flores in one batter too long.

The score was now 7–5, and the Lions didn't look back. They scored two more runs before the fifth was over, two more in the sixth, and one in the seventh against Franklin's very mediocre bullpen. Ethan Sattler gave up a run in the fifth and a run in the sixth before Don Warren came on to finish the game off in the seventh. The final score was 12–7. Hardly pretty, but plenty good enough.

■ ■ ■

There were showers in the Franklin locker room, which was a good thing, because it had been the first really warm day of the spring and everyone was pouring sweat after the game.

Christine and Steve Garland were there for the *Weekly Roar,* but there was little sign of the normal coterie of media or scouts who had been present before Matt's suspension. That was fine with Alex.

"So, Matt texted me and said he thought the hearing went well," Christine said when Alex and Jonas walked out of the locker room.

Instantly, Alex's jealousy began to kick in, but he pushed it aside—if only in the name of self-preservation. "My dad texted too," he said. "But he didn't say anything about how it went."

"Guess we'll find out more when we get to the Palm," Jonas said.

Alex's dad, Matt, Max Bellotti, Stevie Thomas, and a very pretty girl with long dark hair were all waiting at their table when they arrived at the restaurant. Alex wasn't surprised to see Max, but he was surprised to see Stevie. As if reading his mind, his dad said, "I thought maybe we could use a little bit of a push from the media the next couple days, so I asked Stevie to come and discuss strategy."

"And, as luck would have it, Susan Carol's in town, and she's much smarter than I am, so I brought her along," Stevie said.

He introduced them all to Susan Carol Anderson, his friend and fellow teenage reporter. When she stood to shake hands with Alex and Jonas, Alex noticed she was looking him right in the eye. He had heard she was tall but hadn't realized *how* tall.

"Great to meet y'all," she said in a distinctly Southern accent. "Stevie's pretty much filled me in on everything. I'm not sure if we can influence the state high school athletic association, but we've both got some ideas on how we can try."

She actually said "traa." Alex thought the accent was charming. Of course, if she'd had a New York or a Russian accent, he probably would have found it charming too.

As they sat down, Matt said, "You may not have heard, but KOP killed Chester this afternoon, eight to four."

"That's not as bad as fourteen to two," Jonas said, reminding them all of their loss to KOP.

"Let's not worry about that now," Alex's dad said. "Let's get you guys menus, because I'm sure you're hungry. And then I'll fill you in on everything."

Alex liked that idea. Especially the part about getting menus and ordering.

■ ■ ■

After they had ordered—all the boys and Alex's dad ordered the porterhouse, the biggest steak in the house, while Christine and Susan Carol asked for filets—Alex's dad got down to business.

He told them that the appeals board had consisted of five people—four men and one woman, all athletic administrators. They had read his written appeal and had a lot of questions both for Matt and for him.

"It comes down to two basic things," he finally said. "One, Matt's admission that he threw at Twardzik intentionally. From their point of view, that's the smoking gun. He put the kid at risk by throwing high and inside, even if his intent was just to make him hit the dirt. Just inside would have been okay; if he'd said the pitch got away from him, that would have been okay too.

"My argument on that was simple: They're right. He should be punished. And he's been punished. Today was the fourth game he's missed, and if the Haverford Station game is resumed, he's been ejected already. So that makes five in all."

"What was the second thing?" Jonas asked. Alex was pretty certain he knew the answer.

"The PEDs," Alex's dad answered, not surprising Alex at all. "They felt they cut Matt a lot of slack letting him play baseball this spring. As the chairman said"—he reached into his jacket pocket for a small notebook, took it out, and began reading—"'We let him play because he confessed and was clearly contrite about what he'd done and because, technically, he never tested positive. What we've gotten in return is a player who required brain surgery because your client had a temper tantrum.'"

That didn't sound good to Alex. Apparently he wasn't the only one who reached that conclusion.

"*Ouch!*" Jonas said.

"What he said," Max threw in.

"What did the other board members say when he said that?" Susan Carol asked.

Alex's dad pointed a finger at her. "I heard you were smart," he said. "Two of them pointed out that Billy Twardzik was out of the hospital and, according to the medical report they'd received, might play again this season."

"So it's not unreasonable," Christine added, "to say that if Billy can play, then Matt should be allowed to play."

"No law school training, and you made the exact same argument I made," Alex's dad said.

"My guess is she would have been more convincing," Matt said, grinning.

Everyone laughed except Alex—not because it wasn't funny but because he wished he had been the one who had said it.

■ ■ ■

Dinner was unbelievably good. Alex had never seen a bigger steak in his life, and all the sides his father had ordered for the table came on massive plates. Alex had noted the price on the porterhouse—sixty-nine dollars—when he ordered. He did a little math and realized his dad was picking up a huge check.

By the time Alex had failed in his attempt to finish the largest piece of carrot cake—or any cake—he'd ever seen in his life, a plan had been pieced together.

Matt was going to give an "exclusive" interview to Stevie and Susan Carol: Stevie for the *Daily News*; Susan Carol for the *Washington Post*. He would talk about how awful the past couple of weeks had been and how he knew he had only himself to blame. And about how incredibly relieved he was that Billy Twardzik was okay and how guilty he felt for putting his entire team's season in jeopardy.

"The good news is, that *is* the way I feel," Matt said. "I don't have to fudge it to make it sound better. I'll be telling the truth."

Stevie would also talk to Dick Jerardi about getting Matt on *Daily News Live*. There wasn't much going on at the moment: The Final Four and the Masters were both over, and neither the 76ers nor the Flyers were going to make the playoffs. They would shoot for Monday, hoping that the two newspaper interviews and the TV show would engender some sympathy and, perhaps, give the board members something to think about before they rendered their decision the following Wednesday.

"What do you think, Dad?" Alex asked when they had talked it all through for the fifth time.

His dad was signing the credit card bill for dinner.

"I think it'll be a three-to-two vote," his dad said. "I just don't know which side will have the three and which side will have the two."

28

Whether or not they'd have Matt back on Friday, there was still the matter of the rematch with Bryn Mawr on Tuesday. Technically, this game would put them at the midway point of the conference season, although they would have only seven results when it was over since the outcome of the Haverford Station game was still to be determined.

Alex felt great when he took the mound. With each passing game, his confidence was growing. He was spotting his fastball better and was learning how to control his breaking pitches—an occasional curveball and the slider that Matt had taught him.

It turned out the rest of the Lions were feeling good too. Jeff Cardillo hit for the cycle: single, double, triple, and home run. And Oliver Flick, who struck out often but could hit the ball prodigious distances when he made contact, made contact with a pitch in the fourth inning with the bases loaded for a grand slam that gave Chester Heights a 7–0 lead.

Alex pitched solidly with the lead, but he was helped greatly by his defense. Early in the season, the Lions had had three very good defensive players: Jonas, who could run down almost anything in center field and had a very good throwing arm; Matt, when he was in the lineup at shortstop; and Jeff Cardillo, regardless of where he played.

But the fielding drills Coach Birdy had insisted on were paying off. "I know you guys would much rather just take BP," he often said. "But I promise you we'll win as many games with our gloves as our bats if we work on this."

Lucas Mann had probably improved the most. He'd gone from struggling to stop breaking pitches—especially Alex's curves and sliders, which could go almost anywhere—to almost never letting a pitch get past him. When Cardillo had moved back to shortstop, Brendan Chu had stepped in at third base and was just about as good as Cardillo— with a stronger arm. And Oliver Flick was now a very solid outfielder—not as fast as Jonas, but with great instincts that made him look faster than he actually was when running down balls.

Early in the season, Alex had almost closed his eyes when he was on the mound and the ball was put in play. Now he was confident that if there was a play to be made, it would be made.

"God bless you, Coach Birdy," he said to himself when Chu dove toward the foul line to cut off a sure double, ending the sixth inning. That allowed Alex to get through the inning still leading, 8–2, even though he was tiring and was surrendering more rockets than pop-ups.

Don Warren finished up. They were now 6–1 in the conference: a half game behind Chester, at 7–1, and a game and a half behind King of Prussia, which was 8–0. KOP would come to Chester Heights on Friday afternoon.

"We gotta have Matt back to pitch that game," Alex said to Jonas as they sat in the dugout in the seventh inning— Jonas had been pulled too, along with several other starters, to give some of the bench guys a chance to play.

"Yeah, I know," Jonas said. "Of course, he won't have pitched for three weeks even if we do get him back, so who knows what will happen."

"I'd just like the chance to find out," Alex said.

"Amen to that," Jonas said just as Warren threw strike three for the final out of the game.

The media was back, but Matt was nowhere in sight. After he had done his *Daily News Live* interview on Monday as a follow-up to the Stevie and Susan Carol newspaper interviews, Alex's dad had told him to stay away from Tuesday's game.

"You've made your case," he said. "If you overdo it, the board might get upset."

As it was, Alex wondered if the mini publicity tour might have been too much. But he trusted his dad to know what he was doing.

Even Matt had apparently wearied of the whole thing. He had called Alex the night before to tell him that.

"I appreciate what your dad and Stevie and Susan Carol are doing," he said. "But, boy, am I glad it's over. I was beginning to feel like the biggest phony alive."

"You mean you don't feel that bad—"

"*Of course* I do," Matt said, breaking in. "But after a while, you get numb. I got to the point where I almost wanted to say, 'You know what? Whatever they decide, I probably deserve it.' This was worse than the steroids, Alex. At least with the steroids, the only person I hurt was me."

That, Alex knew, was Matt the Old talking. He liked hearing it—even if there was pain in his voice as he spoke.

With Matt not around, the media settled for talking to the rest of the Chester Heights players . . . about Matt.

"This is the fifth game he's missed," Alex said. "That's more than twenty percent of our season. I think anyone who has read or heard what Matt's been saying knows how sorry he is. People deserve second chances—especially good people. Matt's a good person."

Alex wished he could have snatched the "second chances" line back almost as soon as it came out of his mouth. Matt had already been given a second chance. He was asking for a third chance now.

■ ■ ■

Dave Myers flew to Philadelphia that night because he and Matt were due in Harrisburg at ten o'clock the next morning. The board required their presence when it ruled on the appeal.

That meant that Alex and Molly and their dad went to dinner again. The kids decided it was time their father tasted a Tony's pizza.

"It's not Regina's, but it's very good" was his verdict. "For Philadelphia, it's excellent."

"When did Boston become the pizza capital of the world?" Alex asked, surprised that he found himself defending Philadelphia.

"It's not—New York is," their dad said. "But we *do* have Regina's." He smiled. "And Fenway Park."

"Yeah, but Citizens Bank is pretty nice too, Dad," Alex said. "And in Philly we don't have to drive to Foxboro to see the NFL team play."

"You win that round," their dad said, and they all laughed. It was almost like old times again, Alex thought. Or maybe it was the beginning of better new times.

"So what do you think about tomorrow?" Alex asked as he was digging into his fourth slice.

Their father shook his head. "When I plead a case before a jury, I can almost always tell after my closing argument whether I'm going to win or lose. Some of it is watching their eyes; some of it is body language; some of it is just knowing the facts of the case and whether the law is on your side or not.

"I couldn't read these people at all," he continued. "Maybe it's because I've never argued a case like this in the past. I have no experience to draw on."

He took a long sip of the coffee he'd ordered and for a moment said nothing. "And some of it, I honestly think, is that they really hadn't decided, either. *They've* never had a case like this. I think it will come down to one thing in the end: Do they like Matt? I mean, do they think he's a good kid who made a couple of bad mistakes, or do they think he's just a bad kid?"

"He's not a bad kid," Alex said.

Their dad held up a hand. "I know that, Alex," he said. "I wouldn't be trying to help him if I didn't think he was a good kid, and honestly, all I needed on that was your word. Having spent time with him, I know why you like him so much—in spite of his flaws."

"So," Molly said finally. "Up or down tomorrow? Win or lose?"

Their dad smiled. "If this was a baseball game," he said, "I'd say we're heading for extra innings."

He looked at Alex. "Should we order a small pizza? I'm still hungry."

That was the best idea Alex had heard in a good long while.

■ ■ ■

Alex wasn't usually one to break school rules—at least not knowingly. But he made an exception the next morning by slipping his cell phone into his pocket before heading for his first-period class. Jonas saw what he was doing and smiled.

"When will you hear?" he asked.

"They're supposed to be there at ten," Alex said. "Shouldn't take them long to tell them what they've decided. There's no formal appeal once they've ruled, but if it's bad, my dad said he would ask to see a written verdict of some kind and would ask the panel what Matt might be able to do to soften the ruling, whatever it is."

"Sounds like a long shot," Jonas said.

"More like no shot," Alex said. "But he'll go down swinging."

"So to speak," Jonas said as they headed down the hallway.

"I should know by the end of third period," Alex said.

Third period ended at ten-thirty.

"You have English third period, right?" Jonas said. "I'll come find you right after. I'm just down the hall."

Alex nodded. He hadn't seen Christine or Max yet, but he figured they'd want to know too. He kept his phone off for two periods, then ducked into a stall in the boys' room en route to English and turned it on to silent mode. Even though he couldn't look, a vibration in his pocket during class would tell him the verdict was in.

He didn't hear a word Mr. Conway was saying in English class. Then again, he rarely heard a word Mr. Conway was saying. Jonas, who had him for fifth period, had once said, "If Mr. Conway taught English in Shakespeare's day, no one would ever have heard of Shakespeare."

Alex was vaguely aware of Mr. Conway trying to tell the class that *Romeo and Juliet* was *not* a good play—he had some weird theory about Mercutio being a more interesting character than Romeo—when he felt his pocket vibrate. He almost jumped out of his seat and was relieved to see that Mr. Conway was looking in the other direction. There was no clock in the classroom, but Alex was certain class was almost over. It *had* to be almost over.

It didn't end soon enough. Alex was trying to calculate how much time was left when he heard Mr. Conway say, "Mr.

Myers, if you don't mind taking part for a moment, can you tell me why this is a flawed play?"

Alex had read the play. He loved it. He had envisioned himself as Romeo to Christine's Juliet—except for the part where they both died.

"I don't think it's flawed, Mr. Conway," he said. "I think it's great."

"Really?" Mr. Conway said, folding his arms. "Apparently, you haven't been listening today. Can you explain to me why you disagree with what I've been saying?"

Alex was about to answer that and get himself into trouble when the bell rang.

"Well, Mr. Myers—saved by the bell," Mr. Conway said. "I would advise you to be better prepared tomorrow."

Yeah, Alex thought, *and I'd advise you to try another profession.*

He pushed those thoughts aside, packed up his backpack, and bolted for the door. Jonas, Christine, and Max were all waiting outside the room.

"Do you guys have jetpacks or something?" Alex asked.

"Forget that," Jonas said. "Did you hear anything?"

Alex didn't want to take out his phone in the hallway.

"Let's go outside real quick," he said, nodding in the direction of the door that led to the school's backyard.

"Hurry," Christine said. "We've only got seven minutes."

■ ■ ■

They all walked briskly down the hall, Alex slipping the phone out of his pocket as they went outside. He opened his messages, and there it was. He read it aloud to the others: "'Good news—and bad news. Good news: Matt is reinstated, effective right away.'"

Jonas, Christine, and Max all let out yells of happiness.

"What could possibly be bad news about any of that?" Christine asked.

Alex had looked up for a second in response to their cheers. He looked back down at the screen and read: "'Bad news: He can't pitch or play the field for the rest of the season. He can be the designated hitter—but that's it. They said this was their compromise—no negotiating. On our way back now. Matt will be at practice.'"

Alex stopped reading and looked at his friends. They had gone from ecstatic to stunned in a matter of seconds.

"Can't pitch?" Jonas said finally. "That's like saying Tom Brady can play football, only not at quarterback."

"Well, it *is* better than not playing at all," Christine said.

Alex was about to ask her if she was sure about that when the bell rang. He stuck his phone into his pocket. There was nothing to be done right now—except try to make it to fourth period without being late.

■ ■ ■

Alex got another text from his dad during lunch: *Coach Birdy asked that I come to practice and explain to everyone what's going on. I'll see you there.*

Matt wasn't in the locker room when everyone arrived, but the word had spread about the decision made by the board. Alex was a little surprised at how mixed the reaction to it was from Matt's teammates.

"They're like King Solomon," said Brendan Chu, the one guy on the team with a 4.0 GPA. He was going to Yale in the fall.

"Who's King Solomon?" asked Jonas—a relief to Alex because he was too embarrassed to ask himself.

Chu and the other seniors laughed. "You'll find out next year," Chu answered. "He was asked to resolve a dispute between two mothers over who a baby belonged to, and his solution was to cut the baby in half. That's what this is—they just cut Matt in half."

"Actually, he's lucky he can play at all," said Jeff Cardillo, someone who never had anything bad to say about anyone. "He *could* have killed that kid. He's lucky he didn't. That's the way I would have looked at it."

"Yeah, but we need him to pitch," said Patton Gormley.

They were still arguing as they walked across the soccer and lacrosse field. Matt, Alex's dad, and Coach Birdy were waiting for them when they got to the dugout. It was spitting a little bit of rain—which, Alex thought, was appropriate under the circumstances.

"Guys, I know you've all heard about the outcome in Harrisburg," Coach Birdy said. "I thought it would be good to have Mr. Myers explain how the board reached its decision."

He looked at Alex's dad, who had taken off his suit coat and his tie but still looked quite formal in his button-down shirt. Matt was still in his street clothes too—no jacket, no tie, but also a dress shirt.

"I'm a believer, as I told Matt in the car coming back here, that you should try to look at the glass as half full," he said. "That's what this is. The board was very close to keeping the season-long suspension fully intact. Two board members were adamant about that. Two others felt he deserved to play. The swing vote—the tiebreaker—was a man named Jonathan Showalter. If the last name sounds familiar, that's because his cousin is Buck Showalter, the Orioles' manager.

"He gave us a rather lengthy speech about how he understood the emotion of competition and that pitching inside was, for better or worse, part of the game. But he went on to say he was also a parent who had two sons who played the game and he couldn't imagine how Billy Twardzik's parents felt that night when they had to go to the hospital because of Matt's reckless action. That's the phrase he used, 'reckless action.'

"He looked at Matt and said, 'Young man, I simply can't justify putting you back on a mound again this season. But I don't think you threw that pitch with malice or intent to injure. So I have suggested the following compromise to the board.'

"Then he told us what it was. Rather than vote on whether the penalty should be upheld or reduced, the board voted unanimously in favor of Mr. Showalter's suggested compromise. So here we are. Matt can be your DH, but only your DH."

There was silence when he finished. "Any questions, guys?" Coach Birdy said.

More silence.

"Okay, then. Matt, go get dressed. The rest of you guys, warm up. Mr. Myers, on behalf of all of us, thank you for all the work you did. Can you guys give Mr. Myers a round of applause?"

They did. As Matt jogged in the direction of the locker room, Alex walked over to his dad and gave him a hug.

"I think you did a great job, Dad," he said. "More important, thanks for just taking all the time to be here and to help Matt."

"Did the best I could," his dad said. "I think Matt's happy to be part of the team again. Maybe you guys won't win the league this year, but you'll be better with him in the lineup."

He looked at his watch. "I'm trying to catch a four-thirty flight. I have a lot of work to catch up on. But I'll be back in two weekends."

"You will?"

"Absolutely."

He didn't say "I promise." This time, though, Alex believed him.

29

King of Prussia came to Chester Heights on Friday afternoon.

Matt, having taken a lot of batting practice on Wednesday and Thursday, was back in the lineup, hitting third as the DH. Alex had pitched Tuesday, so Bailey Warner got the start. The bullpen was fresh, since Alex had gone six innings. Alex hoped they wouldn't be needed too early. But KOP was a formidable team—especially those Herman brothers. . . .

The first hint of trouble came when the KOP players began taking the field to warm up. The Lions were stretching in front of their dugout, and Alex was standing next to Warner when he heard him say, "Oh my God!"

For a split second, Alex thought Warner might've hurt himself again, but when he looked up, he saw that he was staring in the direction of the third base line, where the Chargers were starting to loosen up. Apparently he had just gotten his first look at the Herman brothers. Warner hadn't made the trip the first time the two teams played.

"You guys told me they were big, but . . . *my God!*"

"Just keep the ball down and away from them and you'll be fine," Alex said. He was staring too. He'd *seen* the Hermans before and was still a little bit in awe of them.

"How'd that work out for you?" Bailey asked.

Alex didn't answer because he knew Bailey already knew the answer: not so good.

Coach Birdy gave them a quick pregame pep talk in the dugout, something he rarely did.

"Bailey's healthy and ready," he said. "Think how well you guys played when Matt was out of the lineup—we didn't lose a game. Now we have Matt back. We win today, we're in a virtual first-place tie. We don't need to score seven in the first. Just let the game come to you."

Actually, as it turned out, they could have used seven in the first, because by the time they got up to bat in the bottom of the first, KOP was up, 6–0.

As experienced as he was, Bailey Warner looked like a scared freshman from the first pitch he threw—which went about two feet over Lucas Mann's head to the backstop. He walked the leadoff hitter on four pitches, then walked the second hitter on five. Jake Herman came up, and Warner looked like he wanted to crawl under the fence and escape. His first pitch hit Herman in the arm, and Alex wondered if the baseball had been damaged. Herman dropped his bat, looking like he'd been hit by a feather, and jogged to first.

Coach Birdy didn't even bother to send Coach Bloom out.

He sprinted to the mound to try to calm his pitcher down. Later, Bailey would tell Alex that the message was direct: "You gotta throw strikes. Find the plate. Make them earn it!"

Warner followed the instructions—at least he tried to. His first pitch to Joey Herman was a strike—but it was right down the middle of the plate. Apparently figuring that Warner had been ordered to throw strike one, Herman was sitting on the fastball. Alex took one step as the ball soared over his head and stopped. If he had been playing somewhere close to the Delaware state line, he might have had a play on the ball. Otherwise, no chance.

Bailey gave up two more runs before the inning was over and the Lions slumped into the dugout.

"Hey!" Matt yelled. "We can score too, you know. It's just the first inning!"

He was right—they did score. Matt hit a long home run of his own in the fourth for the first run, and Cardillo singled in two runs in the sixth. But it wasn't nearly enough. Each Herman hit another home run, and the final score was 13–3.

"Guess we're getting better," Jonas said as everyone lined up for handshakes. "Last time, it was fourteen to two."

Alex was right behind Matt in the handshake line. He heard one of the Hermans—he thought it was Jake—say to Matt, "I wish we'd gotten a chance to hit against you. Least that would have been a challenge."

"Yup," Matt said, "it would have been. Good luck in the playoffs. I hope you guys go far."

KOP hadn't clinched anything yet—they were still just a game ahead of Chester. But Chester Heights' chances had died a cruel death that afternoon. Not only was KOP two games in front of the Lions now, it also had the tiebreaker, since it had won both games between the two teams. Even counting the Haverford Station game as a win, the Lions were 7–2 in the conference, and KOP was 9–0. That meant even if Chester Heights won every game from now on and finished 14–2, KOP would have to go 4–3 the rest of the season for the Lions to catch and pass them in the standings.

"They aren't losing three games," Matt said when Alex asked him about congratulating the Hermans on making the playoffs. "They aren't losing any games. Their whole lineup is good, not just those guys, and their pitchers are pretty good—plenty good enough. Those two guys make them great. You might be able to pitch around one, but not both."

He sighed. "Still, I would like to have had the chance to pitch against them."

"Yeah, I know," Jonas said. "If you'd pitched, we probably would have only lost, like, six to three."

Matt smiled. "Probably right," he said. "Those two guys will be pros someday."

■ ■ ■

Not surprisingly, Matt's return had brought the media back in full force, although Alex also noticed quite a few cameras around the King of Prussia dugout—specifically, around the Herman brothers. Matt had told Alex that each of them now had fifteen home runs for the season—in seventeen games. KOP was undefeated and ranked number twelve in *USA Today*'s high school baseball poll.

Even so, Matt still had a half dozen cameras around him. Alex could see that Christine, Dick Jerardi, and Stevie Thomas were also talking—or at least listening—to him. Alex knew that Matt had been prepared for this by his dad and that he would stick to the script: He was grateful to be playing again; he was pleased the board had understood that he'd made a mistake but that it wasn't part of a pattern of any kind; he just wanted to help the team any way he could.

"I told him it wouldn't change anything for this season, but he has to think big picture," Alex's dad had said when he'd called after getting back to Boston. "College recruiters, pro scouts, even agents will be watching to see how he handles this."

While Alex was watching Matt handle it all, Steve Garland walked over.

"What do you think?" Garland asked.

"About the game?"

Garland shook his head. "I don't need to know what you thought about the game, Alex," he said. "That was men against boys. Nothing to be ashamed of—they're just way better than anyone else playing at this level. No, what do you think about Matt?"

"I wish he could have pitched today," Alex said. "But I'm glad we'll have him in the lineup the rest of the season. We're better with half of him than with none of him."

"Do you think the decision was fair?"

Alex had thought about that long and hard. "I'm biased," he said. "I wanted him back—period. But I'll say this: I think the board tried really hard to be fair."

Garland nodded. "For the record, because I'm going to write it next week, I thought they were more than fair. I think your dad probably saved the day."

Alex knew there was truth to that. With a less competent lawyer, the initial suspension almost certainly would have been upheld. But Alex just said, "Matt said my dad was great. I know he's a really good lawyer, so I'm not surprised."

"Matt said he did all the work pro bono," Garland said.

"True."

"How come? Matt may not be rich, but he's not poor. Your dad must have lost a lot of hours just with the travel alone."

"He did," Alex said.

"So why'd he do it?"

"Because," Alex answered, breaking into a broad grin, "he loves me."

As he said it, it occurred to him that no matter where Chester Heights finished in the standings, the baseball season had not been a total loss. Far from it.

The rematch with Haverford Station took place the following Tuesday. Billy Twardzik still wasn't back in uniform, but Matt was—even if he wasn't pitching. Coach Birdy warned Matt before his first at-bat to expect a pitch inside.

"Coach Meese told me no one is happy that they're letting you play when Twardzik is still out," Coach Birdy said as Matt and Alex both grabbed bats to follow Jeff Cardillo to the plate in the bottom of the first. "Be ready."

Coach Birdy was half right. Haverford Station's starter, a kid named Marshall Bradley, did deck Matt—but only after he had decked both Cardillo and Alex. Cardillo got out of the way, got up, dusted himself off, and singled to left—typical Cardillo. Alex wasn't as lucky: He got plunked in the ribs and went down thinking he was seriously hurt. He lay on the ground for a couple of minutes while Ralph Willard, the trainer, worked on him.

"I think you're just going to be sore," Ralph said. "See if you can get up."

Alex did. He noticed that Bradley hadn't taken a step off the mound to see if he was okay, nor had the catcher even looked at him. He did hear the home plate umpire talking to Bradley as he started to first.

"One more pitch like that, son, and you're gone," he said. "That's enough vigilante justice. Play baseball."

Alex almost smirked. It figured, he thought. He and Cardillo had to hit the dirt, and Matt would come up, keep his uniform clean, and probably hit a home run.

He was wrong. The first pitch to Matt was, as far as Alex could see standing on first base, in the exact same spot as the pitch to him had been. Matt dove out of the way. The umpire was out from behind the plate almost before Matt hit the ground.

"You're gone!" he said to Bradley, who, without a word of protest, walked into the dugout.

"In case you were wondering," Haverford Station's first baseman said to Alex, "that wasn't our real starter. He was just in there to throw at you guys until he got tossed."

"Glad you guys have gotten over something that happened five weeks ago," Alex said.

The first baseman glared at him. "Do you think we *should* be over it?"

Alex didn't have an answer for that. The kid was right.

The new pitcher was a basketball player Alex recognized

named Mike Dunn. He jogged in to warm up while the umpire called the two coaches together for a chat.

Dunn threw his last warm-up pitch, and Matt stepped in. His first pitch was a breaking ball that was way outside, making the count 2–0. His next pitch was a fastball, and it was grooved. Alex thought he saw Matt smile as the pitch reached the plate. He swung and put the ball into outer space. Alex just stared at it as it left the park, not bothering to run because he knew he didn't have to. It was 3–0, and the Haverford Station dugout was losing its collective mind. To his credit, Matt didn't showboat at all; he just put his head down and circled the bases.

Dunn settled down after that. Before Alex went back to the mound for the top of the second, Coach Birdy called the whole team together.

"Guys, here's the deal. Mr. Dale, the home plate ump, has told Coach Meese and me that if anyone on either team throws inside again, he'll eject the pitcher and the coach on the spot. And if it happens a second time, that team will forfeit the game. So, Alex, we aren't getting even, we're just getting outs. You hear me?"

Alex did. He had no desire to escalate things. And staked to a three-run lead, he pitched with confidence.

Mann and Cardillo produced back-to-back doubles in the third to make it 4–0, and Alex rolled through the Haverford Station lineup, except for a slider he hung to Dunn in the fifth with a man on first. The two-run home run made it 4–2, but Alex made up for it by leading off the bottom of the inning with a triple to the right-center field gap. Matt hit a long fly to drive him in to make it 5–2. That was the final score after Don Warren pitched the seventh.

The handshake line was a little bit tense. Both umpires lingered to make sure no trouble broke out, and the coaches stood nearby too. Several of the Haverford Station players leaned into Alex and said, "Hope you're okay, man. It wasn't personal."

Alex wanted to say, *Then why did you throw at me, you dopes*, but resisted the urge. They'd gotten the win, and unless the suspended game somehow meant something in the standings—almost impossible with King of Prussia firmly in control of the conference race—they wouldn't have to lay eyes on these guys again. That, Alex thought, was a relief.

■ ■ ■

Maybe being out of contention kept them relaxed, because the Lions rolled through their next four games. Bailey Warner's shoulder was at a hundred percent, and with some help from Patton Gormley, who was emerging as a very good relief pitcher, Warner handled his starts with ease. Alex had no trouble with either Jefferson or Franklin. Coach Birdy even let him stay in to finish off a 5–0 shutout against Franklin because the last two games of the season, against Chester, weren't until the following Thursday and Friday. That would give Alex plenty of rest, no matter which game he started.

After the Franklin game, Coach Birdy told everyone to wait in the locker room after they had finished talking to the media. That didn't take long because the Matt story had run its course and King of Prussia had already clinched the conference title earlier that day by beating Chester. That gave KOP a 14–0 conference record—the Chargers were 22–0 overall and now ranked ninth in the USA Today poll— with two games to play. Chester was 12–2, and Chester Heights 11–2. Even if KOP somehow lost its last two games to Haverford Station, they had the tiebreaker with both of the teams chasing them, since the Chargers had swept them both. The conference announced that the suspended Haverford Station–Chester Heights game wouldn't be completed because it was now official that KOP would represent the conference in the playoffs.

So the media pretty much consisted of Steve Garland and Christine and a couple of bloggers who were following Matt's hitting exploits. He had gone three-for-four in the Franklin game, including his eighteenth home run of the season— even though he had missed five games.

"I heard both Hermans hit their twentieth today," Jonas teased as they walked into the locker room.

"I'd have more than twenty if I hadn't missed those five games," Matt replied quickly—clearly not amused. "And if we'd played more nonconference games."

"Cool it, Matt," Alex said, a little weary of Matt's total self-involvement. "If not for my dad, you wouldn't have played at all after you nailed Twardzik."

Matt stared at Alex for a second, and Alex thought Matt the New was about to make another appearance. Fortunately, he was wrong.

"You're right, Goldie," he said. "There I go again. It's just been so frustrating not to be able to pitch that I wanted to try to hit a hundred home runs, instead of just being a good hitter. And I've let you down by not being there to help you work on your pitches. When we get a chance, I promise I'll show you the splitter. You get that working by next year and you'll be unhittable."

Alex was about to open his mouth when they all heard Coach Birdy calling for quiet.

"Listen, fellas, I just wanted to take a minute to tell you how proud I am of all of you," he said. "We've been through a lot of ups and downs this spring. We had a rough start. We turned four-and-three into fifteen-and-five, and that's not counting the Haverford Station game or the fact that we didn't have our best player for five games—and won all of them.

"I know it's disappointing that we won't be in postseason"—he paused and looked at Alex and Jonas—"especially for Myers and Ellington. They got spoiled by foot-ball and basketball."

Everyone laughed.

"But I don't want you guys to show up next week and think the season's over. Chester is our archrival, and we can still finish second if we sweep them. They're good—we're good. So it should be fun. I'm going to pitch Bailey on Thursday, because he deserves to start his last home game. Alex, you'll go on Friday. I know it's hard, but I want you guys to show up Monday as if you're preparing to play for a championship."

He looked around the room. Everyone was nodding, but

if the rest of the guys were feeling the way Alex was, their hearts weren't really in it. Coach Birdy was right—he *was* spoiled. He agreed with something Tiger Woods had once said when he was still the world's dominant golfer: "Second place sucks."

Third place, he supposed, was worse.

Alex was sitting at lunch with Christine, Max, and Jonas on Monday when Matt came racing into the cafeteria as if he were being chased by armed gunmen. He had a wild look on his face that Alex couldn't begin to figure out.

"What in the world?" was all Christine got out as Matt pushed his way through people in the aisles to reach the table. He was completely out of breath when he arrived.

"Matt, what the heck is going on?" Alex managed to say before Matt held up a hand to stop him. Still out of breath, he reached into his pocket and pulled out a crumpled print-out. He unfolded it and handed it to Alex.

"What is it?" Christine asked.

"Just . . . read it," Matt said. "Coach Birdy said it just went up on the website a few minutes ago."

Alex looked down at the unfolded paper. At the top it said "By Steven Thomas—Special to the *Daily News*."

"Just *read*!" Matt ordered. "Aloud!"

As Alex began, the table went completely silent. Even as he read the words, Alex found them difficult to believe.

"'According to sources at the South Philadelphia Athletic Conference and King of Prussia High School, baseball superstars Jake and Joey Herman have been declared ineligible because they were found to have taken payments from an agent earlier in the season. As a result, King of Prussia, which clinched the conference championship last Friday, will be forced to forfeit all fourteen of its conference victories . . .'"

"Oh my God!" Jonas yelled.

"Hang on," Matt said. "There's more."

"'. . . meaning that the two-game series later this week between second-place Chester and third-place Chester Heights will decide the conference title. As a result of the forfeits, Chester is now fourteen-and-oh in league play and Chester Heights is thirteen-and-oh—its game against Haverford Station earlier this season having been suspended and never completed.'"

By now, kids from other parts of the cafeteria, hearing the commotion, had surrounded the table.

"'According to conference sources,'" Alex continued, "'the Herman brothers both accepted cash from an agent named Benjamin Anderson. Anderson also co-signed paperwork for both that allowed them to buy cars—each purchasing an Audi Q5 from a dealership in King of Prussia in mid-April. In return, the brothers signed a contract with Anderson guaranteeing that he would represent them after the Major League Baseball draft in June. Both are considered likely first-round picks.'"

Alex stopped reading. "How in the world did Stevie Thomas get all this stuff?" he asked.

Matt had his breath back now. The fact that half the school was listening to him apparently didn't bother him. "From what I heard, the twins decided they didn't want to turn pro right away; they wanted to go to college. I guess they told Anderson that's what they were going to do, and he said he'd go public if they did. They called his bluff, and he ratted them out to the school and the conference."

Bailey Warner, who had joined the crowd around the table, asked the question Alex was going to ask: "Doesn't this make them ineligible to play in college?"

Matt shook his head. "They'll have to file an appeal, and they'll probably have to return the cars and give Anderson back any money he gave them. But if they do that, there's a good chance they'll get to play. But the important thing is—"

"We're playing for the championship!" Jonas said.

"Exactly," Matt said. "We're going to be playing for the championship."

He sat down, smiling the way he had smiled back in football season, when all had been right in his world.

■ ■ ■

Once the crowd had dispersed, Alex asked the question he hadn't wanted to ask in front of half the school.

"This Anderson guy is *your* Anderson guy, isn't he?" he said.

Matt nodded. "Oh yeah."

"Did he offer you money?" Max said. "Or a car?"

"Both," Matt said. "I turned him down. I *knew* that was against the rules."

He looked at Alex and Christine. "I listened to you two," he said. "I gotta say, the money was tempting, but I wanted to keep my options open. If I'd taken anything from him, I would've had to go in the draft this summer. That was the deal."

"What do you think made the Hermans change their minds?" Jonas asked. "They would've both gone in the first round, right?"

"Maybe," Matt said. "Pitchers generally get drafted higher out of high school than hitters because teams try to take a lot of pitchers and hope one or two pan out. I'm guessing some of the colleges recruiting them explained that to them."

"But why not go in the draft, see what happens, and then make a decision?" Christine asked. "That's allowed. Players do it all the time."

"I'm guessing Anderson told them there wouldn't be that option," Matt said. "He wanted the money from repping them *now*, not later."

"Well, now he's got nothing," Alex said. "Nice move on his part."

"Nice move for us," Christine said. "But I do feel sorry for everyone else at KOP. They didn't do anything wrong."

"How sorry do you feel for them?" Alex asked.

"Well," she said, giving him her smile. "A little bit sorry."

"They didn't seem too sorry when they were killing us," Jonas said. "I think I can live with it."

"And now we have two games that matter this week," Alex said. "Amazing."

■ ■ ■

Coach Birdy's concern that the team might be flat with nothing to play for was long gone by the time they got to practice that afternoon.

"Listen up, fellas," he said before they went out to stretch. "I know you all know about what happened to the Hermans and King of Prussia. Honestly, I'm sorry for them. I talked to their coach a little while ago, and he told me the twins are hurting financially and just got sucked in by this agent. Still—I hope all of you are paying attention—this stuff is serious, and it affects all of us.

"That said, KOP's misfortune means we've been handed a second chance. I know you guys are all fired up right now, but let's all take a deep breath and remember we don't play until Thursday. Let's save our fire for then."

"Let's go out and kill Chester!" Oliver Flick yelled.

Jonas looked at Alex. "So much, I guess, for saving our fire."

■ ■ ■

Alex was trying very hard to focus on explaining D'Artagnan's courage in joining the Musketeers that night when his phone rang. It was his dad.

"I just talked to your mom," he said. "She said that as long as you've got your homework done, I can take you and Molly to Tony's for dinner on Wednesday."

"Wednesday?" Alex said. "You're coming to town *Wednesday?*"

"Yup," his dad said. "I'm going to meet with some new clients Thursday morning, and then I can stick around for your game on Thursday."

"New clients? You have new clients in Philadelphia?"

"Jake and Joey Herman," his dad said. "Their coach—his name is Arneke—called me today. He knew I'd worked for Matt, and he said these two kids desperately need legal help and they've got absolutely no money—"

"Hang on, Dad. You aren't going to try to get their eligibility back, are you?" Alex said—panicked one second, sheepish the next, because he realized that was a truly selfish thought.

His dad laughed. "No, Alex, don't worry. That ship sailed. These kids both really want to go to college. Their dad, who hasn't been around for years, showed up all of a sudden when they looked like potential moneymakers. He was the one who did all the dealing with this agent—what's his name?— Anderson. Same sleaze who tried to take advantage of Matt. I'm going to see what I can do about making sure they're eligible to play in college."

"You doing it for free?" Alex said.

"Yes," his dad said. "I enjoyed the way it felt to help Matt out. Plus, it gives me an excuse to see you guys."

"Your partners don't mind?" Alex said.

His dad laughed again. "Actually, they think it's good publicity for the firm—which it is. They're fine with it. So, you think you can get your homework done to go to Tony's on Wednesday?"

"You bet," Alex said.

He wasn't sure what sounded better—the pizza or seeing his dad again.

■ ■ ■

The next couple of days at school were almost a letdown.

Alex had gotten spoiled by the buzz in the hallways before big football games and before the conference-championship-deciding basketball game against Chester. Of course, there had been all sorts of controversy leading up to those games. Now the controversy was centered on King of Prussia, and no one at Chester Heights seemed all that fired up about the possibility of winning a tainted conference title in baseball.

"It's almost like everyone feels like it doesn't really count if we win," Alex said to Jonas while they were at their lockers on Thursday morning.

"Maybe that's because there's some truth to it. KOP was the best team."

"But they cheated," Alex said.

"Not like Matt cheated in football," Jonas said. "What the Hermans did had no effect on how they played. They were a couple kids with no money and, from what I read, a really bad dude for a father. I feel bad for them."

Alex knew Jonas was right. He hoped his dad would be able to help them. For now, though, his concern was trying to beat Chester. Tainted or not, someone had to finish first, and it might as well be the Lions. Alex felt confident about his chances to pitch well the next day, but they would be playing the game on the road. They needed to win at home today. And that would be up to Bailey Warner.

■ ■ ■

Bailey Warner pitched well in front of a packed house, but Jack Duval, Chester's pitcher, was just as good. The teams were tied, 1–1, after seven innings, and Coach Birdy decided that Warner had gone far enough. Needless to say, Bailey didn't want to come out.

"Coach, I feel fine," he said. "I just struck out two guys last inning."

"Bailey, we agreed when you came back that your pitch count wasn't going above eighty-five the rest of the season," Coach Birdy said. "That's what your doctor and I agreed to, right? Well, you're at ninety-four. I can't send you out there again. I'm not going to put your future at risk—no matter how big the game."

No one wanted to see Warner come out. Alex had found his comeback inspiring. He wasn't throwing as hard as he had before his injury, but he was getting guys out. Alex didn't lack faith in the bullpen; he just had more faith in Warner.

Sure enough, Don Warren came in and gave up a scratch run in the top of the eighth. A walk, a sacrifice bunt, a stolen base, and a sacrifice fly gave Chester a 2–1 lead.

Duval came out to pitch the bottom of the eighth. The Lions had the top of the order coming up.

Cardillo worked a walk on a 3–2 pitch that could have gone either way. Alex, standing in the on-deck circle, had a pretty good view of the pitch and wouldn't have been surprised if it had been called strike three.

"About time we caught a break with an umpire," he said to himself as he walked to the plate. He was expecting a bunt sign, but apparently Coach Birdy didn't want to give up an out with only three left in the game.

Alex took two pitches for balls, then lined a single to left. Cardillo held up at second. As Matt walked to the plate, Chester's coach, who Alex knew was one of their assistant football coaches, walked to the mound. Alex figured that was going to be it for Duval. He was wrong. The coach jogged back to the dugout. Matt stepped in, and at that moment, Alex was convinced the Lions were going to win. Duval had done a good job on Matt—he'd gotten him out twice on fly balls and walked him once—but he was tiring. A three-run home run right now would be a perfect way to end the home season.

Neither of Duval's first two pitches came close to the plate. Alex knew Duval didn't want to pitch around Matt and load the bases. He'd have to throw a strike here. Matt stepped out to see if he had the hit sign. He did. What's more, Coach Birdy wanted both Jeff and Alex to take off with the pitch. No doubt he was thinking a ball hit in the gap would end the game if both runners were already in motion.

Alex saw Cardillo repeat the sign to him to make sure he had it. He nodded to let him know he understood. Matt stepped in. Duval took his stretch, paused for a long moment, and threw. Alex put his head down and took off. He glanced back to the plate in time to see Matt uncurling the swing that had become so familiar to him.

The ball took off in a screaming line, headed in the direction of the left-center field gap, just as Coach Birdy had hoped. But then, suddenly, Alex saw Chester shortstop Mike

Jaynes take one step to his left, leap in the air, and somehow stab the rising liner in his glove. His momentum carried him right across the second base bag—doubling off Cardillo, who was halfway to third.

Too late, Alex realized what was happening. He stopped dead in his tracks and tried to scramble back to first. He had no chance. Jaynes swept across the second base bag and in one motion flicked the ball to first—well ahead of Alex's desperate attempt to get back. Alex ended up with a faceful of dirt as a result of his wild dive, which came up well short of the base.

It was a triple play . . . a stunning, game-ending triple play. While the Chester players mobbed one another, Alex got to his knees and stared in disbelief at the celebration. He noticed Matt, who had gotten two steps out of the batter's box, standing with his hands on his hips. Coach Bloom came to help Alex up.

"That was nobody's fault, Alex," he said. "One of those crazy plays. Matt hit it right on the nose, but right at somebody."

"Not exactly," Alex said. "The guy made a great play."

"Yup, he did," Coach Bloom said. "But we'll get 'em tomorrow. *You'll* get 'em tomorrow."

Alex could only hope that he was right.

There were plenty of media people on hand, in part because the two games would decide the conference champion but also because of the circumstances that had made the two games important. The players stuck around to talk and then made their way to the locker room. Coach Birdy told them he wanted to talk to them before they hit the showers.

Alex stopped for a minute to talk to his dad, whom he had spotted climbing into the stands in the third inning, and also to his mom and Coach Archer, who had been sitting several rows away. He figured it would be pretty awkward for the three of them to sit together.

"Tough one, I know," his dad said, giving only a hand-shake since Alex was caked with dirt and sweat and he was still wearing a shirt and tie. "But you've still got tomorrow."

His dad had already told him at dinner the night before

that he had to be in Chicago on Friday. In the past, that sort of excuse had sounded pretty weak to Alex. Now he understood—and said so.

"How'd it go with the Herman brothers?" Alex asked.

"They're nice kids," his dad replied. "But, boy, did their father make a mess of things. This won't be easy."

He decided to ignore all the dirt and give Alex a hug. "I have to run to the airport. The meeting's at seven tomorrow morning. Text me as soon as the game's over. I know you'll get it done."

His mom and Coach Archer said essentially the same thing. "We were in worse situations during basketball, and you came through," Coach Archer said. "We've got faith in you."

Coach Birdy's message in the locker room wasn't all that different.

"We're not in a bad position at all," he said. "Remember, if we win by more than one run tomorrow, we win the title because the first tiebreaker is score differential. So if we outscore them by two tomorrow, we're going to be champions."

"What if we outscore them by one?" Brendan Chu asked.

"Then it comes down to runs on the road. So if we win by a run and score at least three at their place, we still win."

"What if," Jonas asked, "we win by two to one? Then we've both got three runs total and two on the road."

Coach Birdy nodded. "Yeah, we'd like to avoid that because then it comes down to a coin flip."

"Coin flip?" they all said almost at once. "*Coin flip?*"

"Hey," Matt said. "It won't come down to that. They got

lucky today. We'll kick their butts tomorrow. Bailey was great today; Goldie will be great tomorrow too."

"Greater!" Warner shouted.

One other question suddenly occurred to Alex.

"Coach, even if we win tomorrow, we're still technically a half game behind because of the Haverford Station game," he said.

Coach Birdy nodded. "The league commissioner just filled me in on that a few minutes ago," he said. "Since it's now possible that game might mean something, they've finally decided that we'll go over there on Monday to finish it *if* we win tomorrow and *if* we win the tiebreaker."

"Or the coin flip," Cardillo said.

Coach Birdy nodded. "Right. Remember, we were leading that game five–nothing in the sixth before it got suspended."

"Anyone got a two-headed coin?" Matt said.

They all laughed at that and headed for the showers.

"Coin flip?" Alex repeated to Jonas.

"No worries, Goldie," he said. "Like Matt said, we got you pitching. We're not losing."

■ ■ ■

Alex hadn't pitched for a week, but he felt great from the minute he went out to warm up. Chester had seating for even fewer people than Chester Heights did, and by the time Alex walked in from the bullpen, there wasn't a seat to be had or, for that matter, any open space for standing.

He felt even better after the top of the first. Chester's coach, Wayne Tribbett, had gone with Duval—his best guy—the day before. Frank Chamblee, their number two starter, wasn't bad, but he wasn't Duval.

Chamblee began the game with a walk to Cardillo. Alex, seeing the infield playing deep, bunted on the first pitch and easily beat it out for a hit. Then, on a 1–1 pitch, Matt hit one of his out-of-sight home runs. As he rounded the bases ahead of Matt, Alex couldn't help but think that it would've been nice to have had that home run the previous day in the eighth inning.

Matt took a different view. As he crossed home plate and high-fived Alex and Cardillo, he said, "That takes care of one tiebreaker—we've already scored more road runs than they have. It's up to you to do the rest, Goldie."

As it turned out, Alex had plenty of help. Matt hit another home run in the third inning, and Oliver Flick and Lucas Mann produced another run with back-to-back doubles in the fourth. The lead was still 5–0 in the sixth, and Coach Birdy told Alex he wasn't going out to pitch the seventh.

"But, Coach, I'm fine," Alex said in protest.

"I know you are," Coach Birdy said. "But I'm pretty sure between Patton and Ethan and Don, we can get three outs. And I may need you Monday." He smiled. "We're going to have another game to play, remember?"

Alex hadn't forgotten. But still . . .

"Coach, we're up five–nothing in that game too—remember?" Alex said.

Coach Birdy smiled. "How could I forget? But they have runners on first and second in the sixth. We need six outs there. We only need three here. I hope I won't need you, but just in case, I want to save that inning for then."

Alex knew he was right, but he would have liked to have closed the season with a shutout. Any debate ended when the Lions scored three more runs in the top of the seventh. The Clippers were completely lifeless against Patton Gormley in the bottom of the inning, and the final score was 8–0. The Lions celebrated as if they'd won the title—which they believed they had.

After they'd talked to the media and made the short trip back to Chester Heights, Coach Birdy stood up in the front of the bus before they all got off.

"You guys did great work today," he said. "Alex, you were fantastic; Matt, you're the best DH a team could hope for; and the rest of you were terrific. We've now beaten Chester in three sports this year with a championship at stake."

He paused and looked at Alex and Jonas, sitting, as usual, together near the back of the bus. "Must be Myers and Ellington, right?"

They all laughed and cheered for Alex and Jonas.

Coach Birdy put up a hand.

"I don't want any wild celebrating this weekend," he said. "Have fun tonight, but take it easy tomorrow and Sunday. We still have to wrap up the Haverford Station game to be fifteen-and-one and win the league. If we don't, we're fourteen-and-two, and Chester wins it with fifteen-and-one."

It sounded strange to hear Coach Birdy talking about going 15–1 when they had started the week with a conference record of 11–2. But thanks to the two forfeits, they had magically become 13–0 going into the first Chester game, and they were now 14–1, with one game to finish. It had been, to put it mildly, a strange season.

"I know we have a comfortable lead," Coach Birdy continued. "But I want you to keep two things in mind. First, Billy Twardzik came back to play in their two games this week. The doctors didn't want him playing the field, but he was their DH." He glanced at Matt. "Twardzik went four-for-eight in the two games, including a home run. So he can still hit and he's dangerous. Plus, you can bet we're going to face a hostile atmosphere over there.

"We need six outs. Bailey gets the ball first. The rest of you pitchers, be prepared. I don't care if each of you gets one out apiece as long as we get the six we need. Be rested. Remember, we win and we go to Easton for the sectionals next weekend. Let's make sure we get there."

■ ■ ■

In truth, even though Alex followed his coach's orders, he had the best weekend he'd had all spring.

On Friday night, everyone went to Hope's for the first party she'd thrown in several weeks. The weather was warm, and the dance floor had been moved to the veranda on the back side of the house. Alex spent a large chunk of the night dancing with Christine, losing her just once when he went to get drinks and found her dancing—naturally—with Matt. Even that didn't really bother him.

The next day, he and Christine went for a bike ride before everyone met at Stark's. Then the two of them went to the movies and for a walk around the mall. Their goodbye kiss, in front of Christine's house after Alex had insisted on biking her home, was the best and longest of their relationship.

"That was a fun day," she said.

"Yeah, it was," he said. "I hope we won't be able to see each other next weekend because I'll be in Easton. . . ."

"I'll be there too," she said. "Dick Jerardi and Stevie arranged for me to cover the sectionals for the *Daily News*."

"Great! But how will you get there?"

"I'll drive with Steve Garland," she said.

He gave her a look.

"Alex, don't start again," she said. "For one thing, you know he's been dating Lisa Feinberg since they were sophomores. For another, Ally will be in the car too. So just stop." Ally Bachinski was a photographer for the *Weekly Roar*.

"Sorry," he said, feeling sheepish. "Every once in a while, my evil twin jumps out of me before I can stop him."

"I know," she said. "But no backsliding."

She stood on tiptoe and kissed him one more time.

"See you Monday," she said, pushing her bike in the direction of her back porch. "Rest tomorrow. Don't screw up on Monday."

"We won't," Alex said, meaning it.

■ ■ ■

Coach Birdy hadn't been kidding about a hostile crowd at Haverford Station. There were actually hecklers waiting for them when the bus arrived, and Alex could see from the window that there were a number of security guards to escort them to the locker room.

Matt, sitting two rows in front of Alex and Jonas, shook his head when he saw what was waiting outside.

"I shouldn't have come," he said. "I'm red to a bull to all of these people."

"It'll be fine," Alex said. "We wouldn't be playing to clinch a championship if not for you. It wouldn't feel the same winning without you here."

Since Matt had been ejected from the game, he couldn't be in the dugout. He could sit next to the dugout, but not in it and not in uniform.

Matt smiled as they all stood up to get off the bus. "You're a good man, Goldie," he said. "But the fact is, if I hadn't acted like an idiot back in April, we would already have won the championship."

They filed off, surrounded by the security people. It didn't appear that anyone wanted to do much more than heckle them.

"Hey, Gordon, whose head are you going to throw at today?" one heckler yelled, getting just a little too close for comfort.

"He's not even playing, and he hasn't pitched in more than a month, you moron," Alex said, taking a step in the direction of the man.

"Easy, Goldie," Matt said, pulling him back. "Let's just go get six outs."

That proved easier said than done. The game resumed with Haverford Station runners on first and second and no one out in the sixth. Eddie Kenworthy, whose bunt had so infuriated Matt that he had thrown the fateful pitch at Billy Twardzik, was on second, and Twardzik, having been hit by Matt's pitch six weeks earlier, stood on first, looking just fine.

Bailey Warner was on the mound. He promptly made things worse by walking the first hitter, Bobby Kotlowitz, to load the bases.

Coach Birdy came out right away to talk to Warner. Alex remembered what he had said about all the other pitchers needing to be ready because he would have a quick hook if anyone appeared to be struggling.

Alex looked around the stands and noticed that everyone was on their feet. It occurred to him that for everyone at Haverford Station—friends and families of the players, students, even teachers—this wasn't just about winning a baseball game. They were still angry because of what Matt had done to Twardzik. Alex understood. He closed his eyes for a moment and tried to imagine how he would have felt if an opposing pitcher had done to one of his teammates what Matt had done to Twardzik. What if he'd spent a week wondering if Jonas would live, much less play baseball again?

He opened his eyes to see Coach Birdy trotting back to the dugout. Bailey had pitched well since his return. Clearly, the coach had faith that he would get his act together.

Warner settled down and struck out the next two hitters. Alex breathed a sigh of relief. If they got out of this jam with a five-run lead, they were probably home free. The next hitter was another basketball player Alex recognized—Pete Cowen, the catcher. He looked like a catcher, short and stocky, the kind of hitter who didn't make contact a lot but had plenty of power if and when he did.

He also hit left-handed. Coach Birdy decided to get his one left-handed pitcher, Don Warren, in to face him. Alex wasn't sure about the move. Warner had looked good getting the two strikeouts. But it wasn't his call.

Warren jogged in, took his warm-up pitches, and promptly sailed his first pitch over Cowen's head. It went to the back-stop, advancing all three runners. Six weeks after his life-changing bunt, Kenworthy scored. Twardzik moved to third, Kotlowitz to second. It was now 5–1. The crowd booed Don Warren's wild pitch—even though it hadn't come close to Cowen—and Cardillo went to the mound to settle Warren down. Alex could see Warren nodding his head the way a pitcher did when he wasn't listening. His body language said, *Get off the mound and let me pitch.*

Cardillo did.

Not surprisingly, Warren tried to throw strike one on the next pitch—a fastball right down the middle. Cowen swung smoothly, and the ball took off in a high arc toward left field. Alex started to sprint back but realized after a few steps he had no chance. The ball sailed well over the fence. He watched it bounce on the other side and roll up against a tree. The crowd was going nuts as Cowen, having shown remarkable opposite field power, circled the bases.

It was 5–4. And Chester Heights still needed four more outs.

Coach Birdy was back on the mound, waving Ethan Sattler in. The lefty-lefty move hadn't exactly worked out. Alex felt his heart thumping in his chest. This wasn't good, he thought. They'd given Haverford Station life. He could see that everyone in the home dugout was on the top step, leaning over the railing.

Sattler managed to get the final out on a routine ground ball to Cardillo. Alex breathed a sigh of relief as they all ran in, with the lead now only 5–4.

Everyone was chattering about getting a couple of insurance runs.

"We're fine, fellas," Coach Birdy said. "Three outs to go, and we're still in front."

He turned to Alex. "You've got the ball in the bottom of the inning, Myers. Just get three outs and let's get out of here."

Alex felt his heart pumping almost through his chest again.

"You've got this, Goldie," Matt said, just like he had said to him during football season. "Go be the hero. It's what you do."

The Lions went down one, two, three in the top of the seventh. It looked to Alex as if each guy who came up was trying to hit a six-hundred-foot homer. Instead, they got nothing but air.

Before he left the dugout, Coach Birdy put his arm around Alex. "You've been through this before in football and in basketball," he said. "No need to do anything special. You're plenty good enough to get these guys out."

Alex nodded. He was still trying to control his breathing and his heart rate. For some reason, this felt different from the way football and basketball had felt. There, once he was on the field or the court, all his nerves went away. He had simply focused on what he needed to do and, for the most part, had done it.

He felt fine warming up and got lucky when the Hornets'

first hitter, overeager, jumped at a fastball that was low and outside and hit a one-hopper right back to him. Easy out. Two to go. Alex could feel himself relaxing just a little.

The next hitter was a lot more patient. He worked a 2–2 count, fouled off several pitches, and then hit a long fly ball to center field. Jonas took a few steps back and made an easy catch.

One out to go. Now Alex was in his own world. He didn't hear the crowd, and he didn't hear his teammates yelling encouragement to him.

The batter was Kenworthy. *This*, Alex thought, *is the way to end it.* Alex saw Coach Birdy signaling Brendan Chu, the third baseman, to play in a couple of steps in case Kenworthy decided to bunt again. Alex was pretty sure Kenworthy wouldn't try it with one out left in the season, but he thought moving Chu in was a good move.

Alex was dimly aware of the crowd screaming at Kenworthy to keep the game alive. He threw a fastball that he thought was on the corner. Kenworthy took the pitch. Ball one.

No matter, Alex thought. He threw the same pitch. Strike one. Kenworthy backed out and said something to the umpire, who simply pointed at the batter's box, as if to say, *Get in there and hit.*

Alex had gone outside twice; now he aimed for the inside corner. Kenworthy swung viciously and fouled the pitch back. It was 1–2. One strike away. Alex had thrown three fastballs. It was time to throw a breaking pitch—to try to fool Kenworthy into a bad swing.

It worked, almost. As the pitch dipped away, Kenworthy started to swing, then held up. Alex thought he saw the umpire's arm start to come up to signal strike three. It didn't.

From the dugout, Alex heard Coach Birdy yell, "That wasn't a swing?" His teammates were shouting too.

The umpire took his mask off and glared into the dugout. Everyone quieted down quickly.

The count was 2–2. Lucas Mann wanted a fastball. *No*, Alex thought, *Kenworthy will be looking fastball*. He shook him off. Mann signaled for the slider—the same pitch as the last one. Alex liked the idea. This time, though, Kenworthy wasn't fooled. He could see the pitch breaking out of the strike zone, and he let it go by. It was 3–2.

Now Alex agreed with Mann's fastball signal. He reminded himself not to overthrow the pitch, to just go through his motion and put the pitch where he had put the first two—just above the knees, toward the outside corner. He reminded himself to avoid *too* fine so as not to throw ball four.

He wound up, kicked, and threw. The pitch was perfect—so perfect that it froze Kenworthy, who simply watched it go by. Alex was about to throw his arms into the air when he noticed the umpire had not put his right arm up to indicate strike three.

Even Kenworthy looked surprised.

"What's the call, Ump?" Alex asked, coming down off the mound, shouting to be heard.

"Did I move my arm, son?" the umpire answered.

"Where was the pitch?" Alex asked.

"Below the knees," the ump answered.

"*No way!*" Alex said, more stunned than anything.

Kenworthy, still looking surprised, dropped his bat and jogged to first base. Alex turned his back from the plate. He knew he couldn't afford to get ejected.

He took one more deep breath and turned back to face the plate. Billy Twardzik was walking into the batter's box.

■ ■ ■

Alex had been so focused on Kenworthy that he'd completely forgotten that Twardzik was on deck. Now, as Twardzik stepped in, Alex was suddenly out of the bubble he'd been in. The noise was almost deafening.

He looked into the dugout to see if Coach Birdy might be coming out to talk to him. He was standing with one foot on the top step, hand on his chin.

Alex was on his own, which made sense. What could Coach Birdy say at this moment?

Twardzik stood close to the plate, clearly not concerned about getting hit again by an inside pitch.

Alex was confident Twardzik would take a pitch. So he threw a fastball just off the middle of the plate. He had guessed right. Twardzik never moved a muscle. Strike one.

With an 0–1 count, Alex decided to see if Twardzik might go fishing for a pitch off the plate. He threw another fastball, but this one was low and outside. Again, Twardzik didn't move. He was going to wait for a pitch that he liked. Now it was 1–1.

Time for a breaking pitch. Alex had thrown sliders to Kenworthy, so he decided to throw a curve to Twardzik, even though he knew that if he hung it, Twardzik might hit it into outer space.

It broke perfectly, dropping through the strike zone to Twardzik's knees as he flailed at it. One strike away . . . again.

Twardzik backed out and picked some dirt up and rubbed it on his hands. "Good pitch," he said, mouthing the words carefully so Alex could understand him over the din.

Mann had liked that curve so much, he called for another one. This time, though, Alex missed outside. It was 2–2.

Now Alex backed off the mound to gather himself. He glanced at the on-deck circle. Johnny Strachan, the cleanup hitter whom Warner had walked to restart the game, was swinging a bat. Alex wanted no part of facing him, especially with the tying run in scoring position.

He walked back onto the mound and looked in for the sign. Mann wanted another curve. *No*, Alex thought, *I can't chance hanging one*. He shook him off.

Mann called for a slider. *Okay*, Alex thought. *Let's try it.*

It was the worst pitch he had thrown—in the dirt. Mann did a great job blocking it to keep Kenworthy at first base.

Now it was 3–2. Again. *Why*, Alex thought, *does each of these at-bats have to stretch to the bitter end?* He pawed at the dirt with his foot. He knew that if this were a movie, Twardzik would hit a home run on the next pitch to end the game and the season. From surgery on his brain to a season-ending home run to ruin the chances of the team whose pitcher had put him in the hospital.

For a split second, almost comically, Alex thought of a *Peanuts* cartoon his dad had shown him when he was a kid.

Linus had been telling Charlie Brown about a ninety-nine-yard run on the last play of a football game for the winning touchdown. "You should have seen it, Charlie Brown!" he said. "The whole team and all their fans were celebrating!"

To which Charlie Brown had said, "How did the other team feel?"

Alex didn't want to be the other team.

Mann was signaling for a fastball. Alex had thrown three straight breaking pitches and knew he had to throw a strike. He nodded.

He checked Kenworthy at first, kicked his leg, and fired, putting everything he had into the pitch. Twardzik was sitting on a fastball. He swung, and the ball took off like a rocket, heading for the center field fence. Alex turned, convinced the Lions had just become the other team.

Jonas, playing deep to try to cut off a game-tying extra-base hit in the gap, took off, angling into the gap and back toward the fence. He was in a full sprint as he reached the warning track. One step onto the track, he leaped and stretched his body as far as it could go, his glove reaching across his body and above his head.

Alex could see that his glove was above the top of the fence as the ball finally came down. At the last possible second, just before he began to descend, Jonas twisted his glove back *over* the fence and reached for the ball. He came down to the ground, and everyone in the park held their breath.

Jonas looked inside his glove and smiled. Then he pulled the ball out and held it over his head. Somehow, he had pulled the ball back into the field of play and held on to it.

The second base umpire, who had run into the outfield to make a call, put his right arm up, signaling the out.

Alex threw his arms into the air and was starting to sprint in Jonas's direction along with the rest of the team when he saw Billy Twardzik, who had been between first and second bases when Jonas finally caught the ball. He was bent over, hands on knees, staring at the ground.

Alex stopped running. He walked over to Twardzik and put an arm around his back. "You crushed that ball," Alex said. "You couldn't have hit it harder."

Twardzik looked up, saw Alex, and smiled. "I needed to hit it one inch harder," he said. Then he stood up and put out his hand. "You guys won, fair and square."

Alex shook his hand, and then they hugged. Matt, who had come out of the stands, was standing right behind him.

He didn't say anything. Neither did Twardzik. Instead, they just hugged one another. There was really nothing left to say.

■ ■ ■

When they finished celebrating and came off the field, Alex found a welcoming party waiting to greet him.

Christine was there, and so were his mom and Coach Archer. Standing a few feet away was his dad.

"Dad! When did you get here?" Alex asked.

"Just as the game restarted," his dad said. "I had a gut feeling you were going to end up on the mound. But I never figured the game would end *that* way. I'm proud of you. But if Jonas hadn't made the catch, I'd have been proud of you anyway."

"Amen to that," his mom said.

A few yards away, Jonas was surrounded by cameras and notebooks, which was as it should be. There were some other media members talking to Billy Twardzik and Matt, who were being interviewed together. Twardzik had his arm around Matt. That, Alex thought, was pretty cool.

"Don't you have work to do?" Alex asked Christine.

"Not yet," Christine said. "I asked to do the Myers sidebar." She smiled. "But I think I can get him to talk to me later."

Alex smiled. As usual, she was right.